WHAT THE REVIEWERS SAID ABOUT

THE MACGREGOR BRIDES

'A splendiforous reading treat... It would be hard to pick any one book as Ms Roberts' best—such a feat defies human ability—but for many readers their favourite character might well be named MacGregor.'

—*Romantic Times*

'...witty and well done...a fun read.'

—*Publishers Weekly*

'Fast-paced, warmly romantic, and filled with deftly portrayed characters.'

—*Library Journal*

AND WHAT THE READERS HAVE TO SAY!

'...reading *The MacGregor Brides* [is] like visiting old friends...I love your books and await each new one anxiously. I can't put it down until I finish. Then I'm sorry because the characters become a part of my life and I miss them. Thank you for all the suspense, love and laughter you have brought into my life.'

—*J. Alvarez, California*

I laughed, I cried, I enjoyed. Oh, to know [people] like the MacGregors. I am so looking forward to the next MacGregor book. Thank you for all the enjoyment.'

—*E. McCarthy, Illinois*

NORA ROBERTS

The MacGregor *Grooms*

SILHOUETTE®

Silhouette and Colophon are registered trademarks of Harlequin Books S.A., used under licence.

First published in Great Britain 1999
Silhouette Books, Eton House, 18-24 Paradise Road,
Richmond, Surrey TW9 1SR

© Nora Roberts 1998

ISBN 0 373 48369 4

82-9910

Printed and bound in Great Britain
by Caledonian International Book Manufacturing Ltd, Glasgow

NORA ROBERTS

is one of the most prolific and popular authors writing for Silhouette®, as well as a *New York Times* best-selling author in both hardcover and paperback. Nora was the first author inducted into the Romance Writers of America Hall of Fame and has received awards for her fiction, her creativity, her sales and her contribution to the genre. She has received lifetime achievement awards from the Romance Writers of America and from *Romantic Times* magazine, and best-selling title and series awards from booksellers, readers and peers.

The MacGregor Grooms brings back one of her best loved and most requested characters, Daniel MacGregor, as he tries out his matchmaking skills on a new generation.

For Mom and Pop

THE MACGREGORS

Daniel Duncan MacGregor
m.
Anna Whitfield
(FOR NOW, FOREVER)

Alan
m.
Shelby Campbell
ALL THE POSSIBILITIES

Grant Campbell
m.
Genevieve Grandeau
ONE MAN'S ART

Adria   Matthew   Cybil
(twins)

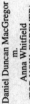

Daniel
Campbell
'D.C.'
*THE
MacGREGOR
GROOMS*

Julia
m.
Cullum
Murdoch
*THE
MacGREGOR
BRIDES*

Travis   Fiona Joy

Caine
m.
Diana Blade
TEMPTING FATE

Laura
m.
Royce
Cameron
*THE
MacGREGOR
BRIDES*

Daniel   Blake

Ian
*THE
MacGREGOR
GROOMS*

Serena
m.
Justin Blade
PLAYING THE ODDS

Robert
MacGregor
m.
Darcy
Wallace
*THE WINNING
HAND*

Duncan
*THE
MacGREGOR
GROOMS*

Gwendolyn
m.
Branson
Maguire
*THE
MacGREGOR
BRIDES*

Amelia

Anna   Lauren

More *MacGregors* coming in 2000!

CONTENTS

From the Private Memoirs
of
Daniel Duncan MacGregor

At my stage of life, the years pass quickly, with season rushing into season. Every moment should be savored and lived to the fullest.

Of course, I felt the same way when I was thirty!

Now, in the last handful of years, I've watched four of my beloved grandchildren find love, marry and start families. Laura, then Gwen; Julia, then Mac. Happiness beams out of their eyes; contentment shines in their voices. Each has built a home and a life with the mate of their heart.

So why, I ask you, did it take them so damn long?

Hah! If it hadn't been for me they'd still be floundering around, and there wouldn't be a single great-grandchild for Anna to cuddle and spoil, would there? But do I ask for gratitude? No, indeed. As long as I'm head of this family I'll do my duty without the need for thank-yous. It's my duty, and my pleasure, to see that my chicks are comfortably—and properly—roosted.

It would seem, with all this marital bliss going on, that the other grandchildren would get the hint and follow the fine example of their siblings and cousins. But no, no, the MacGregors are a stubborn and independent lot. And God bless them for it.

Thankfully, I'm still around to see that things get done. I saw three of my girls to the altar and gave my first grandson his nudge. Some say it's interference. Bah. I say it's wisdom. I've decided it's time to apply a little wisdom to my namesake, Daniel Campbell MacGregor.

Now he's a fine boy—sharp as a whip-

lash, if a mite temperamental. Handsome, too. Looks a bit like I did at his age, so he doesn't lack for female companionship. That's part of the problem, as I see it. Too much quantity and not enough quality.

We've found a way to fix that.

D.C.'s an artist, which he comes by naturally enough. Though for the life of me I don't understand half the things he paints, he's made a fine success out of his work. Now what the boy needs is a woman to share that success, his life, and give him children to center it.

Not just any woman, mind. A woman with backbone, a woman with brains and ambitions—and breeding. The woman I picked out for him while they were both still children. I've been patient, bided my time. I know my boy and just how to handle him.

A bit perverse is my D.C. The type of man who too often goes left if you tell him he'd be better off turning right. Comes, I suppose, from the eight years of childhood when his father was president and there were so many rules that had to be obeyed.

Well now, with a little help from an old and dear friend, we'll get young Daniel Campbell turned in the right direction—and let him think he did it all by himself.

A wise man doesn't need thanks— just results.

Part One

D.C.

Part One

B.C.

Chapter 1

The light poured through the tall windows and splashed on the violent slashes of sapphire and ruby. It washed over the man who stood before the canvas like a warrior at battle, wielding a paintbrush like a claymore.

He had the face of a warrior—tough, intense, with knife-edged cheekbones adding hollows, a mouth that was full but firmed in concentration. Eyes brilliant blue and icy cold beneath knitted brows the color of old mahogany.

His hair waved over his ears, curled over the collar of the splattered denim shirt he wore in lieu of a smock. He'd rolled the sleeves up, and the well-toned muscles of his arms rippled as he slashed the brush on canvas.

He was built like a warrior—broad of shoulder,

narrow of hip and long of leg. His feet were bare, his wide and clever hands smeared with paint.

In his mind he saw explosions of emotion—passion and lust, greed and hunger. And all of this he fought onto the canvas while mean-edged rock pumped out of the stereo and thumped against the air.

Painting was a war to him—one he was determined to win, battle after battle. When the mood was on him he would work until his arms ached and his fingers cramped. When his mood was otherwise, he could and did ignore his canvases for days, even weeks.

There were those who said D. C. MacGregor lacked discipline. To those, he said who the devil wanted it?

As he clamped the brush between his teeth, switched to a palette knife to smear on a bold emerald, his eyes glittered in triumph.

He had it now. The hours of waging this battle were nearly done. A thin line of sweat slid down the center of his back. The sun beating through the windows was fierce now, and the studio was viciously hot because he'd forgotten to turn on the air-conditioning or open a window to the warm spring air.

He'd forgotten to eat as well, or check his mail, answer the phone or so much as glance out any of the wonderfully tall windows in his apartment. The energy swirled through him, as potent, as primitive as John Mellencamp's edgy, streetwise vocals blasting through the room.

When D.C. stepped back, the brush still clenched

like a pirate's blade in his teeth, the palette knife like a dagger in his hand, that firm, somewhat forbidding mouth curved.

"That's it," he murmured. He put the brush in a jar of solution, began to absently clean the knife as he studied his work. "Need," he decided. He would call it simply *Need.*

For the first time in hours he realized the room was stuffy, the clashing and familiar scents of turpentine and paint thick in the air. He crossed the unpolished hardwood floor and shoved open one of the tall windows, took a deep gulp of fresh air.

It had been the windows, and this view of the C & O Canal, that had sold him on this apartment when he'd decided to come back to Washington. He'd grown up here, with eight years of his life spent in the White House as first son.

For a space of time he'd lived and worked in New York, and enjoyed it. He'd also lived and worked in San Francisco, and enjoyed that as well. But all through his restless twenties something had tugged at him. He'd finally given in to it.

This was home.

He stood by the window with his hands shoved in the back pockets of ragged jeans. The cherry blossoms were in full, glorious bloom; the canal sparkled in the afternoon light. Joggers plugged away along the towpath.

D.C. wondered idly what day it was.

Then, realizing he was starving to death, he left the music blaring and headed to the kitchen.

The penthouse was two levels, with the top designed for a master bedroom suite. D.C. had made it his studio and slept on a mattress tossed on the floor in the spare room. He hadn't gotten around to dealing with bed frames.

Most of his clothes were still in the packing boxes they'd been shipped in nearly two months before. He figured they worked efficiently enough as dressers until he found time to buy the real thing.

The main floor had a spacious living area ringed by more windows, still undraped. In it, there was a single sofa—the tags still on—a glorious Duncan Phyfe table with a half inch of dust coating its surface, and a floor lamp with a dented metal shade. The random-width pine floor was bare and desperately needed vacuuming.

The dining alcove off the kitchen was empty, the kitchen itself in shambles. What dishes and pots weren't heaped in the sink were still in boxes. He went directly to the refrigerator and was bitterly surprised to find it empty but for three beers, a bottle of white wine and two eggs.

He could have sworn he'd gone shopping.

Rummaging through the cupboards, he came up with a few slices of very moldy bread, a bag of coffee, six boxes of cornflakes and a single can of soup.

Resigned, he ripped open a box of cereal and ate a handful while debating which he wanted more, coffee or a shower. He'd just decided to make the coffee and take it with him into the shower when the phone rang.

He noted without much interest that his message light was blinking, and, munching dry cereal, he answered.

"Hello."

"There's my boy."

And those ice blue eyes went warm, that hard mouth went soft. D.C. leaned against the counter and grinned. "Hey, Grandpa, what are you up to?"

"Some would say no good." Daniel's voice boomed out. "Don't you return your messages? I've talked to your bloody machine half a dozen times in the last few days. Your grandmother wanted to fly down to make sure you weren't dead in your bed."

D.C. only lifted a brow. It was well known that Daniel used his serene wife whenever he wanted to nag the children.

"I've been working."

"Good. That's good, but you can take a breath now and then, can't you?"

"I'm taking one now."

"I've a favor to ask you, D.C. I don't like to do it." Daniel let out a heavy sigh and had his grandson's brow knitting.

"What do you need?"

"You won't like it—God knows I can't blame you. But I'm in a bit of a fix. Your aunt Myra—"

"Is she all right?" D.C. straightened from the counter. Myra Dittmeyer was his grandmother's oldest and dearest friend, his own godmother and an honorary member of the Clan MacGregor. D.C. adored her, and remembered guiltily that he hadn't been to see her since he returned to Washington six weeks before.

"Oh, she's fit and fine, boy. Don't you worry about that. The woman's just as feisty as ever. But, well, she has another godchild. I doubt you remember the girl. You'd have met her a time or two when you were a lad. Layna Drake?''

Concentrating, D.C. got a vague image of a spindly little girl with hair like dandelion fluff. ''What about her?''

''She's back in Washington. You know Drake's— the department stores. That's her family. She's working in their flagship store there now, and Myra… well, I'm just going to say it straight out. There's a charity ball tomorrow night, and Myra's fussing because the girl doesn't have an escort. She's been at me to ask you—''

''Damn it, Grandpa.''

''I know, I know.'' Daniel used his most long-suffering sigh. ''Women, boy—what else can I say? They'll peck away at us like ducks until we just give in. I told her I would ask you. It would be a big favor to me if you'd see your way clear for this one night.''

''If you and Aunt Myra are trying to set me up—''

Daniel interrupted with a hearty laugh that had D.C. frowning. ''Not this time, boy. This girl isn't for you, take my word. She's pretty enough, and well mannered, but she'd never do for you. Too cool, to my way of thinking, and a bit of the nose-in-the-air sort. No, no, I wouldn't like to see you looking in that direction. And if you can't spare the evening, I'll just tell Myra I reached you too late and you already had plans.''

''Tomorrow night?'' D.C. scooped his fingers through his hair. He hated charity functions. ''Is it black tie?''

''I'm afraid so.'' At the muttered oath in response, Daniel made sympathetic noises. ''Tell you what, I'll just call Myra back and tell her you can't make it. No use wasting your evening with a girl who's likely to bore you to tears, is there? I doubt the two of you have a single thing in common. Better you start looking for a wife. It's time you were married and settled, Daniel Campbell. Past time. Your grandmother worries you'll end up starving in your studio, a lonely old man without a single chick or child. I've got another girl in mind. She's—''

''I'll do it,'' D.C. interrupted, purely in reflex. If Daniel didn't think much of Myra's goddaughter, it meant he wouldn't be on the phone constantly asking for relationship updates. Perhaps after this favor, his grandfather might ease off his relentless dynasty building—and though D.C. didn't hold out much hope for that outcome, it was worth a try. ''What time tomorrow, and where do I pick what's-her-name up?''

''Oh, bless you. I owe you for this one. The affair's at eight, at the Shoreham Hotel. Layna's taken over her parents' town house on O Street.'' Examining his nails, Daniel rattled off the address. ''I appreciate you getting me out of this little fix, D.C.''

D.C. shrugged, upending the cereal box into his mouth as he traded family gossip with Daniel. And he wondered fleetingly where the hell he might have packed his tux.

''Oh, Aunt Myra, really.'' Layna Drake stood in her underwear, a waterfall of white silk over her arm and a mortified expression on her face. ''A blind date?''

''Not really, sweetheart.'' Myra smiled. ''You've

met before—when you were children. I know it's an imposition, but Daniel rarely asks me for anything. It's just one evening, and you were going anyway.''

"I was going with you."

"I'll still be there. He's a very nice young man, darling. A bit prickly, but still very nice." She beamed. "Of course, all my godchildren are wonderful people."

Myra continued to smile as she sat and studied her goddaughter. Myra was a small woman with hair as white and soft as snow. And with a mind as sharp and quick as a switchblade. When the moment called for it—as it did now—she could adopt a fragile and helpless air. The aged Widow Dittmeyer, she thought with an inner chuckle.

"Daniel worries about him," she continued. "And so do I. The man keeps too much to himself. But honestly, who would have thought when I was just casually mentioning tonight's affair and how you'd come back to Washington, that Daniel would get this idea in his head? I was just…" Myra fluttered her hands helplessly. "I didn't know how to say no. I realize what an imposition it is."

Because her adored godmother suddenly looked so unhappy, Layna relented. "It doesn't matter. As you said, I'm going anyway." Gracefully, she stepped into her gown. "Are we meeting him there?"

"Ah…" Gauging the timing, Myra rose. "Actually, he'll be here shortly to pick you up. I'll meet you there. Goodness, look at the time. My driver must be wondering what happened to me."

"But—"

"I'll see you in an hour or so, darling," Myra

called out, moving with surprising speed for a woman of her age. "You look gorgeous," she said once she was safely halfway down the stairs.

Layna stood in the unzipped column of white silk and heaved out a breath. Typical, she thought. It was just typical. Her godmother was forever shoving men into her path. Which left her with the sometimes irritating job of having to push them out again.

Marriage was something she'd firmly crossed off her life plan. After growing up in a house where manners took precedence over love, and casual affairs were politely ignored, Layna had no intention of finding herself in the same sort of relationship.

Men were fine as decoration, as long as she ran the show. And at the moment, her career was much more important than having someone to dine with on Saturday night.

She intended to continue her steady climb up the family's corporate ladder at Drake's. In ten years, according to her calculations, she would take over as CEO.

It was another show she intended to run.

Drake's wasn't just a department store, it was an institution. Being single, and remaining that way, insured she could devote all her time and energies to maintaining its reputation and its style.

She wasn't her mother, Layna thought with a faint frown marring her brow, who thought of Drake's as her personal closet. Or her father, who had always been more concerned with bottom-line profits than innovations or traditions. She was, Layna thought, herself.

And to her, Drake's was both a responsibility and a joy. It was, she supposed, her true family.

Some, she mused, might find that sad. But she found it comforting.

With a quick move, she zipped the dress. Part of her responsibilities to Drake's was to mingle, to attend social functions. To her, it was simply a matter of changing gears, from one kind of work to another. The after-hours work called on training she'd received throughout her childhood and was second nature to her now.

And the "job" often meant being linked with the proper escort.

At least this time her aunt Myra didn't appear to have any real interest in making a match. It would just be a matter of making small talk with a virtual stranger for an evening. And God knew she was an expert at such matters.

She turned and picked up the pearl-and-diamond drops she'd already set out on her dresser. The room reflected her taste—simple elegance with a dash of flash. The antique headboard of carved cherry, the highly polished surfaces of lovingly tended occasional tables topped with vases of fresh flowers or carefully chosen accessories.

Her home now, she thought with quiet pride. She'd made it her own.

There was a cozy seating area in front of a small marble fireplace and a dainty ladies' vanity displaying a collection of boldly colored perfume bottles.

She selected her scent, absently dabbing it on while she allowed herself to wish, just for a moment, that she could spend the evening quietly at home.

She'd put in a ten-hour day at Drake's. Her feet hurt, her brain was tired and her stomach was empty.

Pushing all that aside, she turned to the cheval glass to check the line and fit of her gown. It was cut straight at the bodice and flowed without fuss to the ankles, leaving her shoulders bare. She added the short jacket, slipped into her shoes and checked the contents of her evening bag.

When the doorbell rang she only sighed once. At least he was prompt.

She remembered D.C. vaguely from childhood. She'd been much too nervous and impressed from meeting the president to notice much else. But she'd heard of him off and on over the years.

An artist, she reminded herself as she started downstairs. Of the modern school, which she didn't pretend to understand. Layna preferred the classics in all things. Had there been some scandal about him and a ballet dancer a few years back? Or had it been an actress?

Ah well, she thought. She supposed the son of a former president would make news over trivialities. And being the grandson of Daniel MacGregor would only intensify the spotlight. Layna was much happier working backstage herself.

And obviously the man couldn't be such a hit with the ladies if he couldn't even get his own date on a Saturday night.

Putting on her company smile, she opened the door. Only years of education by Swiss nuns, and the discipline they'd instilled, kept her mouth from dropping open.

This man—this very dangerous looking man in

black tie, with hair the color of her prized dining-room table and eyes so blue they burned—needed his grandfather to find him a date?

"Layna Drake?" He had to have the wrong house, was all D.C. could think. This shimmering willow stem in white silk was nothing like the spindly little girl he remembered. Rather than dandelion fluff, her hair was spun gold curved sleekly around a face that might have been carved from ivory. Her eyes were a soft and misty green.

She recovered, her how-do-you-do smile never faltering as she offered a hand. "Yes. Daniel Mac-Gregor?"

"D.C. Daniel's my grandfather."

"D.C. then." Normally she would have invited him in, played hostess for a short time and given them both an opportunity to get somewhat comfortable with each other. But there was something not quite safe about him, she decided. He was too big, too male, and those eyes were far too bold. "Well." Deliberately she stepped out and closed the door behind her. "Shall we go?"

"Sure." Cool, his grandfather had said, and D.C. decided the old man had hit the mark. Definitely an ice princess for all her glamorous looks. It was going to be a very long evening.

Layna took one look at the ancient and tiny sports car at the curb and wondered how the hell she was supposed to fold herself into it wearing this gown.

Aunt Myra, she thought, what have you gotten me into?

Chapter 2

She felt as if she were locked inside a mechanical shoe box with a giant. The man had to be six-four if he was an inch. But he seemed perfectly content to drive the toy car—at high rates of speed—through the swirling Washington traffic.

Layna clamped a hand on the padded handle of her door, checked the fit of her seat belt and prayed she wouldn't be crushed like a bug on the windshield before the evening even started.

Small talk, she decided, would keep her mind off that particular image.

"Aunt Myra tells me we met some years ago when your father was president." The last word came out in a squeak as he threaded the little car between a bus and a limo, then careened around a circle.

"That's what I hear. You just relocated in Washington?"

"Yes." Realizing she'd squeezed her eyes shut, Layna lifted her chin and courageously opened them again.

"Me, too." She smelled fabulous, D.C. thought. It was mildly distracting, so he opened his window and let the air whip through the car.

"Really?" Her heart was in her throat now. Didn't he see that light was turning red? Wasn't he going to slow down? She bit back a gasp, nearly strangled on it as he zoomed through the yellow just as it blinked to red. "Are we late?"

"For what?"

"You seem to be in a hurry."

"Not particularly."

"You ran a red light."

He cocked a brow. "It was yellow," he said, downshifting, then screaming past a slow-moving compact.

"I was under the impression one slowed for a yellow light in preparation for stopping."

"Not if you want to get where you're going."

"I see. Do you always drive like this?"

"Like what?"

"Like you're at the wheel of a getaway car after a bank robbery?"

He thought about it, smiling at her description. "Yeah."

He made the turn to the hotel and pulled in with a cocky squeal of brakes. "Saves time," he said easily, then unfolded those long legs and climbed out of the car.

Layna sat where she was, catching her breath, offering up her gratitude that she'd arrived in one piece. She hadn't moved a muscle by the time D.C. rounded the hood, passed the keys to the valet and opened her door.

"You're going to want to unhook your seat belt." He waited while she did so, then took her hand to help her out. It brought them close, made him aware of her scent again, the texture and shape of her hand.

She was a looker, all right, he mused. Sea-siren eyes in a cameo face. An intriguing contrast. Though portraiture wasn't the heart of his work, he sometimes sketched faces that interested him.

He imagined he'd be compelled to sketch hers.

Her legs were still weak, but she was alive. Layna drew one deep, steadying breath. "People like you shouldn't be issued a driver's license and should never be allowed behind the wheel of a car for any reason, particularly that soup can on wheels."

"It's a Porsche." Because she didn't seem inclined to move on her own, he kept her hand and pulled her into the hotel lobby. "If you'd wanted me to slow down, why didn't you just ask?"

"I was too busy praying."

He grinned at that, a quick flash of humor. It didn't detract from the danger of his face by a whit. Layna would have said it only added to it.

"Looks like your prayers were answered. Where the hell are we going here?"

Setting her teeth, Layna turned to the bank of elevators and jabbed the button. Then she stepped in ahead of him and jabbed the proper button for the proper ballroom, simmering.

Behind her back, D.C. rolled his eyes. "You know…" What the hell was her name? "Layna, if you're going to sulk, this is going to be a very long, tedious evening.''

She kept her eyes trained straight ahead and kept a choke hold on her temper. She knew it was a bad one, tending toward blasts of sarcasm if she didn't maintain control. "I don't sulk." Her voice had as much warmth as winter in Winnipeg.

Only deeply ingrained manners prevented her from stalking off the elevator the minute the doors slid open. Instead she stepped off, turned gracefully and waited for him to stand beside her.

Temper put color in her cheeks, D.C. noted as he took her arm. Added passion to a cool and classic face. If he'd had any interest in her, he thought he'd make it his business to put that color there, that snap in her eyes, as often as possible.

But since he didn't, and he wanted to get through the evening as smoothly and painlessly as possible, he would placate. "Sorry."

Sorry, she thought as he guided her into the ballroom. That was it? That was all? Obviously he hadn't inherited any of his father's diplomatic skills or his mother's charm.

At least the room was full of people and sound. Layna wouldn't be stuck making conversation with a graceless oaf all night. As soon as manners permitted, she intended to separate and find someone sensible to chat with.

"Wine?" he asked her. "White?"

"Yes, thank you."

He'd pegged her there, D.C. mused as he got her a glass and selected a beer for himself. He could only be grateful that his adored meddler of a grandfather wasn't playing matchmaker this time around.

"There you are!" Myra hurried over, both hands extended. Oh, didn't they make a handsome couple? She couldn't wait to tell Daniel how striking their babies looked together. "D.C., you're sinfully handsome." She tilted her head as he bent down to kiss her cheek.

"Did you save a dance for me?"

"Of course. Your parents are here. Why don't you come sit with us awhile?" She stepped between them, sliding an arm around each and making them a unit. "I know you have to mingle, and of course you'll want to dance. Glorious music tonight. But I'm entitled to be selfish with you for a few minutes."

With the skill and style of long practice, Myra steered them through the crowd, around groups that had gathered to chat, winding among tables spread with white cloths and decked with bouquets of sunny spring flowers.

She was dying for a chance to watch them together, to study the little details of body language, to see how they behaved. In her head she was already working on the guest list for the wedding.

"Look who I brought us," Myra announced.

"D.C." Shelby Campbell MacGregor sprang to her feet. Her gown of citrine silk rustled as she opened her arms to her son. The russet curls piled on top of her head brushed his cheek. "I didn't know you were coming."

"Neither did I." He held her close a moment, then turned to catch his father in a bear hug.

Alan MacGregor's silver hair glinted under the lights. A grin spread over his strong face as he looked at his son. "God, you look more like your grandfather every day."

Even an oaf could love his family, Layna supposed. But a part of her had softened because the love between them, and their enjoyment of it, was so obvious.

If she'd met her parents under similar circumstances, there would have been impersonal air kisses and a polite "how are you?"

Then Shelby turned, her gray eyes warm, the slim brows over them lifting curiously. "Hello."

"Shelby MacGregor, my goddaughter," Myra said with a lilt of pride. "Layna Drake."

"It's wonderful to meet you, Mrs. MacGregor."

Shelby accepted the hand, pleased that it felt strong and capable. "You'd be Donna and Matthew's daughter?"

"Yes. They're in Miami now."

"Give them my best when you speak to them again. Alan, this is Layna Drake, Donna and Matthew's daughter—and Myra's goddaughter."

"Myra's told us a great deal about you." Alan took her hand, held it warmly. "You've moved back to Washington?"

"Yes, sir. It's good to be back. It's an honor to meet you again. I was introduced to you when I was a child. I was terrified."

He grinned as he pulled out a chair for her. "Was I frightening?"

"No, sir. You were presidential. I'd just lost my two front teeth and was feeling miserably gawky.

You talked to me about the tooth fairy.'' She smiled. "I fell in love with you.''

"Really?'' Alan winked at his wife when Shelby chuckled.

"You were my first crush. It took at least two years before you were replaced by Dennis Riley— and that was only because he looked so very stalwart in his Boy Scout uniform.''

Fascinating, D.C. thought, as he watched Layna chat with his parents. Suddenly, all this warmth and animation. Oh, the coolness was still there, a light sheen on the surface, but the charm and vivacity bloomed under it, like the blush on a new rose.

When she laughed it was like a murmur through fog. Sexy but discreet. He had to admit it was a pleasure to watch her—those smooth, economical gestures; the sleek sweep of gilded hair; the slow curve of soft, shapely lips.

It was entertaining to listen to her—that low, cultured voice. Especially if he didn't have to actually talk to her.

"D.C., for heaven's sake.'' Myra gave him a subtle elbow jab and kept her voice in a whisper. "You haven't even asked her to dance.''

"What?''

"Ask Layna to dance,'' she hissed, fighting impatience. "Where are your manners?''

"Oh, sorry.'' Hell, he thought, but obligingly touched a hand to Layna's shoulder.

She nearly jolted, and her head whipped around, her eyes meeting his. She'd all but forgotten he was there. Ignoring her duties, she realized with an inward wince. She fixed a smile on her face and prepared to shift her attention from the delightful parents to the oafish son.

"Would you like to dance?"

Her heart dropped to her toes. If he danced the way he drove, she'd be lucky to leave the dance floor with all of her limbs intact. "Yes, of course."

Feeling like a woman approaching a firing squad, she rose and allowed him to lead her toward the dance floor.

At least the music was lovely, she mused. Slow, dreamy, heavy on the brass. A number of couples were taking advantage of it, so the dance floor was crowded. Crowded enough that Layna had hope her partner wouldn't feel compelled to plow through it, stumbling over her feet and wrenching her arms out of their sockets.

Then he stopped near the edge of the dance floor and turned her into his arms.

It was surprise, she decided, sheer surprise that had her mind fogging. Who would have believed that such a big man could move so well? The large hand at her waist wasn't rough or awkward, but it was very, very male. It made her outrageously aware there was only a thin barrier of silk between it and her skin.

The lights twinkled down, dancing over his face, over that not-quite-tamed mane of richly colored hair. His shoulders were so broad, she thought numbly. His eyes so blue.

She struggled to clear such ridiculous thoughts out of her mind and behave. "Your parents are wonderful people."

"I like them."

She was slim as a willow, he thought. A long-stemmed rose. He watched the lights play over her face, hardly aware he'd drawn her closer. Their bodies fit like two pieces of a complicated puzzle.

Her pulse quickened. Without thinking, she slid her hand over his shoulder so her fingers brushed the back of his neck. "Um…" What had they been talking about? "I'd forgotten how lovely Washington can be in the spring."

"Uh-huh." Desire snaked up his spine, circled in his gut. Where the hell had it come from? "I want to sketch your face."

"Of course." She hadn't heard a word he was saying. She could only think that a woman could blissfully drown in those eyes. "I believe they're calling for rain tomorrow." A little sigh escaped when his fingers splayed over her back.

"Fine." If he dipped his head, he could have that mouth, find out if the taste of it would soothe the edges on this sudden clawing need, or sharpen it.

Then the music ended. Someone bumped them and shattered the thin glass bubble that seemed to have surrounded them.

Both of them stepped back. Both of them frowned.

"Thank you," Layna said, and her voice was carefully controlled again. "That was very nice."

"Yeah." He took her arm, keeping the contact very light, very impersonal. He wanted to get her back to the table, dump her and escape until his mind cleared.

More than willing to cooperate, Layna let herself be guided through. She wanted to sit down quickly before her legs gave way.

Chapter 3

D.C.'s big plan for Sunday was to sleep late, eat an enormous breakfast, which he'd specifically shopped for, and spend a couple hours at his health club. After that his most knotty decision would be whether to while away the afternoon in solitude or to wander down to M Street to the blues festival.

The plan broke apart when he found himself awake and restless just after sunrise.

Annoyed, he tried to sink back into the fitful sleep that had plagued him through the night. But every time he began to drift, he started to think of her. That was more irritating than getting up.

There was no reason for Layna Drake to be on his mind. That one moment of physical connection, of awareness, had been a short side trip in a long and uneventful evening. They'd been scrupulously polite to each other, had mingled, socialized and made tedious small talk, together and separately.

He'd driven her home—deliberately keeping his speed under the limit, signaling for every turn, and braking gently. They had exchanged lukewarm handshakes and goodbyes at her door. And, he was certain, had each been desperately relieved to have parted company.

So it was ridiculous for her to keep chasing through his brain, for him to remember exactly the way it had felt to hold her, to smell her, to watch her eyes go soft and dreamy in the dance.

It was her face, that was all. He was intrigued by it. In an artistic sense, of course.

So he went to the gym early and spent a couple hours trying to sweat out the restlessness. He told himself he felt better, more alert, more clearheaded. By the time he got back to his apartment, he was ready for that big breakfast.

He turned the stereo up to blast, pushed up the sleeves of his black sweatshirt, then put bacon on to fry. Feeling a great deal more cheerful and in control, he sang along with John Foggerty and mixed eggs for scrambling.

When the phone rang, he answered one-handed as he scooped crisp bacon out of the pan.

"So, you're up and about," Daniel boomed out at him. "Turn that music down, boy. You'll have no hearing left."

"Hold on."

D.C. spent a few seconds looking for the remote control—he could never find the damn thing when he needed it—then jogged into the living area to turn down the music manually. On his way back through the kitchen, he snagged a piece of bacon.

"Yeah, I'm up and about," he said into the phone. "I've already been to the gym and I'm about to clog my arteries."

"Bacon and eggs?" Daniel sighed wistfully. "I remember when I used to sit down to a Sunday breakfast like that. Your grandmother, she's so strict. Frets about my cholesterol, so I'm lucky if I'm allowed to look at a picture of bacon these days."

"I'm eating some now." With a wicked grin, D.C. crunched, loud and deliberate. "Fabulous."

"You're a sadistic young man." Daniel sighed again. "And to think I called you up to thank you for doing me such a favor. Now I hope you had a miserable evening entertaining Myra's goddaughter."

"I got through it."

"Well, I appreciate it. I know you've better things to do with your time. Not that she's not a sweet-enough girl, but just not the type who'd interest you. We're looking for a livelier lass for you."

D.C. frowned at what was left of his slice of bacon. "I can do my own looking."

"Well, why aren't you? Locked away in that place with your paints and canvases. Hah. Ought to be out romancing some suitable woman. Do you know how your grandmother frets? Picturing you there, by yourself in that stuffy apartment, with all those paint fumes?"

"Um-hmm." So accustomed to the lecture he could recite it himself, D.C. grabbed another slice of bacon.

"It's a fire trap is what it is, that place you live in. At your age you need a nice house, a good woman, noisy children. But I didn't call to remind you of a duty you should already have seen to," Daniel rushed on. "I appreciate what you did. I remember, before I found your grandmother, the evenings I spent cross-eyed with boredom with some girl who didn't have a single interesting thing to say. What you need is common ground, and a spark. Can't waste your time with someone without those things. You wouldn't have them with little Linda."

"Layna," D.C. muttered, irritated for no good reason. "Her name's Layna."

"Oh yes, there you are. Odd name, don't you think? Well, it's neither here nor there. It's done now, and you won't have to waste any more of your evenings on her. When are you going to come up and see your grandmother? She's pining for you."

"I'll come visit soon." Scowling, D.C. tossed the rest of the bacon back on the platter. "What's wrong with Layna?"

"Who?" In his office in his fortress in Hyannis Port, Daniel had to cover the mouthpiece on the phone until he was certain he'd controlled the bark of laughter.

"Layna," D.C. repeated through his teeth. "What's wrong with Layna?"

"Oh, nothing, nothing at all's wrong with her. Pretty young woman. Fine manners, as I recall. She's just not for you. Chilly sort of thing, isn't she? Her parents are cold fish and stiff as two boards, if I remember right. Well, you eat your breakfast, lad, and make time to come see your grandmother before she nags me to distraction.''

"Okay, yeah. Give her my love.''

"Oh, that I'll do.'' And Daniel hung up, wondering how long it would take his grandson to pay a call on pretty Layna Drake.

It took under an hour—particularly since D.C. found he'd lost his appetite and had poured his egg batter down the sink. He put his sketchbook and his pencils and charcoals in a battered leather bag and slung it over his shoulder. He decided to walk to give himself time to think.

His grandfather was right, of course. That grated a bit—the idea that the old man would so confidently eliminate her. It grated just as much, D.C. discovered, as it did when Daniel tossed selections of proper candidates for marriage at his feet.

He'd damn well make his own choices.

He certainly wasn't thinking about Layna in that manner. He just wanted to sketch her face. And since they'd more or less agreed he could come by and do so that day, he might as well get it done.

She didn't answer his knock. Vaguely peeved, he shifted his bag and told himself he'd be smarter to walk down to M Street, after all, and do some sketching there. But he could hear the light and liquid notes of a Chopin concerto drifting through the open windows.

With a shrug, he tried the door, found it unlocked and stepped inside. "Layna?''

He glanced around, interested, as she hadn't let him over the threshold the night before. The foyer had polished wood floors and walls the tone of lightly toasted bread. An antique gateleg table held a vase of white tulips.

Two pencil sketches on the wall caught his eye—street scenes, cleverly done with a fine eye for detail and movement. He moved to the steps, laid a hand on the glossy newel post and called up. He considered going up and searching her out, then decided it was wiser to look through the main floor first.

She wasn't in the parlor, with its dignified furnishings, or the book-lined library, which smelled of leather and roses. By the time he'd poked into the sitting room, the dining room and the kitchen, he had a solid grip on her taste and life-style.

Elegant, traditional, tidy—with occasional and surprising touches of splash. A conservative woman who liked beautiful things, preferred classics in furnishings, reading and music, and kept everything in its logical place.

He saw her through the kitchen window. The postage-stamp patio beyond was outlined with flowers. Layna was underplanting more white tulips with sunny-faced yellow pansies.

She wore buff-colored garden gloves, a wide-brimmed straw hat and a brown gardening apron over simple beige slacks and a thin summer sweater.

She looked, he thought, like a picture in some country style magazine article on the proper attire for casual morning gardening. Competent elegance.

The light was good, D.C. determined, filtering nicely through branches just starting to green with new leaves. He stood where he was and did three quick sketches.

It amused and intrigued him how precisely she worked. Turn the earth with the spade, mix in fertilizer, carefully tap out the plant, place it exactly in the center of the prepared hole, gently fill in the hole, tamp.

She was lining them up like little soldiers.

He was grinning when he stepped outside.

Because all her concentration had been focused on making a success of her first attempt at gardening, the sound of the screen door slamming was like a bullet in the heart. The spade went one way, the pansies another as she jerked up and spun.

"Startled you, sorry."

"What? How did you get out here?" She had a fist pressed against her racing heart as she stared at him.

"I walked through the house. You didn't answer the door."

He set his bag on the wrought-iron table centered on the patio, noted the thick gardening book set there and open to instructions on the planting of annuals, then walked over to pick up the pansies that had gone flying.

"You can't just walk into someone's house."

"Yes, you can." He crouched beside her, offered the plants. "When the door's unlocked. I told you I was coming by."

He smelled of soap, she thought fleetingly, and he moved like a big, sleek leopard. "You certainly did not."

"Last night. You ought to plant these in a sweep instead of a line, and crowd them some. More pizzazz." With his eyes narrowed, he took her chin, turned her head to the left. "I said I wanted to sketch your face."

She jerked free, as irritated with his touch as with his critique of her novice gardening attempts. "I don't remember anything about that."

"When we were dancing. It's a nice light out here. This'll be fine." He rose to get his pad. "Just keep gardening if you want."

When they were dancing? Layna sat back on her heels and tried to think. She couldn't remember anything that happened when they were dancing except that she'd gone momentarily insane.

Now he was sitting there, dwarfing the curvy little patio chair, his long legs kicked out and a pencil in his hand.

"You don't have to pose," he told her, shooting her a smile that went straight to her gut. "Just pretend I'm not here."

It would be like ignoring a big, sleek panther crouched in the drawing room, she thought. "I can't work while you're staring at me. I want to get these planted. They're calling for some rain this afternoon."

"You don't have more than a dozen left, so take a break." He nudged the other chair away from the table with his foot. "Sit down and talk to me."

She got to her feet, dragging at her gloves. "Didn't we establish that we have nothing to say to each other?"

"Did we?" He knew how to charm a reluctant model, and used his smile ruthlessly. "You like music. So do I. Let's talk music. Chopin suits your style."

She shoved the gloves into the pocket of her apron. "I suppose wailing bagpipes suit yours."

He cocked a brow. "You have something against bagpipes?"

She only huffed out a breath, then gave in enough to sit. "Look, D.C., I don't mean to be rude, but—"

"You'd never be rude unless you meant to. You're too well bred. Nice smile," he commented, drawing quickly as he spoke. "Too bad you're so stingy with it."

"I'm not—when I like someone."

He only grinned. "See, you meant to be rude."

She couldn't help it. She laughed. But the laughter ended on a stutter of annoyance when he leaned over and plucked off her hat.

"It's shading your eyes," he said as he dropped it on the table.

"That was the idea." Puzzling over him, she leaned back. "Correct me if I'm wrong, but in my opinion you and I didn't hit it off in any particular fashion last night."

"So?"

She opened her mouth, shut it again. Ridiculous, she told herself, to feel insulted because he agreed with her. "So, what are you doing here, sketching me?"

"I like your face. It's strong, all-female. Sexy eyes and classy bones. I don't have to be attracted to you on a personal level to want to draw you."

"I appreciate your honesty," she said coldly.

"No, you don't. It ticked you off." He'd flipped over a page and started a fresh study. "That's female, too. Why get irked because we agree we're not each other's type? It doesn't mean you're not beautiful. You are. Turn your head to the left a little. You need to tuck your hair back."

He leaned forward to take care of it himself, skimming his fingers over her cheek. As he did, both of them went very still.

Her heart fluttered in her chest, continued to dance no matter how firmly she told herself it was a foolish, knee-jerk reaction. The gilded, filtered sunlight was suddenly too hot. Her throat was abruptly too dry.

"You've got great skin." He said it softly, slowly, as if the words were foreign to him. He trailed his fingers down to her chin, along her jaw, then down so that he felt the pulse in her throat beat hard and erratic.

He wanted his mouth there, just there, tasting that wild beat.

Simple, keep it simple, he ordered himself, and picked up his pencil again. Though he wondered how the devil he was supposed to sketch when his fingers seemed to have gone numb.

"I thought…" She had to clear her throat. "I thought you painted shapes—the modern school."

"I paint what appeals to me." His eyes stayed on hers as his pencil began to move again. "Apparently you do. On some level."

Relax, she ordered herself, and unballed the hands she'd fisted under the table. "You had a show in New York a couple of years ago. I didn't see it, but one of my friends did."

"That's all right. I don't do a lot of shopping in Drake's, but my mother does."

Layna chuckled, and the smile stayed in place long

enough to make his mouth water. "Well, I suppose we've exchanged subtle insults now. What next?"

"We could try a conversation. How do you like being back in Washington?"

"Very much. I've always loved this house, this area." She glanced back toward the pansies she'd planted. "I'm going to enjoy making a home here." Her brow creased. "What did you mean, plant them in a sweep?"

"Hmm? Oh, the flowers. More of a flow, less rigid lines. Something like what Monet did in Giverney."

"Yes, you're right." And her eyes went soft, her lips curved again as she imagined it. "I tend to follow directions exactly when I'm learning. You make fewer mistakes that way." She angled her head, and the dappled sunlight flickered over her face, turned it dreamy again, soft again. "But then you'd look at things with an artist's eye. And I don't imagine you worry overmuch about making mistakes."

"Not usually." But he realized he was worried about making one now, with her, here where the light was lovely, the music soaring and the air carrying just a shimmer of scent that was her, turned earth and young flowers.

"I do, so I plan things carefully and very rarely deviate." Something about him tempted her to make an impulsive turn, almost demanded it. And she imagined the trip would be just as wild and fast as the ride they'd taken the night before.

The kind of ride, Layna reminded herself, where a woman could end up crashing very abruptly, and very hard.

"I guess that's enough for now." He shoved his

pad in the bag. He had to go, before he did something stupid. Like touch her again. "I appreciate it."

"You're welcome." She got to her feet when he did, intending to see him out. But they only stood there, a bit too close for comfort.

"I know the way out." He took the first step back. He had a feeling if she walked inside with him he'd be unable to stop himself from doing that stupid thing. Like pulling her against him, taking a good long taste of that mouth. Then dragging her to the floor to take a great deal more of her while Chopin crashed around them.

"All right. Well...goodbye."

"Right." He picked up his bag, turned. He'd nearly made it into the house and away before he was compelled to turn back. She was still standing there, the sunlight on her hair, those misty green eyes watching him.

"There's a Dali exhibit at the Smithsonian. Opens Wednesday. I'll pick you up at seven."

No, absolutely not. "All right," she heard herself say, with some surprise. "That'll be fine."

He merely nodded and strode into the house. He made it to the front door before he started cursing himself.

Chapter 4

He thought of a dozen reasons to break the date. He'd have preferred to go alone, enjoy and absorb the exhibit. Then perhaps find an interesting woman to discuss it with. Over coffee or a late supper.

That was, D.C. reminded himself, the way he operated.

But he didn't break the date. Or the next one he found himself making with her. It baffled him that he enjoyed her company. It made absolutely no sense. She liked art to express something specific in tangible terms. She preferred her music subdued and her movies with subtitles.

They ended up debating half the time, sitting over steaming cups of espresso or glasses of wine. Somehow they'd managed to have three fairly civilized dates. He wondered if she was as surprised as he that they'd enjoyed themselves.

They were about to have a fourth. Four dates in two weeks, D.C. mused. It was…bizarre.

He stepped back from the canvas, frowned at it. He often worked in watercolors for a change of pace. He hadn't intended to do a portrait. The sketches he'd done of Layna had simply been an exercise. But they'd nagged at him until he'd given in and begun to commit the image to paper.

Watercolors would suit her. Cool tones, soft lines. He hadn't selected a sketch of her smiling. Again and again, he'd been drawn to his quick study of her looking straight ahead, mouth soft and serious, eyes aloof.

Frosty sex, he thought now. It was the expression of a woman who challenged a man to chip through the ice to the heat. And if he did, what then? Would it be a flash or a simmer, a slow burn or an explosion?

The wondering was maddening, D.C. decided. And erotic.

Painting her this way was both intriguing and frustrating. He had to know. He'd never bring that face to life until he knew what went on behind it.

When that realization struck him, his shoulders relaxed, his mouth curved up. Of course, that was it. That was why he kept going back. He wanted to paint her, and he couldn't until he knew her.

Pleased that the puzzle had been solved, he set his brush aside. He picked up his coffee, drinking deeply before he realized it had gone stone cold. With a grimace, he started downstairs to brew a fresh pot.

When his buzzer sounded, he switched directions and found his mother on the doorstep.

"I've caught you at work," Shelby said instantly.

"No, on a break." He gave her a hard, one-armed hug. "And now you can make the coffee."

"Fair enough. I promised myself when you moved back I wouldn't start popping in unannounced." She smiled up at him as they walked back to the kitchen. "But Julia sent me new pictures of Travis, and your father's not home. I had to share them with someone."

"Let's see."

He shoved unopened mail, a few dirty dishes and a sketch pad into a pile on the table. Shelby dug a pack of snapshots out of her purse and handed them over as she turned to hunt up coffee beans.

Her son, she thought, with an eye roll at the state of his kitchen, lived like the clichéd starving artist. But if it suited him, it was fine with her.

"Damn. He's great, isn't he?"

"He looks very much like you did at that age."

"Yeah?" Foolishly pleased, D.C. glanced up from his nephew's grinning face.

"Those MacGregor genes. Good blood," she said in a fair imitation of Daniel. "Strong stock. And speaking of The MacGregor, have you heard from him lately?"

"Mmm. Just a few days ago. He wanted to thank me for doing him a favor, then nag me to come up for a visit. Grandma's pining again."

Shelby laughed as she ground fresh beans. "You'd think he'd come up with a new one. To hear him say it, you'd think Anna sat around moping all day." Angling so that she could see D.C. as she measured out coffee, she cocked her head. "What favor did you do for him?"

"Layna Drake," D.C. answered absently, as he studied the snapshots. "Aunt Myra was badgering him about her—asked him to have me escort her to that deal the other night."

Shelby tucked her tongue in her cheek. "Oh really? And you bought that, did you? Foolish, foolish boy."

"Huh?" He blinked, then shrugged. "No, it's not his usual marry-the-girl-and-make-babies-for-your-grandmother deal. He doesn't think she's my type—told me straight-out it was a one-shot to get Myra off his back."

Shelby opened her mouth, shut it again. Very, very foolish boy, she thought, amused. "I see. And what did you think of her?"

"She's all right. Great face. I want to paint her."

"You—" Shelby nearly bobbled the clean cup she'd found in the cupboard. "You don't do portraits."

"Now and then." In fact, he was debating which snapshot he'd use to paint little Travis as a gift for his sister.

Once again Shelby decided to keep her mouth closed. Her son had indeed done some portraits. Of the family, she thought now. Of people who mattered most to him.

Just what, she wondered, did Layna Drake mean to him?

"You've asked her to sit for you?"

"No, I'm working from sketches."

"Then you've been seeing each other."

"Off and on. A few times." He glanced up. "Why?"

"Just curious," Shelby said lightly. "I know her parents slightly. She doesn't seem a great deal like them."

"And is that a good thing or a bad thing?" He moved his shoulders restlessly. "She doesn't have much to say about her family."

"Well." Shelby turned, leaned back on the counter. "I suppose I'd call them surface people. Lots of gloss. She has the polish, but there seems to be more under it. I prefer undertones, don't you?"

"Yeah." Appreciating the fact that his mother could always put her finger on the pulse, he grinned. "I'm working on getting down to them with her. I like her—haven't figured out why yet, but I do."

"She isn't your usual. That wasn't a complaint," she added with a laugh when D.C.'s grin turned into a typical MacGregor scowl. "Or a criticism. Just a comment that your usual choice of women lean toward the bohemian or the flamboyant. And she's neither."

"I didn't say she was my choice, I said I liked her." Now he grinned again. "And I'm told my mother was a flamboyant bohemian."

Shelby lifted her eyebrows. "I heard that somewhere. What ever happened to her?"

"She made it fashionable, and she's still the most important woman in my heart."

"Oh." Touched and delighted, she moved over to fold her arms around him, to rest her cheek on the top of his head. "I'm so glad you moved back, so glad, D.C., that you're here where I can pretend I'm not going to drop in on you."

"Dad pretended not to drop by yesterday." He wrapped his arms around her waist and squeezed. "Don't stop."

"Can't." She sighed. "But we won't hover."

"You never did. You were both just always there—even when you weren't."

"That's our job." She kissed the top of his head, then turned back to pour the coffee.

"Can I keep this one?" he asked, holding up a shot of Travis showing off his two teeth in a grin.

"Sure. Sketches in here?" Casually, she flipped open the book on the table, browsing through until she came to several studies of Layna Drake. "She's lovely," Shelby murmured, and a little part of her heart sighed. "You're very attracted to her."

"She's got a great face." When his mother's gaze shifted to his, held, he shrugged. "It's no big deal. Grandpa's right, she's not my type."

"Yes, The MacGregor rarely misses a step." Cagey old goat, she thought as she sat down to enjoy her coffee. He was probably already planning the wedding reception.

She decided then and there it was time to go shopping. She'd take a look at what Drake's was showing in the new spring lines.

Layna's assistant was all awed eyes and reverent whispers as she popped her head into Layna's office. "Ms. Drake, there's a Mrs. MacGregor to see you."

"MacGregor?" Layna glanced up from her sample book. "Shelby MacGregor?"

"Yes. The former First Lady. She's right out there. I couldn't believe it."

"Oh." Flustered, Layna ran a hand over her hair, scanned her office to be certain everything was in place. "Show her right in."

Layna rose quickly, smoothed her skirt, hitched at the line of her jacket, then rubbed her lips together to see if she'd chewed off her lipstick again. The answer was yes, but she didn't have time to dive for her bag and repair the damage. She moved forward with a smile as Shelby came in.

"Mrs. MacGregor. What a pleasure."

"I know I'm interrupting your work, but I was shopping and thought I'd just drop in for a moment."

"I'm delighted you did. Please sit down. Can I get you anything? Coffee, tea?"

"No, no, don't fuss." Shelby smiled easily as she surveyed the woman and her office. Tasteful, she decided, choosing a high-backed chair with a petit point seat. Cool but not cold, controlled but not rigid. "I won't keep you long. I was just browsing through casual wear. You have a lovely selection."

"Thank you. Of course, I'm already focused on next fall." Though puzzled, Layna smiled as she sat. "Plaid's the big news."

"That will delight my father-in-law. You haven't met Daniel, have you?"

"Yes, actually. My godmother wanted to visit and didn't feel up to making the trip to Hyannis alone. I went up with her for a couple days last fall. It's an amazing house, and your in-laws are delightful people."

"Yes, indeed." And the plot thickens, Shelby

thought. "Of all the grandchildren, D.C. most resembles Daniel."

And she saw it, that flicker in the eye, the faint rise in color. Oh my, Shelby thought. She's hooked.

"Yes, I suppose so. They're both a bit larger than life, aren't they?"

"The MacGregors are all a bit larger than life. They're demanding, charming, frustrating, generous. Being married to one, I can say that boredom ceases to be part of my vocabulary. And very often chaos becomes the key word."

"You must handle chaos very well."

"Oh, Layna, I adore chaos." With a laugh, Shelby rose. "I'd love to have lunch sometime."

"I'd like that, very much."

"Then I'll check my calendar and we'll set it up." Shelby took her hand, held it a moment. "When the man is larger than life," she began, "the woman has to be smart and clever. You strike me as a smart and clever woman, Layna."

"Ah...thank you."

"I'll call you," Shelby said as she breezed out. But first, she decided, she was going to call Daniel. After she'd blistered his ears for meddling in her son's life, she'd tell him she very much approved of his choice.

That, she mused, would throw the old devil off balance a little—long enough, she hoped, for D.C. and Layna to figure out they were falling in love.

Crowded, noisy clubs were stimulating. That was why D.C. enjoyed dropping into one occasionally. He could listen to the music, the chatter, watch the movement. Most of all, he could see the shapes of thoughts and emotions. When he sketched in a place like Blues Corner, he didn't sketch faces or bodies, but feelings.

Layna watched him, studied the slashes and splots and squiggles he drew on his pad. She didn't understand them, but they were fascinating just the same. Just like the man who created them.

He had kicked back and was lounging at their tiny table, shoulders braced against the wall behind them. He wore jeans and a black T-shirt, and had yanked his hair back with some thin string of leather. The lights were a dim, hazy blue; the tables around them jammed with bodies. On the stingy slice of stage a man with hair down to his shoulders plunked deep notes from a bass guitar, while another wearing tiny sunglasses blew aching tenor notes from a sax. A painfully thin young man caressed the keys of a scarred piano.

Seated on a stool was an old black woman with a face as wrinkled as a raisin. She sang in a voice like whiskey and cream about the miseries of love.

Layna didn't understand the music, either, though it pulled and stroked at something deep inside her. It made her sad. It made her want. For somehow the singer made the idea of love worth all the misery that came with it.

Layna sipped her wine, or what the club pretended was wine, and slanted a look toward D.C. He'd barely spoken to her since he'd brought her into this place. He looked like some kind of bohemian god— the tumble of rich hair, the ripple of muscle against black cotton and denim.

What was she doing there? What was she doing with him?

This was definitely the last time, she told herself. Absolutely the last. She couldn't have been more out of place.

Under the table her foot tapped time with the bass, and her heart was being torn to pieces by the slow and liquid voice of the singer.

"She's great, isn't she?"

"Yes." Layna waved absently as smoke drifted in front of her face from the next table. "But why does it have to be so sad?"

"The blues reach inside you, grab ahold of what's sinking your heart. Most times it leaves it lighter for it."

"Or shatters it," she murmured.

He looked over then, let his pad slide onto the table. "Music's supposed to touch you, affect you, bring on a mood or end one."

"Is that what you're drawing? Moods?"

"Yeah. And the music." He tilted his head. She'd swept her hair back tonight, twisting it into some sort of clip in the back. It changed her look, he noted. Added a hint of fragility. "What mood are you in, Layna?"

"A fairly relaxed one."

"You never look really relaxed. You know what you look?"

"No, but I'm sure you'll tell me."

"Perfect. Just a little too perfect. I've never seen you mussed." On impulse he reached out, and in one quick move nipped the clip out of her hair. "There, not quite perfect now."

"For heaven's sake." She skimmed her fingers through her hair in an attempt to smooth it, then made a grab for the clip. "Give me that."

"No. I like it down better, anyway." Grinning, he raked his fingers through it to disorder it again. "That's a good look for you. Just a little tumbled. Very sexy, especially with that bite of temper in your eyes and a pout on your mouth."

"I don't pout."

"You're not the one looking at your mouth." His gaze lowered to it, lingered there for one long moment. In one long moment her pulse began to shimmy. "I really like your mouth," he murmured. "In fact…"

"Wait." She pressed a hand to his chest. It was foolish, she knew. Hadn't she wondered why he'd yet to kiss her? Hadn't she wondered what it would be like when he did? Yet she found herself almost frightened, taking this minute to draw her defenses together, certain she would need them to survive intact.

"We've already done the waiting part." He closed a hand around hers, then cupped his other around the back of her neck. "We have to get to this sooner or later—see what's there. Or what isn't."

He lowered his head just enough to catch her bottom lip lightly between his teeth, to feel her breath shudder out.

"Let's see what mood we make."

He took her mouth slowly, wanting to savor and absorb. The tastes, the textures, the movement. Dark tastes, with a hint of cool, light wine. Smooth textures. Fluid movements.

More.

Her lips parted, in a quiet moan that vibrated under the weeping of the sax. He slipped his tongue between them, taking his time, and when she began to tremble, he shifted angles and lazily took the kiss deeper.

God, why had he waited so long for this? was all he could think. And drawing her closer, he steeped himself in her.

She was drowning, sliding down where the air was too thick to breathe and the music seeped into the blood and pulsed.

She hadn't expected this, not this. Gathering her defenses had done nothing to protect her from this endless and dreamy onslaught. Her mind clouded, and her body took over, a sweet and steady ache.

Her heart tripped once, then fell with barely a sound.

It cost him to draw back, to force himself to remember where they were. Her hand was still caught in his.

"Now what, Layna? Do we finish this, or do we stop it?"

"I don't know." How could she be expected to make a rational decision when her head was spinning?

"If you're going to leave it up to me…" His smile flickered, wicked around the edges, before he rubbed his lips over hers again.

"No, no, I'm not," she said quickly, pulling away. "We need to step back and look at the overall picture."

"What I see are two unattached adults who have a basic attraction for each other."

"I'm not sure what I see yet." More than a little panicked, she snatched up her purse, shoved back from the table and rushed outside.

Chapter 5

He caught up with her on the sidewalk, and was just churned up enough to grab her arm and spin her around. "Look, what's the problem? All you have to do is say, 'no thanks, pal, not interested.'"

She tossed her hair back, suddenly furious that it was messy. "No thanks, pal. Not interested."

"Liar."

"Jerk." She turned on her heel and strode down the sidewalk. It didn't surprise her when he fell into step beside her. It irritated, but didn't surprise.

"You weren't exactly fighting me off in there, baby."

She inhaled sharply, had to remind herself the sidewalk cafés were full of people. She would not, absolutely not, be pushed into creating a scene. "I was mildly curious," she said in a voice like January frost. "Now my curiosity is satisfied."

"Pardon me, but I believe I was involved in that same little experiment. You melted like butter."

"It was a simple kiss." Had to be, she told herself with a new sense of rising panic. She didn't want to feel what she'd felt, want what she'd wanted.

"A simple kiss is what you give your grandmother on her birthday." He hitched his bag to his other shoulder and asked himself why he was pursuing this. A lady put up a stop sign, you put on the brakes. End of story.

But damn it, he could still taste her.

"Layna."

This time she shook off the hand he put on her arm, then sharply turned toward home. "I will not be backed into a corner this way."

"You're making your own corners. If you'd just stand still a minute…" He swore when she only lengthened her stride. "Just hold it." He took both her arms this time, held her in place. And got a good look at her face.

Her cheeks were too pale, her eyes too dark. And there was more jittering in them than temper.

"You're scared. It scared you." He knew realizing it should make him feel sorry, but it didn't. It made him want to grin. "I figured you for more spine than that."

She jerked back, and for the first time in her life found herself actually tempted to strike another human being. "I have absolutely no interest in continuing the conversation. Now if you'll excuse me, I'm going in."

"We can end the conversation. Let's try this instead."

She saw his intention. Thrill wrapped in fear pounded at her heart. "I don't want—"

But his mouth was already on hers. No lazy exploration this time, no slow, smooth seduction. He possessed, then conquered, then devoured. Lights exploded in her head; heat swam through her blood. All she could do was hold on and ride that high and savage wave.

He hadn't realized he'd lifted her off her feet, that he'd lost himself in the taste of her, until he felt his heart ram brutally against his chest. He was always, always, aware of his size, of the strength of his hands. Now realizing he hadn't been appalled him.

He dropped her back on her feet, took two steps back. "Ball's in your court." He turned, strode away.

He cursed himself for days. Slept poorly at night. He talked himself into apologizing a dozen times, then talked himself out of it again.

It was best to stay away from her, he told himself. To let it go, let her go before they tangled themselves up again. Every time he came to that decision, he felt better. He'd work like a demon for hours. Then somehow she'd sneak into his brain again and leave him miserable, itchy and angry.

Nothing could have pleased him more than the call from his father telling him his grandparents had come down for a quick visit.

It would do him good to have an easy family dinner, he thought. To spend an evening with people he loved and understood. In fact, he could go back north with them. Spend some time with Julia and Cullum and little Travis, see some of his cousins.

He could toss a few clothes in a bag, pack up some canvases and paints and be on the road whenever he wanted to. That, he assured himself as he walked to his parents' home, was the beauty of his life-style.

It was simple, it was basic. It was his.

The last thing he needed was a woman clogging up the works. God knew women like Layna Drake were major complications. High maintenance, he decided, as the breeze fluttered and sent a shower of fading cherry blossoms flying.

Across the street a leggy brunette in bicycle shorts jogged along with a sleek black Lab on a silver leash. The dog barked happily; the woman gave D.C. a long, slow smile. He watched her long enough to note she tossed a look over her shoulder that radiated invitation.

And he cursed himself for not having the slightest interest in following up on it.

Leggy brunettes with slow, hot smiles had always been his style, hadn't they? So why the hell was he hung up on a cool blonde who never had a hair out of place?

A change of scene, he told himself, was definitely in order. He'd spend a couple of weeks in Boston and Hyannis Port, play with the kids, do some work and get rid of this ridiculous obsession over a woman.

He climbed the short set of stairs to the walkway. Vivid red impatiens were spreading on either side of the doorway. His mother would have planted them, he knew. She liked strong colors. They added a touch of flash to the dignity of the town house. Dignity and flash. It was a perfect description of his parents. It made him smile to think of it.

The potter and the politician.

Together they'd made marriage, home and family mean something. Mean everything, D.C. mused, then smiled again when he heard his grandfather's laugh boom through the open windows.

He didn't knock, but walked in. He smelled flowers and lemon oil, heard more laughter, and the murmur of voices from the parlor. His uncertain mood lifted and steadied.

So when he stepped in, he was totally unprepared to see Layna sitting knee-to-knee with Daniel, or the two of them grinning at each other.

"There's the lad!" Daniel surged out of his chair, moving with a speed that laughed at more than ninety years of living. His shoulders were broad, his hair a snowy mane that matched his beard. His eyes as they met D.C.'s twinkled blue with delight.

Daniel hugged him like a bear trap, thumped him on the back with sledgehammer blows and noted—with pleasure—that D.C. had yet to stop staring at the lass Daniel had picked out for him.

"About time you got here. These women have been pouring tea down my throat when any fool can see I need a whiskey. The lad wants a whiskey, Shelby, and I'll join him."

"Two fingers, Shelby, no more." Anna Mac-Gregor's quiet voice held authority. Smiling as her husband complained bitterly about a bairn being able to handle two fingers, she opened her arms to D.C.

"Grandma." He folded himself down until their

cheeks rubbed. As always, he found both softness and strength. And closing his eyes, breathed her in.

Layna looked away before it undid her. There was complete, unquestioning, unconditional love in that welcoming embrace. So much love it sparked both envy and need.

She didn't want to see it, didn't want to feel it.

"You look tired," Anna murmured when she cupped D.C.'s face in her hands.

"Been working." He kissed her again, then deliberately looked past Layna. "Nice to see you, Aunt Myra."

When he kissed her cheek, Myra made certain she had a good strong grip on his hand. "You remember Layna, don't you?"

"Yeah." He looked at her now, straight on, measuring. "How's it going?"

"Very well." Her hands wanted to tremble, so she kept them neatly folded in her lap.

"Sit down and keep Layna company, darling." Myra was up and nudging him to the chair. "I need to ask Daniel about…an investment," she improvised.

"I'm terribly sorry." Keeping her voice low, Layna struggled to fix a casual smile on her face. "I didn't realize you'd be here. Aunt Myra asked if I'd bring her to see your grandparents. We're supposed to stay for dinner, but I can make an excuse."

"What for?" He leaned back and wished to God he'd gotten the damn whiskey before he'd sat beside her. "It doesn't bother me."

That stung. She'd been suffering for days. "I don't

want to spoil your evening with your family. I realize
the last time—we were angry with each other."

"I got over it." He lifted a brow in challenge.
"Didn't you?"

"Of course." She lifted her chin, cloaked with
dignity. "I simply thought since you stalked off like
an irritable child you might be uncomfortable having
me here."

"As I recall, you're the one who ran out of the
club, like a scared rabbit." His lips curled in a sneer.
"You don't make me uncomfortable, Layna."

"Just look at them, Daniel." Myra spoke out of
the corner of her mouth as she pretended not to watch
the couple across the room. "You can practically see
the air sizzle around them."

"Don't know what's taking them so long," Daniel
complained. "Boy's just scowling at her. I tell you,
I worry about him."

"Oh, they've just had a tiff, that's all. It's just as
I told you, Layna's been sulking for days. I'm just
glad you decided to come see for yourself. This
might give them the next little nudge."

"I've got my work cut out for me." Daniel sighed
and sipped lovingly at his whiskey. "Don't you
worry, Myra, we'll have the two of them wedded and
bedded by summer." He tapped his glass against her
teacup. "You have my word on it."

And being a man of his word, Daniel didn't loiter.
He got to work on D.C. the minute Myra lured Layna
out of the room to look at Shelby's studio.

"Pretty young thing," Daniel said casually, and

pricking his ears for his wife's voice, pulled out a cigar. "Could be sturdier, though. Needs some meat on her bones."

"Her bones look fine to me." D.C. cocked his head. "If Grandma comes back in while you're smoking that, she'll scalp you bald."

"She won't catch me." Content, Daniel puffed out smoke and wiggled his eyebrows at his son. "Alan, I'll have a real glass of whiskey this time."

"It's not worth my head."

"Coward," Daniel muttered, but settled back with his cigar. "Myra's telling me the girl's too buried in her work just now. No social life."

"Her choice." D.C. shrugged, and catching Daniel's sorrowful look, sighed and handed over what was left in his own whiskey glass.

"You're a fine, respectful lad." Daniel sent his son a beetle-browed look that made Alan laugh. "At least we've got one here who isn't afraid of his poor old granny. Now, as I was saying…that young lass has Myra fretting day and night. Glad I got down to get a good look at her again, see what she's made of. Girl needs the right man beside her. A banker, I'm thinking, or an up-and-coming executive."

"What?" D.C. stopped sulking long enough to tune in. "A banker? What the devil are you talking about?"

"Why, seeing that Layna has some proper companionship. Happens I know a young man right here in Washington. He's already worked his way up to department manager. Good head on his shoulders has Henry," Daniel continued, pulling a name out of his hat. "Got a future ahead of him. I'll just give him a call."

"Hold on, just hold the hell on." Lurching out of his chair, D.C. stared at his grandfather. "You're going to call some stiff-necked banker named Henry and try to fix him up with Layna?"

"He's a good lad, comes from a nice family." Daniel blinked innocent blue eyes. "It's the least I can do for Myra."

"The least you can do is stay out of it. Layna's not interested in being bartered off to some banker."

"What a thing to say. Bartered indeed." As glee danced in his heart, Daniel scowled at his grandson. "I'm speaking of arranging a perfectly acceptable social connection between two young people." He jabbed the air with his cigar. "And if you'd concentrate on finding the proper woman for yourself, you wouldn't have time to get on your high horse about someone else's business. What's Layna Drake to you, I'd like to know."

"Nothing!" D.C. threw up his hands and shouted it, pleasing his grandfather enormously. "She's nothing to me."

"Glad to hear it." The boy's hooked good and proper, Daniel decided, and thought he'd just reel him in a bit more. "Couldn't be more ill suited to each other. You don't want to be casting your eyes in that direction, lad. What you need is a fine, sturdy girl, one who'll give you lusty babies and won't be worrying if her nail polish chips. That lass is too elegant for you, when you're needing more the earthy sort."

"I think I'm the best judge of what I need," D.C. said coolly.

Daniel got to his feet, shot D.C. a narrow-eyed stare. "You'd do best to listen to the wisdom and experience of your elders."

"Hah!" was D.C.'s response to that, and it took all Daniel's willpower not to laugh out loud and kiss his grandson with soaring pride.

He watched steely-eyed as D.C. stalked into the hall and shouted for Layna.

"What are you up to, MacGregor?" Alan murmured.

"Watch, see and learn, boy." He remained standing and stone-faced as Layna came down the hall. The ice in her voice could have frosted glass at fifty paces.

"What in the world are you shouting about?"

"Come on." D.C. grabbed her hand, pulling her down the hall.

"What? Let go of me."

"We're leaving."

"I'm not leaving."

He solved the problem in a way that made Daniel's heart swell with family pride. D.C. scooped her off her feet and carried her out the door.

"Now that's a MacGregor. He's—sweet Lord, here comes your mother." Daniel shoved whiskey and cigar into his son's hands and bolted for the side door. "Tell her I've gone to take a turn around the garden," he ordered, and escaped.

Shelby came in first, pushing a hand through her hair. "What's all the shouting?" she demanded, then scanned the room. "Where's D.C.? Where's

Layna?'' And her eyes narrowed. ''Where's your father?''

''Well...'' Alan contemplated the cigar, decided he might as well enjoy it. ''The best I can tell you is...'' He smiled, puffed on the cigar as his mother and Myra came into the room. ''My father told D.C. that Layna wasn't suitable, which naturally put D.C.'s back up—as intended. After snarling at The MacGregor, he carried a very annoyed Layna out of the house.''

''Carried her out?'' Myra put her hand over her heart as her eyes filled with romantic tears. ''Oh, I'm so sorry I didn't see. I just knew one more little push would...'' She trailed off as she caught the bland stares of her companions. ''What I mean to say is...hmm.''

''Myra.'' Anna puffed out a sigh. ''I can't believe, after all these years, you'd actually *encourage* Daniel this way. And you,'' she said to her son. ''Who do you think you're fooling with that cigar? Go get your father.'' She sat and serenely folded her hands. ''And then let's hear the whole story.''

Chapter 6

"You've lost your mind." Shock prevented Layna from struggling until they were out the door and heading down the sidewalk. Even when she snapped back, the best she could do was gape at him. "Put me down." She spoke calmly, certain that a raised voice would make things worse. "Put me down, D.C. Get a hold of yourself."

"It's for your own good," he muttered, striding down the sidewalk and staring straight ahead with grim eyes. "If I hadn't gotten you out of there, the next thing you know you'd be married to some banker named Henry."

She'd never heard a whisper of a rumor about insanity in the MacGregor family. Then again, she supposed, such things could be hushed up.

"All right, that's enough." Children were starting to point at them and giggle. A woman watering the petunias in her window box stopped to stare. "I told you to put me down, and I mean it."

"You're not going back there. You have no idea what that old schemer's got in store for you. First it'll be, 'I'd like you to meet my young banker friend, Henry,' and next you'll be picking out china patterns. He's ruthless."

"I will not be carted down the street like a parcel." Which, she realized, was exactly what it felt like. He'd marched down two blocks and wasn't so much as breathing heavily. He had arms, she realized—reluctantly—like steel beams. "Put me down and I'll forget this ever happened—forget you embarrassed me in front of your family and Aunt Myra, forget the inconvenience and the mortification. Most of all I'll forget you, you dunderhead."

"He's a sly one," D.C. continued, as if she hadn't spoken. "Sly and sneaky, and he's taken an interest in you now. God save you."

Her temper—and she felt she'd been admirably restrained in that area up to this point—snapped. She punched his shoulder, which did no more than give her sore knuckles. "What the hell are you talking about?"

"He did the same thing to my sister. And she's married with a son already. And my cousins, too. Three of them. Now he's got delusions of grandeur. Thinks he's some supermatchmaker. And he's got his eye on you, baby."

She hit him again, flat handed this time on the side of the head. As expected, it was like slapping granite. "Who are you talking about? Damn it, if you don't put me down—"

"The MacGregor, of course. Here, we'll talk about it inside."

"Inside?" She'd barely blinked before he shouldered open a door. "Inside where? I want you to *put me down!*"

"It's my place. Obviously you don't see what he's up to. Thousands wouldn't. You'll thank me when we straighten this out."

"Thank you? Oh, I'll *thank* you all right, Daniel Campbell MacGregor." The roaring in her head nearly blocked out the fact that he carried her onto an elevator. An occupied elevator. Hot color spread up her neck as the tidy middle-aged couple beamed at them.

"Hello, D.C., how are you?"

"Well enough." He tossed a smile at the woman as the couple stepped out into the lobby. "And you?"

"Just fine. Such a beautiful day."

Layna simply closed her eyes as the elevator door slid closed. Obviously, she decided, the man made a habit of hauling women bodily up to his apartment. His neighbors were used to it. Why be embarrassed when she was just one of a crowd?

"I think it's clear that your life-style and mine are dramatically opposed." She heard herself speak in a calm, clear voice, and blocked out the thunderous beat of her heart. "And though we have some family connections and live in the same neighborhood, I don't think it should be a problem to avoid each other from this point to the end of our lives."

She drew in a cleansing breath, let it out slowly.

"Now I realize I'm repeating myself, but I want you to put me down."

His temper had cleared just enough for him to become distracted by the way she smelled. Coolly, quietly sexy. And turning her head so that their faces were close, so that their mouths nearly brushed, was her mistake, after all. What was a man supposed to do but take a good, long taste?

So he did, easily fitting his mouth over hers, patiently waiting out her first jolt of shock, greedily absorbing her quick hot burst of response.

Missed you. He muttered it, or perhaps only thought it.

She turned into him, her hands fisting in his hair as her mouth moved under his. A low purr sounded in her throat and shot fire straight to his loins.

The doors opened, remained wide, then started to close again before he managed to think clearly enough to block the movement with his shoulder.

She dragged her hands through his hair, fisted them again to keep his mouth on hers. Her heart had gone wild, pounding some primitive beat through her blood. Need, outrageous need, clawed after it.

When he swore, tore his mouth from hers, her lust-hazed mind tried to clear. "What?"

"Trying to get the damn key." If he didn't unlock the bloody door, get her inside, he thought he might very well end up taking her in the hall.

"What?" she said again, then pressed her hands to her face as reason struggled to surface. "Wait. This is—"

"There." He shoved the door open, then simply

turned and kicked it shut with his foot as he crushed
his mouth to hers again.

"No, wait."

"We'll talk later." He drew back, barely an inch,
and his eyes, burning blue, stared into hers. "Now
we'll finish this."

"No, we'll…" She couldn't get her breath,
couldn't quite get a grip on that slippery edge of
reason. So for the first time in her life, she let it go.
It looked as if she was going to take that wild, fast
ride, after all.

"We'll talk later," she said breathlessly, and
dragged his mouth back to hers.

He had to get his hands on her. He set her on her
feet, braced her back against the door and moved
those wide-palmed artist's hands over her. She was
willow slim, graceful, extraordinary. Then, tugging
the sweater over her head, he traced the same path
with his lips.

Fast and greedy, as if a part of him feared she
would vanish or slip away. He wanted it all—the
balletic curve of her shoulders, the lovely female
swell of her breasts, the long, slender torso. Her skin,
smooth as satin, went hot under his mouth.

He took her hips, hitched her off her feet again
and began to steadily devour.

She cried out, her hands braced on his shoulders.
Somehow her legs had wound themselves around his
waist. Wild fists of need battered at her, pushing her
into a narrow world where the heat was brutal and
there was only one answer.

"Now. Right now." The raw words burned her

throat. Her fingers trembled as she yanked at his shirt. Desperate, she used her teeth on his neck.

Then they were on the floor, grappling, fighting with clothes, panting like animals as they groped for flesh. And flesh was damp, dewed with desire.

In a fierce and sudden move, he twisted, shifting her until they were face-to-face, torso-to-torso. His eyes were wildly blue as he lifted her hips. "Now," he said, watching her face. "Right now."

He filled her. She surrounded him. Time spun out, no movement, all sensation. Light poured through the windows, wide beams where dust motes danced. His heart pounded against hers, beat to beat. She tried to hold herself there, just there on that dangerous and delicious edge.

But her body craved more. She began to move.

She arched back, lost in the flood of fresh pleasure, moaning when he leaned in to lick at her skin, shuddering when his mouth closed hungrily over her breast.

As the pace quickened she rode with him, and gloried in it.

He couldn't get enough. His hands raced up her back, then down again. The taste of her exploded inside him and only heightened a craving for more. Every moan or ragged gasp brought him a fresh thrill. Then her nails bit into his back; her body arched back like a drawn bow. He was helpless to stop himself from tumbling over the edge with her.

He could have slept for a week. The thought slipped into his mind as he lay back, cushioning her.

With his eyes closed, his body blissfully relaxed, he
stroked a lazy hand over her hair.

Who would have thought, he mused, that there had
been a wildcat pacing around inside the coolly com-
posed Ms. Drake? He was delighted to have broken
the lock on the cage door.

She was appalled. Or she badly wanted to be. She
was naked, lying on the floor where her clothes were
scattered. She had just had crazed and mindless sex
with a man she wasn't entirely sure she liked.

Mindless was precisely what it had been, she admitted. Her mind simply shut off whenever he
touched her. She'd never in her life behaved that
way. Torn at a man's clothes, used nails and teeth
on his flesh, let him touch and take and take again
until she was biting back screams.

And she felt…fabulous.

Just a physical reaction, she told herself. She kept
her eyes closed, struggling to find her common sense
somewhere inside the glow that seemed to surround
her. She'd been celibate for…well, a very long time,
she thought. Her body had simply betrayed her con-
victions. She was human, after all, and susceptible to
certain basic needs.

And this…experience had certainly been as basic
as basic could get.

Now it was time to put things back in some kind
of order.

She cleared her throat and sat up. "Well." It was
the best her muddled brain could think of as she
reached for her sweater. Where in God's name, she
wondered, was her bra?

D.C. slitted his eyes open to study her. Her hair

was tumbled, her skin rosily flushed. "What're you doing?"

"Getting dressed."

"Why?"

The hell with the bra, she thought. She would not go crawling around the floor hunting for it. "I've never…I haven't ever… This was just sex."

"This was really great sex."

She drew a breath, braced herself and looked at him. She'd known he'd be grinning at her. And there he was, a huge, fabulously built male with a disordered mop of rich hair, impossibly blue eyes and a smug grin.

Her treacherous system yearned. The fascinating idea of crawling onto him and nibbling away flashed brilliantly in her mind. "I don't do things like this." She snapped it out and yanked the sweater over her head.

Cocking a brow, he sat up. "Ever, or as a rule?"

"Ever. This was just…spontaneous combustion, so to speak. As you said, we're single, unattached adults, so no harm done. But…" She started to turn to find her slacks, and his hands slipped slyly under the sweater. "I'm leaving." But her voice had gone weak.

"Okay." He scraped his teeth gently along her jawline, felt her tremble.

"We don't understand each other. We can't… This was a mistake."

"And you don't like to make mistakes, so we should try it again." He drew the sweater over her head, gathered her closer. "Until we get it right."

* * *

And just how, she asked herself, had she ended up in his bed? If you could call a mattress on the floor of a room stuffed with boxes a bed.

Stupefied, Layna stared up at the ceiling. She'd let it happen. She was responsible for her own actions—even for allowing herself to be seduced. She'd certainly been a willing participant and had no one to blame for the current situation but herself.

And what the hell *was* her current situation? She had no real experience with this kind of irresponsible, impromptu and reckless behavior. She was a sensible woman with a well-conceived, sensible life plan mapped out.

This kind of detour could only lead to sheer curves and sudden drops.

"I have to go."

Beside her, D.C. groaned. "Baby, you're killing me." Every time she claimed she had to leave, he was compelled to convince her otherwise.

"No, I mean it." She slapped a hand on his chest as he rolled on top of her. "This has to stop."

"Let's call it an intermission." Cheerfully, he kissed the tip of her nose. "I'm starving. You want Chinese?"

"I said I have to go."

"Okay, let's have pasta. More energy."

How could he make her want to tear out her hair and laugh at the same time? "You're not listening to me."

"Layna." He sat up, rolled his shoulders. It crossed his mind that he hadn't felt so relaxed and content in weeks. "We both know by now we're good in bed. And on the floor. And in the shower. If you leave now, we're both going to wish you were right back here in an hour. So let's just get something to eat.''

Because the sheets were on the floor, she grabbed a pillow and pressed it to her as she sat up. "This isn't going to happen again."

"Fettucini with red sauce okay with you?"

"Yes, that's fine."

"Good." He picked up the phone, punched in some numbers, then gave the order to a local Italian place that delivered. "Be about a half hour," he told her. "I've got a bottle of merlot downstairs."

He got up, tugged on a pair of jeans and strolled out.

She sat where she was for a full minute. She'd let it happen again, she realized. With a sigh, she pushed back her hair. All right, she would do the sensible thing. She'd go down, have a civilized meal with him and discuss the status.

Then she would leave and never see him again.

Chapter 7

"**Y**ou live like a pig." Layna sat in the kitchen, sipping merlot and sampling pasta.

D.C. merely grunted, broke a hunk of garlic bread in two and passed her half. "I keep thinking about getting a housekeeper, but I don't like people around when I work."

"You don't need a housekeeper, you need heavy equipment. How long have you lived in this apartment?"

"Couple months."

"You still have things in packing boxes."

He jerked a shoulder. "I'll get to them sooner or later."

"But how can you think with all this mess? How can you work?"

He flashed that quick grin at her. "My sister says it's because I was forced to accept order throughout a large chunk of my childhood. Somebody was always tidying things up in the White House.''

She arched an elegant brow. ''Don't you think you should be over that rebellious period by now?''

''Apparently not. You like things in their place, don't you?''

''Things were always in place when I was growing up. It makes life simpler.''

''Simple isn't always satisfying.''

''I think we can agree that we have little to no common ground. Which is why this…situation is a mistake.''

''Being lovers isn't a situation, it's a fact. And just because you like tidy and I don't doesn't have much to do with the fact that I want the bloody hell out of you.''

''We can't possibly develop a relationship.''

''Baby, we *have* a relationship.''

''Sex isn't a relationship.'' Brows knitted, she wound more pasta around her fork.

''Seems to me we had something next door to a relationship going before we had sex.''

''No.'' But it worried her because it was uncomfortably true. ''I don't want a relationship, not a serious one. I don't like what they do to people.''

''Oh?'' He might have cocked a brow casually, but his eyes had sharpened. Some underlayer here, he thought, that made her soft green eyes cool again. ''Such as?''

''People don't stick. And because they can't, they deceive each other, or ignore the deceptions.''

She hesitated, then decided the circumstances called for simple honestly. ''My family isn't good at maintaining healthy relationships. My parents have an arrangement that suits them, but it's not the kind of thing I'm looking for. The Drakes tend to be…selfish,'' she decided, for lack of a better term. ''Being with someone on a serious level requires a certain amount of compromise and unselfishness.''

''You had a rough childhood?'' he murmured.

''No. No.'' She let out a breath. It was boggy ground, trying to explain to someone else what you'd never fully understood yourself. ''I had a very good childhood. I had a wonderful home, opportunities to travel, advantages, access to an excellent education.''

D.C. shook his head. If anyone had asked him the same question, those items would have been bottom of the list. Even being raised in the fishbowl of world politics, he'd had love, warmth, attention and understanding from his family. ''Did they love you? Your parents.''

''Of course.'' But because she'd often asked herself the same question, she picked up her wine to wet her throat. ''We're not like you, your family. We don't have that…openness of heart, or that ease with displaying affection. It's a different way of being, that's all. Very different,'' she added, looking at him again. ''I remember seeing pictures of your family, you with your sister, your parents, on the news. You could see the devotion. That's admirable, D.C., it's lovely. But it's not where I come from.''

She would wonder later if the wine had loosened her tongue or if it had simply been the fact that he listened as well as he watched. ''My parents' marriage suits them. They lead their lives, together and separately. And they keep their affairs discreet.

Drakes don't court or tolerate scandal. I understand that, and I prefer avoiding entanglements.''

He wondered if she knew that her family made her sad, or if she actually believed that what she was saying, what she was feeling, was inevitable. ''You didn't avoid this one.''

''That's exactly what I'm trying to do.'' And she wasn't doing a particularly good job of it, Layna admitted. Not when she was sitting in his ridiculously messy kitchen, wearing his ridiculously ragged robe. ''It's like the flowers,'' she began.

''What flowers?''

''The pansies. My instinct was to plant them precisely. Just so.'' She used her hands to demonstrate. ''Because it was ordered, it was logical. Yours was to sweep them out, crowd them together, tangle them up. Maybe you were right—they look better your way, more creative. But I deal with things better if I have a specific plan.''

She was, he thought, so earnest just then. It made him want to snuggle her on his lap. ''But you can change plans when you see the advantage of a different direction.''

''And I avoid changing them if I see as many disadvantages. My plan is to concentrate on my career without distractions. I like being single. I like being solo.''

''So do I. I also like being with you. I don't have a clue why. You're not my type.''

''Really?'' Frost edged her voice. ''And what would your type be?''

Amused, he watched her as he enjoyed his meal. ''You're cultured, sophisticated, controlled, opinionated, with tendencies toward snobbery and aloofness." He continued to smile as her eyes flashed. "You could say my type's the opposite."

"You're controlling, sloppy, arrogant, with tendencies toward irrational behavior and selfishness. You could say *my* type's the opposite."

"See, we cleared that up." Unoffended, he topped off her wine. "But I still want you. I even like you, for some odd reason. And I damn well know I have to paint you."

"If you think that flatters me——"

"It wasn't meant to flatter you. I could flatter you," he said thoughtfully. "You'd have heard it all before, though, and I don't like to waste my time. You're a beautiful woman, and that restrained sexuality is compelling—it's damn near brutal now that I know what's under it. We're both free, healthy adults with a basic attraction for each other. We're acting on it. It doesn't have to be any more or less than that, unless we want it to be."

She said nothing for a moment. What he'd outlined was perfectly sensible. She couldn't have said why it made her feel afraid, and a little sad. "And if we continue to act on it, we'd both have to recognize the limitations."

"I don't like the word *limitations*." It irritated him to have her use it just then when she was sitting across from him in his kitchen, wearing the ancient and ratty robe his mother had given him for Christmas years ago. When the scent of the shower and the sex they'd shared was still haunting his senses.

"While we're sleeping together, we don't sleep with anyone else."

Both of her eyebrows arched now at the edgy tone of his voice. "I wouldn't call that a limitation, but common courtesy."

"Call it whatever you like. Nobody puts his hands on you but me."

"Just one damn minute."

"And if The MacGregor pushes Henry the Banker at you, you just toss him right back."

"I don't know anyone named Henry." Frustration began to surface again. "And I have no idea why you think your grandfather would push a banker on me. I don't need a new banker."

"It's a husband he'd be pushing on you."

She choked, grabbed her wine and drank hastily. "I beg your pardon?"

It gave him some dark satisfaction to see the baffled shock on her face. "I was going to explain it to you, before we got distracted. He's taken to you."

"Henry?"

"No, for God's sake, you haven't met Henry, have you? My grandfather."

Layna set down her wine, lifted both hands. "I'm confused. Your grandfather is a happily married man in his nineties."

D.C. narrowed his eyes. "You're not being deliberately softheaded. Let's try again. The MacGregor likes you—he thinks you're a fine young woman, and that alone is enough for him to decide you need to have a fine young man beside you. You need to be married and having babies. It's all the man thinks about, I tell you. He's obsessed."

"Well, he never mentioned anything of the sort to me. He did say something in passing about your grandmother fretting because you had yet to settle down and raise a family.''

"Hah!"

She jolted a little as D.C. slammed down his glass, then jabbed a finger at her.

"Hah!'' he said again. "There you have it. My grandmother has nothing to do with it. It's him. He uses that to guilt us into doing just what he wants us to do. And before you know it, you're buying diapers. I've seen it happen before. He focuses in on one of us at a time, like a project. Then he drops the perfect match into our laps, pretends he had nothing to do with it. My cousins are dropping like flies into wedding bliss, but it's not enough for him. As long as there's one of us left unmarried, he'll be at it. The man's relentless.''

She waited for the tirade to pass. "All right, I won't argue with you. You'd know him best. Though I really can't see that he could maneuver intelligent adults into making a commitment like marriage. But be that as it may,'' she continued as D.C. sputtered. "I have no intention of marrying anyone, ever. So it has nothing to do with me.''

"There's where you're wrong—and that's just how he'll get you.'' D.C. picked up his fork, wagging it at her before he scooped up more pasta. "He's taken an interest in you, Layna. It's a relief to me, as he's shifted his focus for a bit, but it's only fair to warn you. He'll be sly, just casually mention to you that he knows this bright young man. Then he'll find a way to arrange for the two of you to meet.''

"And this would be Henry.''

"It would. So you just tell the old meddler you're not interested in any Henrys."

She couldn't resist and smiled sweetly. "A banker, you say? I wonder if he's tidy. Did your grandfather mention what he looked like?"

"Oh, go ahead and joke. See if you're still laughing when you're talking to wedding coordinators."

"I think I can handle a little attempt at matchmaking. And I'm flattered that your grandfather would be interested in my future."

"And that's another way he wraps you up in a bow," D.C. muttered.

Layna considered for a moment, then pushed her plate aside, leaned forward. "So, this is the reason you went berserk, dragged me out of your parents' home and carted me down the street? All because your grandfather said he was going to introduce me to a banker? That sounds suspiciously like jealousy to me."

"Jealousy?" His eyes flashed to hers. "That's the thanks I get for looking out for you. Insults."

Coolly, she rose, took her plate to the already overburdened sink. "Just an observation."

"Then you need to have your eyes checked."

"Whatever you say." She waved a hand in dismissal. "Tell me, have you ever actually run this dishwasher?"

"I wasn't jealous. I was…concerned."

"Um-hmm." She slid her plate neatly into the rack of the empty dishwasher.

"If I'd been jealous I'd have threatened to break Henry into several small pieces."

"I see." Since she was there, and so were they,

Layna began to load the mountain of dishes into the washer.

"Then I would have hunted him down and followed through."

"Well, how exciting. Are you done with your plate?" She knew it was ridiculous, but she enjoyed the quick, wild thrill that whipped through her when he shoved back from the table and spun her around.

"I'm not jealous. I'm territorial."

"Fine. You use your term, I'll use mine."

He snarled, lifted her up to her toes, then caught the glint of amused challenge in her eyes. He felt his lips twitch, then let out a laugh. "The hell with it," he muttered, and was grinning when he kissed her.

But he wasn't jealous, he told himself later, much later, when he lay in the dark with Layna sleeping beside him. He was simply…protecting what he'd decided to take as his.

Temporarily as his.

He liked having her around, even though she'd browbeaten him into cleaning the kitchen before she'd let him talk her back into bed. He liked those cool, measured glances she gave him when they talked, and the hot, greedy stares she sent him when they were tangled up in sex.

He liked the sound of her voice. Cool again while they were discussing some point of art or music. Husky when she said his name in the dark.

And he was touched and sorry for the young girl she'd been who'd had so little affection and fun in her life. Advantages, she'd said, but to his mind she'd had very few of those. And that lack of stability and love had made her cross off the possibility of one day having a family of her own.

He found that terribly sad.

Not that he was in a hurry for such things himself, he thought quickly. But one day, certainly…when the time was right, the woman was right, he'd want a family, children, a house filled with noise and color. He couldn't imagine not wanting all those things.

And he thought that somewhere inside the woman who could smile dreamily over pansies lived a heart that wanted to open and share and be treasured.

He could still see the way she'd looked in his old robe, the ragged sleeves neatly rolled up, her feet bare, her hair brushed smooth, her mouth full and naked.

And that earnest look in her eyes as she'd explained to him why nothing could really begin between them.

Now she was curled beside him, wearing one of his T-shirts against the chilly spring night. They'd discovered at least one point of common ground. They both preferred sleeping with the windows open.

No, he wasn't jealous, he assured himself as he wrapped a proprietary arm around her and drew her close. He was simply enjoying her. For as long as it lasted.

Chapter 8

D.C. stepped back from the portrait and stared, stunned at what had come out of him onto the canvas. He had no false modesty about his work. In fact, more than once he'd been told that he carried an often-annoying confidence when it came to his art. He painted what he felt, what he saw, what he knew or wanted to know. It was a rare thing for him to turn away disappointed from a completed painting.

It was rarer still for him to be overwhelmed with something he'd created with his own heart and hands.

But Layna overwhelmed him.

He hadn't worked from a sketch, but from memory, a moment in time that had lodged in his head, settled there and had refused to be shifted aside until he'd re-created it.

He'd intended to work on another watercolor,

keeping the colors cool, the tone reserved. That was her image, after all. Her style. Her type.

But he'd found himself prepping the canvas for oil, choosing vivid tones, bold hues, sweeping strokes.

He'd painted her in bed, her bed. They'd spent more than a dozen nights together now, some in hers, some in his, and most usually in a frenzy of hunger he'd come to acknowledge baffled them both.

She looked back at him now, the eyes he'd painted were heavy, the mouth soft and faintly curved in female awareness.

Her hair was smooth and sleek. He remembered how she'd combed her fingers through it to straighten it—a habit of hers—as she'd sat up with the tangled sheets pooled around her. And she'd turned her head.

Why that single instant still lived so vividly in his mind, he couldn't say. That simple turn of the head, that hint of a smile, the way the lamplight had slanted across her shoulder. And she'd crossed an arm over her breast, not so much in modesty, he thought, but again in habit.

That moment of sexual punch, of quiet reserve, of casual intimacy refused to leave him. Out of it he'd created something more than he'd ever done before. It lived. It knew him, and even as he looked into it, it looked into him.

"Who the hell are you?" he murmured, shaken because he thought he'd known and was no longer sure.

With something close to fury, he tossed his brush down and stalked to the window. When had she gotten inside him this way? How had he let it happen?

And what the hell was he going to do about the fact that he was falling in love with a woman he wasn't even sure existed?

How much of what he'd painted was Layna, and how much was what he wanted from her?

He wasn't entirely sure of what he wanted from her, but he knew it wasn't just a body in the night. It had never been, no matter how hot the need.

She was already a part of his life, and he of hers, though neither of them seemed able to admit it. She'd nudged him into unpacking boxes. He'd bought her a flat of snapdragons and had pushed her into planting them willy-nilly along the border of her patio.

Then they'd sat, in the fragile light of dusk, and admired the results.

He'd bought a bed, a real one, then had let her convince him to go with the twisty brass headboard, though he'd feared it would look too feminine.

She'd been right—it had suited the room perfectly. And he'd enjoyed thanking her for her perception the minute the bed had been in place.

They went to the opera, a street fair, a ball game and the ballet. For some reason those mix of styles and tastes seemed to slide into a perfect union.

Impossible, he reminded himself. It wasn't the right time, and she wasn't the right woman.

Then he saw her, walking down the sidewalk in long, graceful strides. She'd changed from work, he noted. She habitually wore some trim and stylish business suit during working hours. Now she was in slim linen-colored trousers and a tailored shirt the color of ripe limes. She carried an enormous shopping bag with the Drake's logo. And looked both ways, he saw with reluctant amusement, before she crossed the street.

Even as he told himself he wanted to be alone, he pushed open the window and leaned out.

The sound had her glancing up, stopping. She lifted a hand to shield her eyes from the sun, and though she knew it was ridiculous, suffered a sharp sensory shock from the sight of him.

His shoulders all but filled the opening.

"Hello." She smiled and tried not to squirm. He was staring at her so intensely. "Are you still working?"

He hesitated, knowing if he said yes, she'd politely go back the way she'd come. They didn't tread on each other's working hours. "No, come on up."

She had a key. That was something else he suddenly realized had happened without either of them planning it. Like a man who'd just managed to reach the surface of a dream, he dragged his hands through his hair, rubbed them over his face.

He walked out to the head of the stairs just as she came in the door below. They stood, staring at each other.

God, I want you, was all he could think. *When is this going to stop?*

"I took a chance you'd be home and not busy." Her palms had gone damp and made her want to shift the bag from hand to hand. "I was just going to drop this off for you."

Oh help! her mind screamed. *I don't know what to do about you.*

"What is it?"

"A new bedspread." She worked to perk up her

smile. "Very simple, and masculine enough not to disturb the general ambiance of Army Surplus meets the East Village."

He lifted his brows. She'd already taken to ordering the place. It didn't bother him. He didn't mind living with tidy, as long as he wasn't required to do the tidying. "That's domestic of you. Bring it on up."

"It was on sale," she said, stiffly now. "If you don't care for it, you can use it for a drop cloth. Either way, it's better than that rag you've been using—though of course you never bother to make the bed."

When she reached the top of the steps, she shoved the bag at his chest. "You're welcome."

"I haven't thanked you yet. I would have if you hadn't been so busy lecturing me."

"That wasn't a lecture, it was a comment."

He dropped the bag and grabbed her hand before she could turn and march back down the steps. "Where are you going?"

"Home. And the next time I have an impulse to do you a favor, believe me, I'll resist it."

"No one asked you to buy me bed linens or wash my dishes or pick up fresh fruit at the market."

Fury and embarrassment waged a quick and bitter war, with fury edging out on top. "Point taken," she said with deadly calm. "And I'll be sure not to do so again. Or to drop by without calling, as I'm obviously unwelcome unless you're ready to jump into bed."

His eyes flamed. Temper clawed so viciously at his gut that he forced himself to take a step back.

"This isn't about sex." Unable to trust himself, he turned on his heel and stalked back into his studio.

"Oh, isn't it?" The hurt and anger were huge, pushing her forward and over the threshold of an area of his life where she'd yet to be invited. "What then?" she demanded, striding into the studio behind him.

"I don't know what then." He rounded on her, ready to fight, then found himself staring at her as he'd stared at her portrait a short time before. "I don't know," he said with a sigh, then turned back to the window. "You walked in on a mood, Layna." Wanting to clear his head, he braced his hands on the sill and leaned out. "I have a lot of them."

And this one, she thought, had suddenly shifted from irritable to unhappy. She resented the fact that she wanted to walk to him and soothe. It wasn't her job to soothe him, nor to tolerate his capricious tempers.

She told herself to go, to walk out and cross the last few weeks off her list as a learning experience. But instead she turned slowly and looked around the room.

He was everywhere in it, she thought. From the canvases leaning against the walls, to the absurd disorder of paints and brushes and jars. The scents in here were sharp—foreign and familiar. His scent—that combination of male animal and soap. Others that were turpentine and mixers and fresh paints.

It was a large room, filled with light. Filled with him. She studied canvases, streaks of color here, clashing shapes and textures. Another that was brooding shadows, and yet another that was bright and foolish and joyful.

She couldn't understand them, not really. But they made her feel. That, she supposed, mirrored exactly her reaction to the artist.

"Moods, yes, I see." She wandered to an easel. "You have a number of them. That would be part of what makes you what you are."

He turned back to study her studying his work. "And you, stable, balanced. That makes you what you are. What the hell are we doing together, Layna?"

This was expected, she reminded herself as she continued to stare at the canvas. That he would come to that conclusion after she had convinced herself it didn't have to matter, after all.

"I often ask myself the same thing five minutes after we're not." She shrugged a shoulder, determined to be practical. "It's just what we said from the beginning. Basic attraction. Physical."

"Is it?"

"This is." She gestured toward the canvas he'd completed only hours before she'd come into his life and changed everything. "This is all feeling, all passion. It's raw and dangerous and not entirely comfortable."

"It's *Need*," he murmured.

"Yes. Needs are met, and then they change."

"Even when you'd prefer it otherwise. Come over here." He held out a hand. "And tell me what you see."

She crossed the room, but didn't take the hand he offered. Touching him would be a mistake, she was certain, when they were coming to the end. And the ache in her heart was like a burning.

"Tell me what you see," he said again, and because she wouldn't touch him, he put a hand on her shoulder to turn her toward the canvas, and herself.

Shock came first, causing her to lift her arm, cross it over her body in a near reflection of the pose in the painting. Her heart stumbled, her throat closed.

"It wasn't what I expected to paint," he said quickly. "Or to see. Or to feel. I'd just finished it. Then I looked out the window and watched you walk down the street."

"You…you've made me beautiful."

"You are beautiful."

It was too…intimate, Layna thought with a flutter of panic. The woman in the portrait had no shield, no mask. And the woman he had painted knew things she didn't.

"I'm not like that."

"That's how I saw you, in that moment. Full of power and pleasure. It isn't what I meant to paint," he said again, "but it's what came out of me." He touched her cheek, then slid his fingers down until he cupped her chin. Lifted it. "It staggers me. Why haven't we burned each other out, Layna? Why can't I get enough of you and move on?"

"Was that the plan?"

"Damn right it was. It's not working. You're starting to worry me," he murmured as he lowered his mouth to hers. Gently, softly, barely a whisper of a kiss. It rocked her down to the bone.

"We should take a break from each other."

"You're absolutely right." His other hand lifted until he'd framed her face.

"We've been seeing each other constantly for weeks." She leaned into him, circled his waist. "We should ease back a little, take stock."

"Makes sense."

She sighed, rested her head on his shoulder. "That's not what I want."

"Me, either."

"I don't want to fall in love with you, D.C. I'm not equipped for it, for you. It would be a disaster."

"I know it." With his eyes closed, he rubbed his cheek over her hair. "How close are you?"

"Awfully close."

"Me, too."

"Oh God. We can't let this happen. It'll ruin everything just when—"

And his mouth was on hers, taking her away from reason, muddling her thoughts, driving feelings to the surface where she couldn't escape them.

"Just be with me, Layna."

This time it wasn't a wild ride but a dreamy one. There were no fierce bursts of heat, but shimmering warmth that trembled straight to the center of her heart. Not a seduction or demand, but a joining as he carried her from the studio and to the bed they'd chosen together.

Sweetly, patiently, with the afternoon sun beaming through the open windows, he touched her. And shattered any hope of defense.

Pleasure was quiet, natural as breath, gentle as the breeze that fluttered over her skin as he undressed her.

She reached for him, wanting more of this slow and sumptuous sensation, finding it as she drew him closer, as she lifted her mouth and opened it to his.

His warrior's body was familiar to her now—the bold muscles, the big hands, the wide, strong shoulders. But there was a change in the way he moved to her, moved over her that had her pulses beating thick and slow.

And it was more he wanted as well, more of this silky surrender, those lazy sighs, those long, long shudders. As she gave it, he took care, sliding her slowly to the peak, watching her face in the light as she trembled up, then glided down again.

He slipped into her, staggered by the depth of his own desire to give, his need to see those sea-mist eyes cloud and darken, to hear his name whispered.

He watched her, watched her, until his vision blurred, then he covered her mouth with his once again as body and heart shattered.

It wasn't the answer, she told herself, and stopped before she could follow instinct and curl up against him. If she allowed herself to feel this way, she'd be lost. If she didn't pull back enough to think, to plan, to remember what she wanted, she would make a mistake that couldn't be rectified.

She rose quickly and began to dress.

His eyes still hazed from what they'd brought each other, D.C. watched her. "Why are you doing that?"

She trembled once, fumbled with buttons. "We need to think this through. I'm going home."

"Layna. Stay."

"No, this is just confusing the issue, and it's all moving too quickly."

He rose himself, tugged on his jeans. "You matter to me."

Her head jerked up at that, her eyes swimming with emotions. "I know. I think... That's just it," she said with rising panic. "I can't think. I'm going to take a few days. This could very well be just a matter of mixing emotions into what was supposed to be a simple affair."

"Of course it is." He shoved his hands in his pockets. Otherwise he was going to grab her again, and that wouldn't solve anything but his own frustrated need. "Isn't that the problem?"

"I don't know what the problem is." That, she realized, was what frightened her the most. When she looked at him she forgot things—like her plans, her well-ordered, sensible plans. "But we both have some thinking to do before this...situation becomes any more complicated. We'll just stay away from each other for a few days, and cool off."

He leaned back against the wall, arched his brows. "And what if we don't?"

"We'll deal with that when...whenever."

"I want you, Layna."

"I know." And her pulse leaped hearing it, knowing it. "If that was all, we wouldn't have a problem."

"That doesn't have to be a problem. Wanting more doesn't have to be a problem."

"It is for me. I have to go. I have to think."

She was nearly to the door when he said her name, just her name, and stopped her in her tracks. She didn't turn around, didn't dare. And with a quick shake of her head, ran down the stairs and away.

He thought about going after her. He could catch her before she got outside. Talk her back into his apartment, drag her back, if necessary. Then take her to bed again. They didn't have any complications in bed.

And then what?

He swore, pushed away from the wall and stalked back to his studio. He avoided the window. He didn't want to watch her walk away. Instead he studied the two canvases. *Layna* and *Need*. And wondered how they had come to be the same thing to him.

Chapter 9

She didn't go home. It was odd, when she was so content there, that it was the last place she wanted to be.

Damn it, she'd been happy on her own, thrilled with her life and her work. Her ambitions had been simple and straightforward. She would make Drake's Washington a showplace, cement its reputation for the finest and most glamorous store on the East Coast. By doing so, she would cement her own reputation. Not simply another Drake, not just the daughter. But Layna Drake, in her own right, a savvy businesswoman with a sharp eye for fashion.

She loved the travel. Milan, Paris, London. She adored attending the top shows and working out the fine details of buying just the right lines, discovering new designers.

And she was good at it. Over the past few years

she'd honed her skills, developed her own style and had learned the business well.

Business made sense to her. People simply didn't.

Sighing, she slowed her pace. How would she know if she were in love? She'd never had to face anything like this before. The men she'd allowed into her life were suitable, they were easy, they were... safe, she admitted. Not one of them had ever tempted her to change her direction, to make compromises, to alter her plans.

And not one of them had ever touched her heart.

It was better that way, she assured herself. It had worked for her parents, hadn't it?

Oh God, she didn't want the hollow marriage she'd sprung from. She didn't want marriage at all—wasn't that the point?

Of course it was, she decided, drawing a deep breath. That was exactly the point. All she needed to do was distance herself from him, steady her emotions, and then she could slide right back into her life again.

She'd arrange for a few days off work, take a short trip to anywhere. Anywhere, she thought, finally turning for home, far enough away to prevent her from backtracking to his apartment.

Why the devil had fate put her only a few short blocks away from him?

"There you are!"

Layna's head snapped up, and she forced a smile into place as she saw Myra strolling up the sidewalk toward her. Automatically she closed the distance and kissed her godmother's cheek.

"I was just out for my evening walk," Myra began, "and thought I'd take a chance and stop by." She angled her head, her sharp eyes scanning Layna's face, noting the pale cheeks and unhappy eyes. "Oh darling, what's the matter?"

"Nothing. I don't know. Nothing," she said again, more firmly. "Come in. We'll have some tea."

"I'd love some." Myra slid her arm through Layna's as they climbed the short stairs to the trim walkway. "And while we're having it you can tell me what's made you unhappy. Or should I say who?"

"I'm not unhappy. I just have a lot on my mind." Layna unlocked the door. "Make yourself comfortable in the parlor while I start the tea."

"No indeed. I'll make myself comfortable in the kitchen and watch you brew the tea. Cozier." And it would give Layna less time to fortify her defenses, Myra thought. "Were you out for a walk yourself?"

"No. Well, yes, as it happens."

In the kitchen, Layna put the kettle on to boil, then chose a pretty Dresden teapot. She heated the pot first, as she'd been taught, carefully measured out Earl Grey. "It's a beautiful evening."

"It certainly is," Myra agreed. "Before much longer we'll be sweltering in the usual Washington summer. But May is a gentle month. Romantic. Are you having a romance, Layna?"

"I don't know what I'm having." Layna kept herself busy, setting out cups, pouring cream into a small pitcher. "I didn't want a romance. I *don't* want a romance."

"Why ever not?"

"I'm not equipped for them. Drakes don't deal in romance. They deal in business."

"What a ridiculous thing to say."

"Why?" Suddenly angry, Layna whirled around. "You know my parents, you know my grandparents. Can you sit there and tell me they had romantic, loving marriages?"

"No." Myra sighed and leaned back against the cushions of the pretty breakfast nook. "No, I can't. Your mother was a disappointment to me in that area, Layna. She married your father because she found him compatible, because she believed their life-styles meshed, and because she knew she would enjoy being Mrs. Drake. I won't criticize her," Myra continued. "She got what she wanted and made a life that satisfies her. And she made you."

"I'm not criticizing her," Layna said wearily. "I don't want what she has. I like being single. I like being in charge of my own life." She turned back to deal with the tea. "Marriage and children aren't in my plans. I like things as they are."

"Then why are you unhappy?"

"I'm just confused. But I'm straightening everything out now."

"Are you in love?"

"I don't understand love, Aunt Myra."

"It's not meant to be understood. It's meant to be felt, and celebrated."

"I don't want to feel it." Panic threatened, forcing Layna to level her voice. Her hands were steady enough as she carried the tea tray to the table.

"It frightens you?"

"Why shouldn't it? Don't you think my mother

felt something like love when she had an affair with her tennis pro? Or my father felt something like it when he went off on pseudo business trips with his administrative assistant?''

Myra puffed out her cheeks. "So, you knew."

"Of course I knew. About those, about the others. Children aren't nearly as stupid as adults want them to be. I won't put myself in the position of making a marriage, then cheating, or being cheated on.''

"Not all marriages are like that, darling. Herbert and I had over fifty years of happiness, of love, of faithfulness. I still think of him every day. Miss him every day."

"I know." Touched, Layna reached out and closed her hand over Myra's. "But you're the exception, not the rule. I see it all the time, on my buying trips. The little flings and quick deceptions. The carelessness of it. Or I'll watch a perfectly intelligent woman lose her direction, her sense of worth because she's fallen in love. It so rarely works."

"Fear of failure blocks any hope of success."

"Caution and practicality insure it."

"Oh." Irritated, Myra waved a hand. "You're too young to close yourself off this way."

"I'm old enough to recognize my limitations." Layna chuckled, soothed by her godmother's scowl. "And to be practical. I'm going to take a few days off, find a change of scene, and when I come back, I imagine both myself and the man involved will have realized we've taken this situation as far as it goes."

We'll see about that, Myra mused, and smiled into

her tea. "Well, that's handy for me. As it happens, I was coming by to see if you had any free time. I wanted to take a short trip up north, but I'm just not able to go on my own anymore."

Which was, of course, a lie. Myra Dittmeyer traveled as she pleased and traveled often.

"Actually, I was thinking—"

"I always hate to impose, but since you were planning on taking a trip anyway…" Myra smiled and struggled to look frail. "I get so tired and confused in airports these days. Then I'd have to hire a car and a driver. It's so simple when you're young." She sighed wearily.

"Of course I'll go with you. I'll arrange for the time off tomorrow. We can leave the next day if you want."

"You're so sweet to me. I don't know what I'd do without you. Oh, and you'll love spending a few days in Hyannis Port. Daniel and Anna will love seeing you again."

"The MacGregors?" It took all Layna's control not to choke on her tea. "Oh, Aunt Myra, I wouldn't want to impose on them."

"Nonsense. They'll adore having you for a few days. I'll take care of the tickets." She started to scoot out, reminding herself to move slowly. "I can still use a phone, after all. I'm so pleased you can help me with this, darling. At my age, one never knows how much time one will have with their friends and loved ones." She patted Layna's hand. "I'll just see myself out."

She continued to move slowly until she was out of the house, out of sight, then she quickened her pace. Her face was set in a determined smile; her eyes were bright with challenge.

Twenty-four hours to set things up, she thought. More than time enough—once she called Daniel and got him working on his end.

Daniel peeked out the window of his tower office and scowled. What the devil was taking them so long? He only had a handful of days to settle this matter, and he couldn't begin until the first of the players were on stage.

Oh, it was going to work out fine, no doubt about it. Better yet now that his grandson Duncan had flown up for an impromptu visit. Bless the boy, he was just the hammer needed to nail D.C. into place.

The fates were smiling on this particular scheme. And why shouldn't they? he'd like to know. It was a fine scheme, a loving one. Not that he intended to take a bit of credit for it.

And if things went well, he'd just keep his part in it nice and quiet. His family tended to become irritated at the oddest things.

"Grandpa? You up there?"

Daniel rubbed his hands together in anticipation and turned to smile as his daughter's second son strolled in. A fine looking boy, Daniel thought. Tall and dark like his father, with his grandmother's deep brown eyes and his mother's sassiness.

And, he thought with pride, his grandfather's knack for gambling.

He had plans for young Duncan, oh indeed, he did. But one thing at a time.

Duncan angled his head and flashed his quick and cocky smile as he sniffed the air. "What, no cigar?"

Instantly, Daniel pokered up. "I don't know what you're talking about."

"No." Wise to the ways of The MacGregor, Duncan sat in the deep chair across from the desk, stretched out his long legs and slipped a cigar out of his pocket. Watching Daniel, he ran it under his nose, drawing in the scent.

"Now then." Daniel's face glowed with a delighted smile. "There's a lad."

"It's mine." Duncan clamped the cigar between his teeth, his shrewd dark eyes dancing. "But I might share if you tell me what the hell you're up to."

"I'm not up to a thing. Just waiting to greet my oldest and dearest friend, and her goddaughter."

"The goddaughter." Duncan took the cigar out of his mouth and pointed with it. "Who, I'm sure, is single, of marriageable age. Strong stock, Grandpa? Good blood?"

"And if she is?"

"I'm not interested."

Better and better, Daniel thought, and smiled slyly. "She's a fine lass, Duncan. Pretty as a picture. You'd make fine babies between you, which is something you should be seeing to. Boy of your age—"

"Just put it out of that canny mind of yours, MacGregor." Duncan popped the cigar back in his mouth, pleased to have seen through his grandfather so quickly and easily. "I'm happy just as I am—and I'm having a fine time sampling pretty ladies. I can find my own woman."

"And you've been finding too many of them, puttering around on that gambling boat. Up and down the river, going nowhere.''

"Have you seen the latest accounts? The *Comanche Princess* is a very profitable lady. And the only one who holds my heart."

"Aye, I've seen them. You know what you're about, Duncan Blade, but what you need is a wife beside you and babies at your feet. Now this lass who's coming to visit has a good head for business herself. I expect to see…'' He trailed off as a movement outside caught his eye. "Ah,'' he said as he turned back to the window. "Here they are now. You go down and make your how-do-you-dos." Daniel wiggled his brows. "And see if I haven't picked out a fine one for you."

"I'll go down." Duncan unfolded himself lazily. "But don't buy the orange blossoms." He held out the cigar, then grinning, wiggled his fingers, twisted his wrist and made it vanish before Daniel could take it.

"Smart aleck," Daniel muttered, then grinned fiercely as Duncan walked out. "You're just what we need to get your cousin moving."

Humming the wedding march, he went down to greet his guests.

It couldn't have been more perfect, Daniel decided a few hours later. Duncan fell easily into pattern and flirted charmingly with Layna, made her laugh. It was a fine thing, too, that they were easy together, as they'd be cousins before much more time had passed.

He expected his family to be a loving and happy one.

"Duncan, take the girl out in the gardens. You like flowers, don't you, lass? We've fine ones." Daniel continued beaming at Layna. "They show off particularly well at sunset."

"He's right about that." Duncan rose, sparing one withering look for Daniel before turning to smile at Layna. "Want to walk?"

"I'd love to. Thanks."

Anna waited until they'd gone out the side door, then leaned forward in her chair. "You can get that smug look off your face, Daniel. Those children aren't the least bit interested in each other in the way you'd like. And they couldn't be less suited."

He barely resisted winking at Myra when his old friend muffled a chuckle. "They look fine together."

"Of course they do." Exasperated, Anna threw up her hands. "They're both attractive young people, but your meddling's doomed to failure this time. And if you try to push those two together, Daniel, I'll stop you." She lifted a finger before he could bluster. "They're not right for each other. Any fool can see that poor girl isn't happy."

"Well, she'd be happy enough if she wasn't so stubborn." Daniel sniffed. "Needs to think with her heart for a change—like someone else I knew more than sixty years ago. And we'll see if she isn't smiling when she leaves here in a few days."

After those sixty plus years, Anna knew when to stop beating her head against the stone wall of Daniel's determination. She turned to her friend. "Myra, surely you can see that this is a mistake for Layna."

"I just want her happy, Anna. The child is just waiting to open her heart."

"Not to Duncan," Anna said firmly. "You saw for yourself the way she and D.C. looked at each other. If she's not in love with him, she's well on the way—and the two of you shoved them together hardly more than a month ago. Putting Duncan, who can charm the stars from the sky, in her way just now is a disaster waiting to happen."

At Myra's burst of laughter, Anna's eyes narrowed. She took a deep breath and shifted her gaze from her husband to her friend. "Oh, what have the two of you done?"

"Just set a stage, so to speak," Daniel told her. "And D.C. will be walking onto it tomorrow."

"D.C.'s coming?" Anna shut her mouth, sat back, considered. Then she nodded. "Good."

"Good?" Having braced for a lecture, Daniel goggled at her. "Good, you say?"

"Yes, I do. For once I agree with you. Though I don't approve of your tactics, Daniel, and we'll discuss that later." A smile tugged at her lips. "It's going to be a very interesting couple of days."

Chapter 10

The last thing D.C. expected to see when he stepped out of his car in front of the fortress The MacGregor had built on the cliffs over the restless sea was his cousin with his arm slung companionably around Layna's shoulders.

The misery that had dogged him all along the trip north turned abruptly and viciously to bright green fury.

Layna's hair was windblown, her cheeks flushed. He imagined they'd just come from a walk on the cliffs, and the image infuriated him. Even as he watched them, Layna stopped, stared, and that pretty color that had glowed in her cheeks drained.

"Hey." Delighted, Duncan grinned and moved forward to give D.C. a hard hug and a slap on the back. "I didn't know you were heading up."

"Obviously. What the hell is this?" His eyes, sparking with blue fire, stayed on Layna.

"I—I came up with Aunt Myra for a few days. I had no idea you'd be here."

"You left town without a word."

"I said I was going to take a few days."

"I didn't know where the hell you were."

"It was a quick decision." She straightened her shoulders. "My decision."

"I take it you two know each other," Duncan put in.

"Shut up. This is between me and Layna."

"There's nothing between us," she shot back. "Excuse me, Duncan." She turned and rushed up the steps.

"Got a minute?" Duncan asked, neatly stepping into D.C.'s path before his cousin could bolt after Layna. The picture had snapped clear in his mind. *Grandpa, you wily old bastard,* he thought with amused affection, and decided the least he could do was play out his part.

"Get out of my way." D.C.'s hands fisted at his sides. "And keep your hands off her or I'll break you in two."

Duncan lifted a brow and his smile turned sharp. "Oh, we can go around, D.C. We've been there before. But why don't we make sure we know why we're pounding on each other first?"

"She's mine." He jabbed a finger into Duncan's chest. "That's all you have to know."

And that, D.C. realized, was all he'd had to know himself. She was his. That was that.

"Really? Didn't look to me like she knew that. I

guess Grandpa doesn't know it either, since he's picked her out for me." It would be worth a sore jaw, Duncan thought as he watched D.C.'s teeth clench, to see his cousin on the hot seat for a while.

"The hell he did."

"He thinks we'll suit," Duncan said easily. "He could even be right. She's gorgeous, smart, easy to talk with. Then there's that sexy laugh." He barely blinked when D.C. grabbed him by the shirtfront and hauled him to his toes. It would be wise, Duncan supposed, to remember his cousin outweighed him by a good thirty pounds.

"Have you touched her?"

"I don't generally paw women I've known less than a day. But if you want to put up the boundaries, cousin, you'd better do it fast. You want to put the moves on her, fine, just—"

He had the rest of the words shaken back down his throat, and wondered if playing his grandfather's game was going to land him in the hospital.

"I'm not putting moves on her, you stupid son of a bitch. I'm in love with her!"

"Why the hell didn't you say so?" Duncan shouted back at him, and noting that his cousin looked as though he'd just suffered a blow to the head, he shoved his way free.

"I just figured it out."

"You'd be smarter to tell her than to stand here fighting with me over it." Duncan brushed a hand down his shirt to smooth it. "I'm a damn innocent bystander."

"Fighting with you is easier." Jamming his hands in his pockets, D.C. stalked into the house.

He found them in what the family called the Throne Room in honor of the huge chair where Daniel sat to preside over gatherings. It appeared this gathering was a very civilized afternoon tea. The moment he strode in, fury still vibrating around him, his grandmother rose and hurried toward him.

"D.C.! What a lovely surprise. It's so good to see you."

"I told Grandpa I was coming up to paint for a few days."

"That you did." Daniel beamed fiercely from his chair. "Forgot to tell you, Anna. All this excitement. Well, come in, come in. Maybe now that you're here these women will let me have some whiskey in my tea. Where's your cousin?"

"Outside. Layna, I'd like to talk to you."

She had her composure back, barely. "Certainly," she said, and continued to sip her tea.

"Privately," he said between his teeth.

"It's not convenient now. Mrs. MacGregor, these scones are marvelous."

"Thank you. They're one of our cook's specialties." Anna rolled her eyes at Daniel before she took her seat again. "D.C., they're your favorite. Shall I fix you a plate?"

"No, I don't want anything. That's wrong—I do. I want something very much. Layna, will you come outside with me, or am I going to have to carry you out?"

She sent him a level look over the rim of her cup. The bite D.C. loved was back in her sea-siren eyes. "I suggest you sit down and have some tea. When we're finished, if you have something to say to me, I'll be happy to listen.''

"You want me to sit down and have tea? You want me to sit down and have a nice cup after I come across you hanging all over my cousin?"

She set her cup down with a snap. "I was not hanging all over anyone."

"I'm forced to agree," Duncan said in cheerful tones as he strolled in. "But I had hopes. Scones?" Delighted, he pounced on the tea tray and helped himself.

"I told you to keep out of it, or I'll break that pretty face of yours."

Shocked, Layna gaped, then surged to her feet as Anna calmly poured more tea. "How dare you cause a hideous scene, threaten Duncan, embarrass me and upset your family this way?"

"Let him have it, lass," Daniel shouted, thumping a fist on the arm of his chair.

"I wouldn't have caused a scene, threatened, embarrassed or upset anyone if you'd come outside when I asked you to. It's your hard head that's put us here in the first place."

"Now we'll add insults." Eyes slitted dangerously, Layna stepped forward. "I wouldn't be here if I'd known you were coming. And since this is your family home, I'll be the one to leave."

"You're not going anywhere until we finish this."

"There, we agree. Excuse us," she said grandly, then stalked out of the room.

"Outside," D.C. muttered, grabbing her arm to steer her to the door.

"Take your hands off me, I can get there on my

own.'' She jerked free, then yanked the door open herself. "I thought you'd already humiliated me as much as anyone could be humiliated. Now I see I was wrong. You've topped it.''

She kept going, stalking over the long slope of yard, unaware that inside the house four people had made a beeline for the windows.

"You're humiliated? You? How do you think I felt when I come to visit my grandparents and find you snuggled up with my cousin?''

She whirled on him. "In the first place, I was not snuggled up with anyone. I was having a perfectly innocent walk with a very nice man. And it's none of your business what I do and with whom I do it.''

"Think again, baby,'' he said much too quietly.

"I have thought, which is exactly what I told you I intended to do. And I've decided that whatever we'd started between us is going to stop.''

"In a pig's eye.'' He snatched her up, fisted a hand in her hair to yank her head back, and took out his frustration on her mouth.

"We shouldn't be watching this,'' Anna murmured, even as she shifted at the window for a better view.

"Ah, but look at them, Anna.'' With a tear in the corner of his eye, Daniel draped an arm over her shoulder. "It couldn't be more right.''

"He's hooked,'' Duncan muttered, and bit into another scone. "Pitiful.''

"Your time's coming, laddie,'' Daniel warned.

"Not if I can help it.'' Confident in his evasive skills, Duncan polished off the scone and watched his cousin take the fall.

The kiss changed, heat sliding into warmth. A warmth that undid her. "Don't." Even as she murmured it, Layna skimmed her hands over his face. "Don't do this. It's not the answer."

"It is when my heart's in it. Layna." He rubbed his cheek against hers. "Can't you see you're holding my heart?"

Because suddenly she could see it, right there in his eyes, her own heart stuttered. "I can't do this. I don't know how. It changes everything. Let me go, D.C."

"I thought I could. I wanted to be able to." He did release her, so that they could stand facing each other. The wind whipped through his hair, sent it dancing. "Do you think you're the only one who had plans, who thought they knew exactly where they wanted to go and how to get there? I didn't want this. I didn't want you. Now there's nothing else but you."

"It can't work. It was fine as long as we just wanted each other. As long as it was that simple."

"There's nothing simple about the way I want you. And if you felt that way, why are you crying?" He reached out, his big hand painfully gentle, to brush a tear from her cheek. "I'm holding your heart, too. I won't hurt it."

"You can say that, you can believe that because of what you come from. Your family is so lovely, so loving. Mine's empty. It's a name, it's a way of living."

"You're not your parents."

"No, but—"

"And neither of us are exactly the same people we were when we met, are we?"

She crossed her arms over her chest, gripped her forearms. "No, no, we're not."

"We've already started to make compromises, to build something together. We've already let each other in, Layna. We didn't notice it right off because it was right. It was just right. I love you." He cupped her face gently. "You can look at me and see that."

"Yes." It thrilled, and it terrified. "I want you, too, so much. But what if it doesn't work, if I can't make it work?"

"What if you walk away now and we never try?"

"I'd be back where I thought I wanted to be." She drew a deep breath, let it out slowly. "And I'd be incredibly unhappy. I don't want to walk away from you, or from us."

Joy shimmered just under his heart, and his lips curved. "Then take that walk with me." He closed his hand over hers, linked fingers. "We won't always want to go in the same direction, or at the same pace, but we can end up where we both need to be."

She looked down at their hands. So different, she thought. Hers narrow, his wide; hers almost delicate, his so strong. But look how they fit together.

"I've never been in love." She lifted her gaze, looked into his eyes. "I could always stop it. It never interfered, because I wouldn't let it. But I couldn't stop it with you. It made me so angry, so unsettled that I wasn't able to just step back and say that's far enough. But it's not far enough." Her fingers tightened on his. "I want to go a lot farther."

He lifted their joined hands to his lips. "No one

mattered before you. Marry me. Let's make a life together."

"I think we've already started to." She brought her free hand to his cheek. "It just took a while for me to realize it's exactly the one I want."

"I'd say that's a yes."

Her smile bloomed. "I'd say you're right." She laughed when he scooped her off her feet and spun her in circles.

"Let's tell the family." D.C. kissed her, hard and long, then spun her around again. "It'll do The MacGregor good to see he can't maneuver all his grandchildren into taking the matches he picks out for them. Not my type," D.C. said. "Hah!" And kissed her again.

Inside, Daniel wiped a tear from his eye.

From the Private Memoirs

of

Daniel Duncan MacGregor

*Seasons come and go more quickly af-
ter a man reaches an age. Spring moving to summer so fast you hardly see
the tulips bloom before they fade away
again. Without family, without the love
of them, the passing of time would be
a kind of loneliness.*

I'm a man who's never lonely.

*I'm grateful for that fact every day of
my life. For the fine woman who's spent
all these passing seasons with me, for
the children we raised, the babies
those children gave us. And I realized—*

better than most, I think—that when a man's been given such gifts, he's responsible for caring for them.

Just yesterday I stood in the church where my oldest son married and watched his son meet his bride. Seasons pass, and generations with them almost as quickly. I know what my boy felt watching his boy take that next step in life. The pride, the bittersweet loss, the hopes for the future.

Well, I could have told my Alan he's no need to worry about the future of D.C. and Layna. I'd chosen them for each other, hadn't I? Not that we'll mention that outside the hearing of a few select ears. My grandson can have his smug belief that he did the deed all on his own. He'll be a better man for it, I imagine.

A fine couple they made, the prettiest of pictures as they exchanged their rings in candlelight, D.C. looking more than a bit, I'm thinking, like his grandfather did sixty years back, and Layna elegant with the MacGregor tartan on her dress and the MacGregor veil over her golden hair.

The babies they'll make for me—well, for their grandmother, of course. She's already making noises about it. The woman has no patience.

Now that we've seen them off on their honeymoon, and seen the bond between them, we'll leave them to start to build their life together.

Today I walked on the cliffs with my Anna. Below us the sea tossed, as restless as ever, and above, the sky was a clear summer blue. I felt the wind on my face and Anna's hand in mine.

Many's the time we've walked that walk together.

From the cliffs I could see the house we'd built. Some call it a fortress, or a castle. And it's some of both those things. A bold place it is, made of good native stone, with proud towers and strong lines and the crest of my clan over the front door. A man doesn't forget his roots.

But most of what it is is home. The place Anna and I fought our battles, made love—and our children. Where we raised them and watched them grow. It's a home we share still, though the children have children, and some of them have children of their own.

Thanks to me, of course.

I'm happy to have set those who belong to me on the right path. Home and family. Whatever a man, or a woman, makes in this life, that is the base, the foundation of everything else.

So where are the rest of my great-grandchildren, I'd like to know?

Not that we haven't made some progress there, but a man can't live forever. Not even a MacGregor. I've seen five of the children of my children wedded now. And the babies I—that is, Anna—frets for are coming along. We have four bairns to fuss over, and two more on the way. And a joy they are to us—if only they'd visit more often.

But children must have their own lives, after all. That's what I'm seeing to. In my own fashion.

I'm arranging for young Duncan—the second son of my lovely Serena and our handsome Justin—to make his life. Oh, the lad thinks he has one, and just the way he wants it, too. Sailing up and down the Mississippi on his gambling *boat, free as a bird. Oh, a clever boy is Duncan Blade, and a charmer as well. He runs the* Comanche Princess *with a steady hand, for there's good business sense behind that quick, sly smile. And woe to the man who sees only a pretty face and crosses him, by God. The boy carries MacGregor blood, after all.*

No prim, shy miss would do for him. He needs a woman with grit, someone with sass. And I've just the one.

All I've done—to respond to those who would call me a meddler—is put them together for a time. Just as I did the boy's mother and father so many years back. Makes me sentimental to think of it. And it's like a circle closing, isn't it, to give my daughter's son the same opportunity?

We'll see what he does with it.

And if he doesn't do it fast enough, why, I believe Anna and I might enjoy a few days on the river. I'm a gambling man myself.

Part Two

DUNCAN

Chapter 11

Duncan Blade played the odds. Whether they were long or short didn't matter, as long as he knew them, and the pot was rich enough.

And he was a man who liked to win.

Gambling was in his blood, both from the MacGregor Scot and the Comanche Blade. Nothing suited him better than running the *Comanche Princess*. That in itself had been a gamble. His parents had dealt in hotels, of the stationary sort, all of his life. Atlantic City, Vegas, Reno and more. The riverboat had been Duncan's dream, one he'd conceived, planned and nurtured. He understood his family trusted him to make it work.

He had no intention of disappointing them.

From the docks in Saint Louis, he stood, hands tucked in his back pockets, and studied his true love.

The *Princess* was a beauty, he mused, with long,

graceful lines, wide decks and fussily fashioned railings. She had been built to replicate the traditional riverboats that had once steamed up and down the river, carrying passengers, supplies—and gamblers. Her paint was fresh and blindingly white, her trim a hot and sassy red. Beneath the charm was power. And along with the power was luxury.

Duncan wanted his passengers relaxed and happy. The food would be plentiful and first class, the entertainment top of the line. Cabins ran from cozy to sumptuous. Each of the three lounges provided stunning views of the river.

And the casino…well, the casino was, after all, the heart of it all.

Passengers paid for the ride—and for the chance to win.

The *Princess* would sail from Saint Louis to New Orleans, with stops along the way in Memphis and Natchez. Those who chose to stay on board for the full two weeks from north to south and back again wouldn't be bored. And whether or not they disembarked as winners, Duncan knew they'd have gotten their money's worth.

For now, he had the anticipation of another run. Around him, crew worked to load cargo and supplies in the blistering July heat. He had paperwork to do, details to check, but he wanted to take this moment to watch the action. On board, more crew members were swabbing decks, freshening paint, polishing brass and cleaning glass.

The *Princess* would sparkle by late afternoon, delighting the passengers who streamed up the gangplank.

Everything was in place. Almost.

Behind the amber lenses of his shaded glasses, his deep brown eyes narrowed. The new headliner he'd contracted had yet to show. She was now nearly twenty-four hours late. And if she didn't make it within another four hours, they'd be preparing to sail without her.

Annoyed with having his enjoyment of the moment spoiled, Duncan pulled the flip phone out of his pocket and once again called Cat Farrell's agent.

He paced the docks as he waited for the connection, his strides long and loose. His looks bespoke his heritage—tall and dark with dark gold skin, eyes of deep brown heavily lashed and lidded, and the straight black hair of his Comanche ancestors. His face was narrow, sculpted with high, sharp cheekbones and a long straight nose. The mouth was firm and full, and given to quick smiles.

But he wasn't smiling now. "Cicero? Blade. Where the hell is my talent?"

Brooklyn jangled through the receiver as Cicero whined an answer. "She ain't there yet? Hey, I'm telling you, the kid's reliable. Something slowed her up, that's all. She'll be there, and she'll knock you out, I guarantee."

"Pal, you guaranteed me she'd be here yesterday at noon. She's got her first performance tonight. Don't you keep in touch with your clients?"

"Sure, sure, but Cat…well, she goes her own way. Worth every penny you're paying her, though. More. You got her while she's climbing. Give her another year, and—"

"I don't give a damn about next year, Cicero. I

deal in the now. And right now I don't see your client.''

"She'll get there. She'll get there. Look, your brother liked her fine. She blew them away in Vegas.''

"My brother's a lot more tolerant than I am. You get her here—in one hour—or I start by suing your butt off for breach of contract. And then I'll get nasty.''

Duncan disconnected on the resulting sputters, slipped the phone back into his pocket and started across the docks toward the boat.

His brother Mac had indeed approved of Cat Farrell, Duncan thought. And he trusted Mac's judgment without question. Otherwise he wouldn't have been so quick to take his grandfather's additional glowing recommendation of her and hire her without an audition.

She looked good, damned good, he thought, bringing the image of her photo to his mind. Sleek and sexy—and the demo tape Cicero had sent him proved she had a voice to match.

But that wasn't doing him any good if the bloody woman didn't show.

The teenager striding toward the gangplank caught his attention. Battered jeans, lopsided backpack, scarred tennis shoes. A zebra-print baseball cap was pulled low over her forehead and round-lensed dark glasses were perched on her nose. He let out a sigh. It was a pity, he thought, that kids didn't have more of a sense of fashion.

He lengthened his stride to cut her off before she could board.

"Sorry, honey. You can't go on there. No passengers until after three, and you'll need your parents with you to get on."

She shifted, stood hip cocked, and tipped down the little sunglasses with one finger. He felt a quick jolt seeing the eyes behind them. They were a pure and piercing green, with a thin shimmer of gold circling the pupils.

Put a few years on her, Duncan thought fleetingly, and the eyes alone would drop men to their knees. To his amusement those eyes skimmed up, down, then up again before latching on to his with a bold arrogance he couldn't help but admire.

"And who would you be?"

It should be illegal for a female to have a voice like that before she turned twenty-one, Duncan decided. All that husky promise belonged in a ripe and experienced woman. "I'm Blade. She's mine," he said, with a jerk of his head toward the boat. "And you're welcome to come back when you're legal, darling."

Her lips curved with the same easy arrogance she carried in her eyes. "Want to card me, Blade? I've got my ID in here somewhere." She reached around to pat her backpack. "But since we're running a little behind, why don't we skip it? I'm your headliner, sugar."

She stuck out her hand as his eyes narrowed. "Cat Farrell. And I was twenty-five last month."

He could see it now, he supposed. If he used his imagination. The eyes should have tipped him off. But there hadn't been a dusting of freckles across her nose in the photo, and there had been a wild waterfall of deep red hair. He couldn't see a trace of it now, and wondered how she'd managed to stuff it all up under the ugly cap she wore.

"You're late."

"Got hung up." She flashed a smile. "I shouldn't have let Cicero talk me into that gig in Bakersfield. Missed my flight, had to reroute. Pain in the butt. Listen, I've got a cab back there full of my stuff. You want to take care of that for me? I'll go take a look at the setup."

"Hold it." He took a firm grip on her arm before she could turn away. "Stay." He had the satisfaction of seeing annoyance flicker in those remarkable eyes before he strode over to one of the crew and gave instructions for Cat's luggage to be transferred on board.

"We'll take a look at the setup," he told her, then took her arm again and walked her up the gangway. "And afterwards, we'll have a short lesson on how to operate this new and amazing device called the telephone."

"Nobody told me how witty you were," she said dryly. But because she wanted the job, badly, she bit back another sarcastic remark. "Look, I'm sorry. Sometimes you run into obstacles when you travel, and I ran into a few. I got here as soon as I could."

And damn Cicero, she thought, for not giving her more of a window of time to get from California to Missouri. Missing her flight had meant she'd had to settle for puddle jumpers and delays all the way across the country.

She hadn't slept except in snatches in the last twenty-four hours, hadn't eaten except what she could grab and swallow in a few minutes. And now she had this cover of *Gentleman's Quarterly* razzing her for being a little late.

But he was a Blade and he was a MacGregor. Between the two names was enough power to give her career the exposure and the boost she'd worked for for her entire life.

It would be a good gig. The decks were spotless, she noted, the rails romantically reminiscent of balconies in the French Quarter she'd seen in pictures and movies. Glass gleamed. Obviously Duncan Blade ran a tight and tidy ship.

He pushed open one of a set of double doors painted a glossy red, and gestured. Cat stepped in ahead of him, fisted her hands on her hips and scanned the room.

Like the exterior of the boat, it radiated charm and tradition. Round tables were set close enough for coziness, but with enough room to keep elbows from bumping. The lights in the audience area were dripping chandeliers, and the carpet was that same vivid red.

The bar in the far rear corner was fluidly curved. Stylish, Cat thought, with the added benefit of opening a traffic pattern. Stools gleamed with brass fittings, and the mirror behind the bar glittered.

She walked toward the stage, approving of the polished parquet flooring, noting with a quick shiver of delight her picture on the bill poster set on an easel to the side, in front of a gorgeous Steinway.

Hitting center stage, she turned, shut her eyes, drew breath. And belted out the first two bars of ''Stormy Weather.''

Still in the rear, Duncan had to fight to keep his mouth from dropping open. She had a voice that went straight to the gut and managed to fill the room without benefit of a mike.

"You've got good acoustics in here," she told him.

He had to take a breath himself. "You've got good pipes in there."

She grinned. She knew exactly what she had. Her voice was all she'd ever had, and she intended to ride it to the top. "Thanks, sugar. My little claim to fame. I'll need to run a sound check, a short re-hearsal. You point me to my dressing room, my cabin and a sandwich, and I'll get to work."

"You've got a performance in…" he glanced at his watch "…eight hours."

"I never miss a cue." She slipped off her glasses, hooked the earpiece in the neck of her T-shirt. "I'll do my job, Blade."

He intended to make sure of it. "Dressing room's backstage, between the main lounge and the casino."

"Smart," she said as he came toward her. "Get people buying drinks in here, then wandering out and dumping bucks at the tables. Suckers."

He arched a brow. "I take it you don't drink or gamble."

"Not as a rule. Drinking dulls the brain and gam-bling—when the house holds the edge—means los-ing. I don't like to lose."

"Neither do I." He showed her through another swinging door, turned to the left down a short cor-ridor. "This is yours."

Hers, she thought. It had only been a little more

than a year since she'd had her first personal dressing room. It still gave her a secret thrill. No more days of sharing space with strippers or chorus dancers. No more fighting for a place at the mirror or pawing through a jungle of costumes for her own.

Hers, she thought again, and studied the small, organized space.

Lighted mirror, long counter, padded stool, clothes rack. And God bless America, a neat sofa. "A little cramped," she said with a shrug, because she wanted to dance. "But I'll manage. I could use some help getting my wardrobe in here."

"You'll get it. But let's give you the lay of the land first."

She went reluctantly. She'd have enjoyed sitting on that sofa, locking the door and just grinning for a while. Instead, she followed him out, through the casino with its tables of green baize, its colorful wheels and glittering slots.

This, Cat imagined, was his stage. However casually he was dressed—and she imagined he thought of the tailored slacks and white silk shirt as casual— he was the perfect image of the traditional riverboat gambler.

And she didn't imagine he often walked away lighter in the pocket.

"Two performances a night," Duncan told her as they wound their way through and back out on deck into the brilliant sun. "Your days are pretty much your own, though we encourage staff to socialize and mingle with the passengers. You'll take your meals belowdecks with the crew. Breakfast from six to eight, lunch eleven to one, dinner five to seven. I promise you won't go hungry.''

''That's good to know. I've got a big appetite.''

He glanced down at her. She was wand slim, though the photos had shown off some very attractive curves. Duncan knew and appreciated the engineering of female undergarments and what they could do to augment a figure.

''You can use the health club, also belowdecks. You pay for your drinks, and since you don't drink— as a rule—I shouldn't have to tell you that you get drunk on board, you get one warning. Next time you're off.''

He took stairs leading down, and turned into another corridor. ''Passenger cabins. We can hold a hundred twenty full bookings and another hundred fifty day stops when we're in port.'' He stopped by a door, opened it. ''First class cabin,'' he explained, and let her wander in.

''Well, well.'' It was more spacious than she'd imagined, with a generous bed, plush seating area. The furnishings looked antique—genuine stuff, she imagined. The flowers were fresh, and a neat balcony curved out behind a pair of French doors and offered a view of the river. ''Must cost a bundle.''

''You get what you pay for. People come here to relax, to be entertained, and we give them their money's worth.''

''I bet you do.'' One day, she thought, one fine day she'd stay in a room like this. And when she did, she'd stretch out on the bed naked as a baby and laugh until her ribs cracked.

And she'd forget all the two-bit motels, the

cramped rooms and fleabag hotels that had come before.

"Well, sugar, since I don't think employees get such jazzy digs, where's mine?"

"Down one level." He stepped back, but as she passed through the door, their shoulders bumped.

He even smelled rich, she thought with mild irritation. She imagined she smelled just the way she felt. Like tired rags. If she didn't get that sandwich soon, she was going to pitch forward on her face and humiliate herself.

Been hungry before, she thought as she once again followed Duncan down a flight of steps. Just think about something else. Anything else.

Like what a very fine butt Blade has. Definitely first class all the way. Her quick snort of laughter had him glancing back.

"What?"

"Nothing. Since I keep ending up behind you, I'm just enjoying the view."

His left eyebrow winged up—a skill she'd always admired. Then, like lightning, his grin flashed. Whoa, Cat thought, secret weapon. Very effective.

"Next time we'll switch places," he said easily, then opened a door. "This is yours."

It was less than half the size of the cabin he'd just shown her, and the tiny window afforded light but little else. Still, it delighted her to see the space, the single narrow bed, the spotless floor. Her trunk sat there, filling most of the room.

"We'll have that stowed for you when you unpack. It won't seem as crowded."

"It's fine." More than fine, she thought. It smelled

clean. There would be no drunks hollering at each other in the next room, no need to shove a chair under the doorknob so she could sleep with both eyes shut.

She glanced into the tiny bathroom and found no problem with the doll-size sink or the skinny shower stall. Everything there, no matter how small, gleamed from fresh scrubbing.

For the next six weeks, she thought, it was all hers.

"I'll manage okay. Now about that sandwich?"

"I'll have something sent down." He was already an hour behind schedule. "Take an hour, get yourself settled. I'll arrange for your sound check. We'll keep the main lounge closed until four. That's all the time I can give you to rehearse, so be on time."

"I'll be there, sugar." She walked to the opened door, leaned on it in a silent invitation for him to leave. "And I'll need some bottled water—no bubbles, no flavors, just straight mineral water."

He cocked that brow again. "Anything else?"

"Well." Her lips curved slowly as she skimmed a finger down the front of his shirt. "Time will tell. Thanks for the tour."

If she wanted to play, he mused, he was good at games. He flicked a finger under her chin, leaned down just close enough to see her eyes sharpen. "Sweetheart, you ain't seen nothing yet."

He strolled away, grinning.

Chapter 12

He loved the night best. And the approach of it. July meant long, steamy days with sun blasting off the wide, dark waters of the Mississippi. And it meant hot nights with teasing breezes.

It meant action.

The passengers had boarded, and the cast-off party had set the tone for a fantasy period of enjoyment, of pleasure, of reliving those adventurous times when stern-wheel boats ruled the river.

He'd done his meet-and-greet, gauging faces, from the blissful honeymooners to the sharp-eyed hopefuls who dreamed of beating the odds. As twilight approached, Duncan felt that canny little thrill of beginnings.

A large chunk of his life had been spent in hotels, stationary buildings in cities and resorts. He'd been content, and he'd learned the family business, discovered a knack for it. But he'd also discovered that he preferred freedom of movement, change and the unexpected.

His mother often laughed and said he'd been born a century too late. He'd been born to ride the river.

He rode it now as the *Comanche Princess* glided south, cruising lazily through the water and leaving the restrictions of land behind. He could have piloted the grand boat himself—another thing he'd learned. He wasn't a man to put control in other hands without knowing how to take it back if it became necessary.

But he'd handpicked his captain himself, and his crew. Now he could enjoy the moment, satisfied that what was his ran well.

He passed through the casino with a winking nod to his casino manager. Gloria Beene had a sharp eye, a nimble brain and a dreamy Southern accent that disguised her ruthless efficiency.

And she filled out her trim tuxedo just fine.

Duncan had stolen her from Savannah, hiked her salary and had considered pursuing a more… personal relationship. Until both of them discovered they'd begun to think of each other more as family than lovers.

"Nice crowd tonight," Gloria commented. "Heavy on the slots."

"The cruise packages like to play their complimentary tokens in the machines—to start. We've got two honeymoon couples. You'll spot them. If they breeze in, see they get a free bottle of house champagne."

"Will do."

"I'm going to check out the new talent next door, but I'll be round and about for the next few hours."

He wandered through, appreciating the music of the slots, the ruffle of cards, the clink of dice. Circling, he finished his early evening sweep, then stepped through to head for the main lounge.

He stopped, checked his watch, then frowned at Cat's dressing room door. He hadn't heard a peep out of her since he'd left her hours before. And her track record didn't inspire him to trust she'd be ready on time.

He gave a quick, one knuckle rap on the door. "Five minutes, Miss Farrell."

"Got it. Shoot. Give me a hand, will you?"

Duncan pushed open the door—and discovered exactly how it must feel to take two barrels of a shotgun straight to the gut.

She stood in the center of the room in what he supposed some generous soul might call a dress. What there was of it was the same vibrant green as her eyes. It left her shoulders bare in a kind of frame for a waterfall of smoky red hair.

Baggy, ragged jeans hadn't warned him that she had silky legs that must end somewhere in the vicinity of her ears. But the short, tight skirt and mile-high heels showed them off to marvelous advantage.

"Well," he murmured. "Don't you clean up nice."

Cat stopped tugging on the zipper and turned to give him a delicious view of bare back. "You bought the package, sugar, now help me tie the bow. This damn thing's stuck."

"Let's see what we can do about that." He

stepped toward her, noting that with those glamorous eyes expertly highlighted, that mouth slickly painted, she no longer looked like a teenager.

And she smelled exotic, stunningly sexual.

What was a man to do, Duncan asked himself, but enjoy the moment?

"Sometimes you have to go down—" his knuckles skimmed over her skin as he slid the zipper low "—before you go up."

She didn't shiver, and was more surprised than annoyed that for one slippery moment, she wanted to. Reminding herself she knew just how to handle his type, she turned her head and shot him a sultry smile. "Oh, I've been down, and I like up a lot better."

"Maybe you've never been down in just the right place." Unable to resist, he trailed a fingertip along her spine. "Nice back, Farrell."

"Thanks." Oh yeah, she wanted to shiver. Damn it. "Nice face, Blade. Now you want to get me into this dress before I miss my cue? My boss gets bitchy if I'm late."

"I'll have to put in a good word for you." It amazed him just how much he wanted to peel the dress away, to discover what other miracles had been hidden under the dumpy street-urchin clothes she'd traveled in.

He was close enough, focused enough to see the awareness of that in her eyes. And unless his ego was skewing his vision, a glint of curiosity.

She kept her gaze level, though the skim of those fingertips on her back made her want to turn and find out just how clever they could be.

"It would be a mistake," she said evenly.

"Yeah." With some regret, he slid the zipper smoothly into place. "It would." He stepped back, took a good, long survey. "Looks like it might be worth it, from where I'm standing." But he turned and opened the door. "Break a leg."

"I always try to break both." She started by him, then followed impulse and stopped with their bodies close and framed in the doorway. Very slowly she trailed a finger over his mouth, then smiled. "Too damn bad."

She walked away, counting her heartbeats, stopping behind the turn of the stage. Waiting. Instead of blocking out those low, liquid pulls the encounter with Duncan had caused, she used them, focused on them.

When the stage went black, she moved onto it, hit her center mark. Counting, still counting. And closing her eyes, began to sing, a cappella in the dark.

She started soft and dreamy, just her alone, her voice stroking the words, her heart breaking on them. Then the music slipped in to join her. The key light winked on, spotlighting her face, holding, holding, then spreading to cover her as her voice built.

Seduction, Duncan thought as he watched her. Her voice might have been wistful, achingly sad as she sang of wanting someone to watch over her, but it was all seduction.

And the audience was caught in it.

He imagined the women would weep and the men would want.

God, she could make a man want.

He rubbed the side of his finger over his mouth

where she had stroked. That little flick had gone straight to his loins. Dangerous woman, he decided. Edgy woman. It was his bad luck he had a weakness for edgy, dangerous women.

He listened until the last notes died away, until the audience exploded with applause. Then he turned and walked back into the casino, where he knew the odds were in his favor.

Cat didn't surface until noon. After the second show, she'd stripped out of costume and creamed off her makeup. As the adrenaline rush performing gave her drained, she'd stumbled to her cabin and had fallen facedown on her bed. And had slept like a stone.

She woke to the shimmer of sunlight through her window, the gentle rhythm of the boat. And the desperate demands of an empty stomach.

By twelve-thirty she was showered, alert and down in the kitchens. She'd already made friends with one of the cooks. In every hotel, nightclub or dive she'd worked, Cat had made it a policy to get chummy with the person in charge of food.

You ate better that way.

Charlie from New Orleans was a ridiculously skinny Cajun with a huge mustache, snapping black eyes and three ex-wives. Cat heard all about them as she shoveled in the inspired shrimp étouffée he'd heaped on a plate for her.

She chased it down with mineral water. Caffeine made her jumpy. She chatted and ate in the bustling confusion of the kitchen, barely noticing the wait people rushing in and out.

Lunch, she imagined, was being served on the promenade deck, in the dining room and in the staff lounge. She preferred the kitchen, and helped herself to a warm roll.

"So, Charlie, tell me about the boss."

"Duncan?" Charlie eyed one of his line cooks to be certain the mushrooms were being sliced appropriately. "Good man. Smart. He says to me, 'Charlie, I want food dreams are made on.'" Amused by the memory, Charlie gave a cackling laugh. "He wants food like poetry, so that's what I give. He pays for it, 'cause he wants the best. He don't settle for less than that, *chère*. Not Duncan Blade."

"I bet." Cat munched on the roll.

"Got an eye for the ladies." Charlie wiggled his eyebrows. "Smooth moves. Slick. They don't catch him, no. Not like me. Me, I look at the lady too long, I get a ring in my nose."

She laughed. "But not Duncan."

"Nosiree—he gives them a tickle, then slips away while they're still sighing."

"Not everyone's ticklish."

"Oh, everybody, they got a spot, little girl. Always a weak spot. Me, I got too many."

But she didn't, Cat assured herself as she left the kitchen to stroll out on deck. When a woman had reason enough, she could cover over those weak spots until they hardened like rock. Then she could be the one to slip away.

When you had only yourself to depend on, you had to be quick on your feet.

Leaning on the rail, she watched the flow of the river. It was good to be out of the crowds, she thought, away from the city and the noise. To breathe thick fragrant air, to feel the drowsy heat of deep summer.

She could use a few more gigs like this, with the benefits of a smooth ride and lazy afternoons. And Charlie was right. Duncan Blade wasn't stingy. The salary she'd earn over the next six weeks would nicely augment her savings. A little more of a cushion, a little more distance from those days of scrambling for a few dollars more to make the rent on some dingy little room.

She'd never be poor again, she promised herself. Or desperate again. Or afraid again. Catherine Mary Farrell was on her way up.

From the deck above, Duncan watched her. She had her arms folded on the rail, her hip cocked, her feet crossed at the ankles. She looked as lazy and contented as a cat in a sunbeam.

So why was it that just looking at her made him tense?

She didn't resemble the sultry seductress of the night before—not with that ridiculous cap on her head, her long flow of hair tugged ponytail style through the back loop. Her T-shirt bagged over her hips—what there was of them—and her feet were bare.

Of course, those ragged, hemmed shorts showed off a great deal of leg.

But it wasn't how she looked, he decided. It was...the attitude. She stood there radiating absolute confidence, a woman who didn't give a single damn who looked at her or how. And he supposed that kind of attitude equaled style.

"Hey! Cat Farrell!"

She turned, and despite the bill of the cap and the sunglasses, lifted a hand to block the laser beam of the sun. She saw him above, his dark mane of hair ruffling in the breeze. The khaki slacks and light blue shirt showed off a slim and agile build.

Doesn't the man ever look less than perfect? she wondered.

"Hey, Duncan Blade."

"Come on up?"

"Why?"

"I want to talk to you."

She smiled, cocked her elbows on the rail and leaned back. "Come on down."

It was, he supposed, one of those times when surrendering a little battle could lead to losing the entire war. "Up," he said simply. "My office." He had time to see her shrug before he stepped away from the rail.

He waited, knowing she'd take her time. He knew he would have. Behind him, passengers lounged on the deck or escaped to the cool lounge for the afternoon talk on the history of the river.

Others—many others, he knew—were huddled in the casino, listening to the music of the slots.

When she swaggered up the steps, he simply gestured her up the next flight.

"There a problem, boss?"

"Nope. How was your morning?"

"I don't know. I slept through it." When she reached the top, she looked around. "Good thing I like heights."

"Come on in." He opened a door, waited for her to pass through first.

Obviously he didn't like to be closed in, Cat thought. The office wasn't particularly large, but it was ringed by windows that brought the sky inside. She walked across the room, passed the lovely old mahogany desk, through the small sitting area with its curve-backed chairs and glossy tables, and took in the view.

"It's a killer," she murmured.

"Keeps me from getting cranky over paperwork. Want something cold?"

"Water."

With a shake of his head, he opened a minifridge, selected a bottle. "Is that all you drink?"

"Mostly." She turned back when she heard water hitting glass. "So, what's the deal?"

"I looked over your press kit and materials again this morning." He walked to her, offered the glass.

"So?"

"So, they're very professional, well written, and they don't say a lot." He sat down, kicked out his legs, slipped a slim cigar from his pocket. "Tell me more."

"Why?"

"Why not?"

She sat, kicked out her legs in turn. "You hired me, I delivered. What else?"

He flicked on his lighter, watched her through the haze of smoke. "Doesn't say where you're from."

"Chicago. South Side. The projects."

He lifted a brow. "Rough neighborhood."

"How would you know?" she said with a slow,

sharp smile. "MacGregors don't cruise in their limos through rough neighborhoods."

Ah, sore spot, he mused, and casually blew out smoke. "The MacGregor worked in coal mines and spent a good part of his youth in neighborhoods as rough as the South Side. My father's Blade, part Comanche, and he fought his way out of places that make your projects look like paradise. I come from people who don't forget their roots."

"That's you, Duncan. I've ripped mine clean out." She watched him from behind the shield of her dark glasses as she sipped water. "What are you looking for here?"

"More," he said simply. "Where's your family?"

"My father's dead. Drunk driver killed him. I was eight, he was twenty-nine. My mother's in Chicago. She waits tables. And what does that have to do with my job."

Rather than answer, he leaned forward, quick as a snake, and pulled off her glasses.

"Hey."

"I like to see who I'm talking to." He set them aside, leaned back again, pleased to have put that gleam of temper in her eyes. "I've got a contract with you for six weeks, with an option for six more. Before I decide whether or not to exercise that option, I want to know who I'm dealing with."

Another six weeks, she thought. Steady work, steady income with room and board for three full months. She could nearly double her savings, certainly double the check she sent to her mother every month. And it could very well lead to another contract with another MacGregor-Blade arena.

Not a flicker of the thrill it brought to her, of the
hope it had burning like a torch in her heart, showed
on her face as she slowly smiled.

''Well, in that case, sugar, my life's an open book.
What do you want to know?''

Chapter 13

He'd pushed the right button, he decided. Money was, for some, the sweetest of talk. With another woman, he'd have waltzed around the objective, led her gradually to the point he wanted, and done it all with charm, finesse and a good deal of canniness.

He didn't think any of those would work with Cat. "Is there a man?"

Her brows lifted in mild amusement. "Well, you get right to it, don't you?"

"Just a matter of adjusting my stride to the person I'm walking with, darling. Is there?"

"There's no man unless I want there to be." She sipped again, taking her time and making him certain she spoke no less than the truth.

"No man—at the moment," he continued. "You don't drink—as a rule. Don't gamble. No vices, Cat?"

Now her eyes danced over the rim of her glass. "Is that what I said? You drink, gamble, and I imagine there's a woman when you want there to be. Does that mean you're riddled with vices, Duncan?"

"Good point." Absently, he picked up a coin from the table and began to fiddle with it. "You impressed me last night."

"In the dressing room?"

His grin flashed in sheer appreciation. "Oh yeah. And on stage. You've got a hell of a talent."

"I know."

He inclined his head. "The fact that you do know, and use it, is in your favor. Where do you want to take it?"

"As far as I can go, and then some."

"Why aren't you recording?"

She caught a drop of water from her top lip with her tongue. "Record producers have been beating down my door," she said dryly. "I just ignore them."

"You need a new agent."

She snorted out a laugh. "Tell me something I don't know."

"I can help you."

Slowly, she lowered her glass, set it aside. Those marvelous green eyes had gone cold and brittle. "And just what do you want for your percentage?"

The fingers that had been casually manipulating the coin went still. "I don't barter for sex. I don't pay for it, and I don't play for it."

She said nothing for a moment, a little surprised at how that smooth voice could so suddenly cut like a razor. Then she let out a sigh, because when she was wrong, she believed in admitting it. Even when it stung.

"Sorry, my mistake. Let's just say I haven't had a lot of people offering to help me without some very sticky strings attached."

"Sex is for pleasure. Business is for…a different kind of pleasure. I don't tie one to the other. Clear?"

"Crystal."

Satisfied, he began to flip the coin through his fingers again. "I have some contacts in entertainment. Put together a tape in the next few weeks. I'll pass it on."

"Just like that? Why?"

"Because I like your voice. I like the package."

She hesitated, looking for the strings, the drop-offs, the hidden traps, but couldn't find any. "I appreciate it. A lot." To seal the bargain, she held out a hand, then grinned in pure delight as the coin in his vanished. "Cool. Got any more tricks?"

"Too many to count." Amused by her reaction, he brought the coin back, flipping it between the tips of two fingers. Clamping the cigar between his teeth, he held up two fists, then flashed his hands open, and the coin was gone.

Her laugh was quick, rusty and low as she leaned forward. "Do it again. I'll figure it out."

"Wanna bet?"

Her gaze shifted to his briefly. "I've got a very sharp eye."

"Gorgeous eyes. They had my mouth watering when I still thought you were a teenage delinquent. Then there's this hair." His voice had softened as he reached out to run a hand down the stream of her ponytail. With his eyes on hers, he slipped the cap off, dropped it into her lap. "Fabulous. Where's the coin, darling?"

"What?"

Progress, he thought, and smiled. He leaned back, lifted both hands again, palms out. "Nothing up my sleeve."

When she realized her mind had simply clicked off for a very dangerous moment, she let out a long breath. "You're good."

"Damn right." He picked up her cap. "Hold out your hand," he told her, then, turning the cap over, spilled out the coin. The instant before it dropped into her palm, he snatched it out of the air. And it was gone.

She couldn't help it; she laughed again. "Really good. Well, this has been fun, but I want to run through a couple of new numbers I'm hoping to work in."

She rose, but found her wrists caught in those quick and clever hands. Something bumped inside her, hard, but she tipped her head back, met his gaze straight on.

"Feel that?" he murmured.

"What?"

"The connection."

"Maybe. Let go."

He held on just long enough to worry and irritate, then his fingers loosened, his hands dropped away. "No strings, Cat."

"No strings," she agreed. "And I like my hands free." So saying, she reached up, cupped the back of his neck and pulled his mouth down to hers.

She expected the jolt. She liked a good, hard jolt—or what was the point of a kiss? She'd already concluded there would be heat, and she enjoyed a solid blast of heat.

But it was more than a jolt when it knocked you flat. It was more than heat when it singed and sizzled through the blood.

She wanted to crawl right into it until her bones dissolved, until this fist of unexpected need loosened inside her. But her survival instinct was strong and keen and had her pulling back. "Well," she managed, more than a little shaken when she couldn't quite clear her head.

"Well," Duncan echoed, than clamped his hands on her hips before she could escape. "My turn."

He lowered his head, kept his mouth an inch from hers just long enough to hear her quick intake of breath, to see the gold ring around her pupils shimmer.

Then he rubbed his lips over hers, slow and easy.

She'd taken him by surprise before, and he was afraid it could become a habit. If he didn't stay on his toes, didn't stay in control, she'd be leading him around by the nose before the first week was up.

He didn't intend to let that happen.

He knew how to pleasure a woman. How to give and how to take. His hands slid up, skimming her torso, the sides of her breasts, then curved around her back to bring her closer. Slowly, inch by inch, until their bodies bumped, brushed, held.

"Oh, hell." Her oath was next door to a moan. Accepting the inevitable, she wound her arms around his neck.

Still his mouth did no more than play with hers, tormenting with nibbles, inciting with lazy strokes of the tongue, torturing with gentle nips along her jaw.

And finally, finally, she trembled against him.

His mouth took hers then, hot and hard, strangling the air in her lungs, misting the reason still struggling to surface in her brain. With a low purr of pleasure, she opened for him.

She flooded his senses. Tastes, scents, textures. When his hands fisted in her hair, her head arched back, welcoming him to take them both deeper. But there was no surrender. They met flash for flash now, mouths, bodies, needs fused into one. She strained against him, moved against him, sliding, pressing arousal to arousal.

He felt himself begin to slip, heard the animal inside him snarl and fight against its chain. He clawed his way back, forcing himself to gentle the kiss, to stroke his hands quietly over her before framing her face with them.

He waited for one more delicious tremor, then eased back.

His pulse was wild. A dozen hammers slammed against anvils inside him. Need tore like claws through his gut. But his hands remained gentle on her face as those gorgeous eyes of hers opened heavily.

She ran her tongue around her lips as if to absorb just a bit more of his flavor, and her breath came quickly.

"I guess we could call that a connection," she said.

It made him smile. "Works for me. Come to my cabin after the show tonight. We'll…connect."

She let out a sigh because there wasn't anything she wanted more, or could risk less. "Sugar, you are suicide, and I've got too much at stake to jump off a cliff right now."

His fingers tightened just enough to hold her in place. "This doesn't have anything to do with business, Cat."

"I got that part." She lifted her hands to his wrists. "And maybe we could even make that stick. That's not what I mean." She gave his wrists a quick squeeze before stepping back, reaching down for her cap and glasses. "You're a heartbreaker, Duncan, and I can't afford any cracks in mine."

"I don't break hearts. Don't even bruise them."

She laughed, slipped her glasses back in place. "I bet you believe that." She tapped a finger to her lips, tossed the sassy kiss at him and got the hell out before she let herself believe it, too.

He started to go after her, then stopped himself. It would be, he realized, entirely too much like begging. The fact that he could almost picture himself doing so made his palms sweat.

He had to figure the odds here. Pacing, he slipped his hands into his pockets and fingered the coin. Wanting a woman was easy; it was natural. It was enjoyable.

Seducing one was all that and more.

He didn't doubt he could seduce her. There was too much sizzling between them for either one of them to walk away without seeing it through.

And she was wrong, he thought with a frown. He

wasn't a heartbreaker. He'd never hurt a woman. Inevitably he began to ease away before emotions became tangled and messy and led to hurt on either side.

There was no reason for that to change at this stage of the game. She was more of a challenge than most, certainly more intriguing than any. And that raw, in-your-face sex appeal was like a slim feminine finger beckoning in the dark.

He was more than willing to answer the call—as long as it was on his terms.

All he had to do, Duncan mused, was convince her his terms were acceptable.

Considering, he pulled the coin out of his pocket, flipped it high, caught it nimbly. "Heads, I win," he murmured, and turning the coin between his two fingers, grinned at the twin faces on either side.

He was still grinning when the phone rang. Easing a hip onto the desk, he picked up the receiver. "Blade."

"Say hello when you answer the phone! Where are your manners?"

The grin widened. "Hello, Grandpa."

"That's better. How's the boat?"

"She's…a princess. We're heading toward Memphis and it's hot as three hells."

"Hah! I've got a nice breeze coming off the ocean here, and I'm enjoying a fine Cuban."

"Which means Grandma's out."

"Woman's off at some tea party. She's nagging me about missing you."

Anna MacGregor had never nagged a day in her

life, but Duncan let that pass. "I'll come up for a couple days in the fall."

"I was thinking she might like a little ride on the river on your boat."

"That'd be great. You let me know and we'll roll out the red carpet."

"Your brother was telling her about that new singer you've got there. Got your grandmother all fired up to hear her."

"Cat Farrell." Duncan pressed his lips together and tasted her. "She's worth the price of a ticket."

"Don't I know that? I heard her myself, didn't I? Told you she'd do."

"I appreciate it. She was a hit last night. I heard some of the passengers talking about her show this morning."

"Good, good. Sharp looks, too."

"She makes a package," Duncan murmured.

"The Irish are sturdy stock. Catherine Mary Farrell—Irish as they come."

Duncan's eyes narrowed and he shifted as a thought—as uncomfortable as a tack in the seat—pricked his brain. "Catherine Mary? All I have on her paperwork here is Cat Farrell. How do you know her full name?"

"Ah, your brother," Daniel said, cursing himself. "Mac mentioned it to me, and it stuck with me as it's a pretty name—Catherine Mary."

Duncan drummed his fingers on his knee. "So it is. I imagine she'll keep it even after she marries the piano player."

"What! What piano player?"

"The one she's engaged to," Duncan said easily.

Got you, you meddling old fox. "Dabny Pentwhistle."

"Pentwhistle? Pentwhistle? What kind of a name is that for a smart woman to stick herself with? Where the devil did he come from? She wasn't engaged last week."

"Wasn't she? And how would you know?"

"Because I..." Sensing a trap, Daniel backtracked. "It pays me to know details. I've got an interest in that boat of yours, don't I? Means I have an interest in who works on it and what they're about, doesn't it? Girl wants to marry some piano-playing Pentwhistle, that's her business, but it pays me to know what's what."

"Now you know, don't you? So if you had any half-baked ideas about setting me up with Catherine Mary Farrell, you can put them to rest."

"Half-baked? Half-baked? Is that any way to talk to your grandfather? Why, I ought to take a strap to you."

"So you've said before." Grinning now, Duncan reached for his own cigar and relit it. "When are you going to?"

"Next time you're within arm's reach, laddie. See if I don't. Boy your age sitting on some boat letting a Pentwhistle slip a woman like that out from under you. Why, it's a sin. Girl's got grit. Got guts and don't you mistake it. She deserves the best."

"And I'm the best?"

"Hah! A scoundrel is what you are. You'll break your poor old granny's heart whiling away your time on that river when you should be settling down and seeing to the future."

"And making her babies to bounce on her knee. I know the drill, MacGregor." Even as Daniel blustered, Duncan laughed. "I love you, Grandpa."

"And so you should." With a warm chuckle, Daniel shifted tactics. "Duncan, laddie, I'm only looking out for you. I want to see my favorite grandchild happy and settled before I die."

Duncan was fully aware every one of the grandchildren was Daniel's favorite. "You'll never die. And if you do, you'll come back and haunt the great-grandchildren until they're paired up and procreating. Now go pick on Ian or one of the others. I'm on to you."

"All right, all right." But Daniel grinned fiercely at the phone. "Go play with your boat."

"Exactly what I had in mind. Give my love to Grandma."

"That I'll do. Pentwhistle, hah!" Daniel muttered as he hung up, which made Duncan roar with laughter.

Chapter 14

Duncan Blade believed in romance, in the power and the beauty of it. In its small details and sweeping gestures. His brother often said romance was Duncan's religion. And though he himself wouldn't go quite that far, he did have absolute faith in its powers.

And in his experience, women were suckers for it.

He sent flowers to her cabin when they docked in Memphis, perfume when they stopped in Natchez, a heart-shaped trinket box when they turned into Baton Rouge.

And while they'd glided down the river toward all those places, he'd sought her out at odd moments, to invite her to dinner on his private balcony, for a moonlit walk on deck, for a quiet supper after her show.

Her answer was always the same. Forget it, sugar.

Cat Farrell, Duncan decided, was one tough nut, and she wasn't cracking.

It wasn't just maddening, Duncan thought as he studied the docks of New Orleans out his window. It was unreasonable. They'd sparked something in each other that was impossible to ignore. For him, anyway. Since the moment she'd walked out of his office nearly a week before, she hadn't given him a single opportunity to get his hands on her again.

Not that she had avoided him, he mused. She wasn't the type to shut herself in her cabin or duck into crowds. She was there, always there, wandering around the boat, chatting with passengers or crew, rehearsing in the lounge.

She didn't stutter or look away when they came across each other, but would give him one of those slow, feline smiles, looking him dead in the eye.

She didn't seem the least affected, even when he got close enough to smell the perfume she wore— perfume he'd given her, for God's sake.

It was driving him crazy. *She* was driving him crazy.

But he was far from ready to call it a day.

If the combination of Duncan Blade and New Orleans couldn't soften a woman up, there was no hope for humanity.

In her narrow bed, in her cabin with the thin shade pulled over the tiny window, Cat stretched luxuriously. She knew from the rhythm of the boat that they'd docked. After a week on board, she'd grown accustomed to the movements, the sounds, the feel of the *Comanche Princess*.

New Orleans was outside the window, she thought lazily. Beignets, tumbling flowers, cool jazz and drunken tourists. What more could a woman ask for? She had hours to explore it, to wander the narrow streets, to poke into charming shops, to sample the food the city was famous for and listen to street-corner musicians.

To get off the boat—and away from Dangerous Duncan. Her lips quirked. That was how she was thinking of him these days. A man who paid that much attention to a woman, who was that charming, that gorgeous, that sexy, was every bit as dangerous as a loaded gun.

And she had no intention of taking a stray bullet.

But Lord, she thought as she padded into her tiny bath to shower, the man had a way about him.

A way of looking at a woman out of those fabulous, dark chocolate eyes as if she were the sole focus of his world. A way of talking to her with that smoothly sexy, all-male voice as if he'd waited his whole life to speak to her. A way of touching her with those clever hands so that a simple brush on the shoulder sent echoes of anticipation straight to the core.

The charming son of a bitch was making her crazy.

She couldn't afford even a short side trip into insanity.

Sending her flowers, she thought as she toweled off. It was so clichéd. But she was smart enough to know there was a reason clichés worked. Hadn't she mooned over the blossoms, buried her face in them? Hadn't she thought of him every damn time her gaze had landed on them?

And perfume. Never in her life had she owned real perfume. The kind that came in gorgeous bottles, cost the earth and made a woman feel like a queen. Worse, he'd known exactly what kind of scent would appeal to her, would make that glamorous bottle of fragrance irresistible.

She'd decided he'd been born knowing how to get to a woman.

But the trinket box had nearly done her in. It was so foolish, so useless, so pretty. She'd never had the time or opportunity to indulge in the foolish and useless, hadn't realized such things would give her such pleasure.

Wrapped in a towel, she crossed the tiny cabin and picked up the box from where it sat on her little dresser. It was glossy white on white with a little pink bow at the tip of the heart. And it was empty, as she had no trinkets to put inside.

But it made her smile.

Still, she set it down and began to dress for a day of steamy summer heat. She knew what Dangerous Duncan was up to. It was a kind of campaign, she thought—carefully, strategically planned. And she was the hill he intended to take.

Once he'd won her and planted his flag—so to speak—he'd move on to the next campaign, the next hill.

"That's what heartbreakers do," she murmured.

She shrugged, tucking the hem of a simple white T-shirt into simple black shorts. It was fortunate she knew just how to handle him. She slipped on sandals, stuffed some cash in her pocket, then grabbed her cap and sunglasses.

When she pulled open her door, Duncan was just raising a hand to knock.

"Good, you're up."

It jolted her coming face-to-face with him when he'd been so heavily on her mind, and that was irritating. But she swung her glasses casually by the earpiece and cocked her head. "Why wouldn't I be?"

"Because you rarely climb out of bed until after noon."

She only smiled. "Then why would you be knocking on my door at nine in the morning?"

"To wake you up. But since you're up, dressed and ready, we'll have more time. Let's go."

"Where?"

"Ever been to New Orleans?" In a subtle move, he reached behind her and pulled the door closed.

"No. But that's my current plan."

"Great. We'll start with beignets at Café du Monde like proper tourists. Are those shoes comfortable?"

"Yeah. My current plans were solo, sugar."

"Adjust them," he suggested as he nudged her along to the steps. "I've spent a lot of time in New Orleans. One of my favorite places." He kept right on talking as he steered her up on deck, toward the gangplank. "It shows best at night, but there's a lot to be said for it on a sultry summer day. It's all atmosphere. You like seafood?"

"I like food."

"Good. I know a great place for lunch."

"Look, Duncan—"

He stopped, turned, slid his hands up her arms to

her shoulders and pinned her with one of those long, focused looks. "Spend the day with me."

Oh yeah, she thought with an inward sigh. The man had a way. "Why not, but you're buying."

It was like walking through a hot river, and she loved it. Every steamy step. In the French Quarter, the buildings were grand, elegant, feminine with their fussy balconies and tumbling flowers. The smells were rich, undertoned with the warm smell of decay. The streets were narrow, the parks green, the pace sleepy and slow.

She'd eaten three beignets and had sampled a sip of Duncan's café au lait. She'd listened to the patter of Cajun French and the clip-clop of horses pulling carriages around Jackson Square. With him she'd wandered along, studying the sidewalk artists and their wares and had laughed delightedly at a charcoal caricature of Elvis.

Because the day called for it, they strolled hand-in-hand, under huge, shady trees, along blistering sidewalks.

She stopped to watch three young boys tap-dancing in a square, their faces gleaming with sweat, their feet fast and clever. And she noted that Duncan dropped bills into their cardboard box instead of coins.

Generous, she thought. Carelessly and sweetly so.

"Those kids probably make a killing every afternoon," she commented.

"They earn it. Ready for lunch?"

She laughed. "Sugar, I'm always ready."

She'd expected him to take her to some fancy restaurant where the tables were draped in linen and the waiters were discreetly efficient. She'd been completely prepared to be unimpressed. Instead he steered her into a dimly lit, crowded café where the tables were bare, scarred wood shoved up against one another family style, the napkins were paper and the menu was scrawled on a chalkboard.

It was, Cat thought, two steps up from a dive, and exactly her style.

The woman behind the counter was enormous, three feet wide if she was an inch. The apron she wore was big as a tent and stained with splashes of color and shapes that reminded Cat of an abstract painting.

Her moon-size ebony face was smooth as satin and creased into a huge smile when her eyes lit on Duncan.

"There's that handsome boy! Come give Mama a kiss."

He grinned, leaned over and gave her a hard, smacking one on the mouth. "*Bonjour,* Mama. *Ça va?*"

"*Oui, oui.* It comes, it goes. Who's this skinny girl you bring me?"

"Cat, this is Mama. She's the best there is."

"Cat? Well, she looks like a cat. We gonna feed you up here, *chère.*"

"I'm counting on it." Cat took a deep sniff. "Smells like paradise."

"Paradise." Mama slapped a hand on her belly as if to hold it in place as she let out a rolling laugh. "Go take your skinny girl and sit. I fix you up." She waved them away.

"You don't order?" Cat asked as she sat across from Duncan at one of the wobbly tables.

"I take what she gives me." He flashed a smile. "And I like it. So will you."

He couldn't have been more right, Cat decided, as she plowed her way through barbecued shrimp, a mountain of dirty rice and corn bread. Her only comment when Duncan slid two of his shrimp from his plate to hers was a muffled grunt of assent.

Nursing his beer, he watched her eat. He'd watched her before, and marveled. She had the appetite of a starving trucker.

"Why aren't you as big as Mama?"

"Um. Nothing sticks," she said with her mouth full. "But I keep trying."

He laughed, sipped his beer. "Better save room for dessert. She makes a killer pecan pie."

"Pecan pie?" Cat swallowed and glanced over at the glass-fronted display of desserts. "Ice cream on the side?"

He shook his head in amazed admiration. "Sure, if you want."

"Do." When her plate was all but licked clean, she sat back and blew out a breath. "Good stuff."

"I never miss a trip to Mama's if I can help it." He leaned forward. "Here, you've got a little sauce." He rubbed his thumb at the corner of her mouth, then stayed as he was, looking at her, touching her. Wanting her. "And a great mouth," he murmured. "Let me just…help you out with it."

He kept leaning forward, easing off the chair until he could fit his mouth over hers. His hand slid around, skimming her ear, then cupping her neck, with those long fingers gently kneading.

Her heart dropped down to her toes, then bounced into her throat.

He was doing it to her again. Making her mind fuzz, her skin shiver. The clatter from the late lunch crowd dimmed away, and her system was suddenly full of the scent of him instead of the spices, the sauces.

But she could handle him, she told herself as her lips parted. Later.

"Boy, you let that girl alone till she eats her pie." Mama gave Duncan an affectionate whack on the butt.

Wanting to take just a bit more of Cat's taste with him, Duncan scraped his teeth lightly over her bottom lip before he broke the kiss. He kept his eyes on Cat's as he sat again. "She wants ice cream with her pie, Mama."

"Well, don't I got it right here?" Chuckling, she dumped the plates in front of them and scooped up the dirty dishes. Then she winked at Cat. "Him, he got a fine mouth for kissing, eh?"

"Yeah." Determined not to sigh, Cat picked up her fresh fork. "It's not bad," she said, then took the first bite of pie. "But this," she added, closing her eyes. "This is a miracle."

"She eats good." Mama gave Duncan a bat on the shoulder. "Be smart. Keep this one."

"I really ought to introduce Mama to my grandfather," Duncan commented when Mama glided away. "They think alike."

"Really?" Cat ate more pie and wondered what a

black cook from New Orleans and a staggeringly wealthy Scot from Hyannis Port could have in common.

"Yeah. They both think I should be married and raising a small herd of children. One or the other is always trying to fix me up."

Cat swirled ice cream in pie and lifted her eyebrows as she studied his sharply handsome face. "You don't look like you need help in that area, sugar."

"Tell them." He gestured with his beer, sipped, then decided it would be entertaining to see her reaction to his grandfather's latest scheme. "The MacGregor handpicked you for me."

She blinked, and for the first time since he'd met her, appeared completely at sea. "Huh?"

"My grandfather. He wants me to marry you."

Now she laughed and went back to her pie. "Get out."

"I'm serious. Girl's got grit," he said, dramatically rolling his *r*'s. "Guts. Good blood, strong stock."

"How would he know? I barely met him."

"You'd be surprised how much he knows. The man's uncanny—and tenacious. I figured it was only fair to let you know what he has in mind."

She drummed her fingers on the table, trying to figure the angle, and simply couldn't find it. "Do you do everything your granddaddy tells you?"

"Nope. So rest easy, darling. That wasn't a marriage proposal. I didn't figure it out until he called a few days ago, checking up." Grinning now, Duncan settled into his own dessert. "I got the drift and needled him. Told him you were engaged to a piano player. Dabny Pentwhistle.''

"Pentwhistle? What the hell kind of name is that?''

"Exactly what The MacGregor wanted to know. He was pretty disappointed in you, sweetheart,'' he added with a wag of his fork. "Wasting your time on some piano player. But he didn't buy it for long. The old man's damn sharp. He just married off my cousin D.C.''

"Married off? What is this, medieval Scotland?''

"It's MacGregor Land,'' Duncan said with a grin. "Trouble is, they're perfect together. D.C. and Layna, I mean. The MacGregor hit a bull's-eye with them—and he's done it before, starting with my parents. Makes him cocky.''

She wondered idly if Duncan was going to eat all of his pie. "He arranged your parents' marriage?''

"No, just finagled it so that they'd meet, bump into each other. The rest was up to them. He's been working on the second generation the last few years. And he's batting a thousand. Up to me.''

She was far from understanding it, but she nodded. "And you intend to ruin his batting average.''

"I intend to live my own life, make my own choices.'' His fingers slid over the table to toy with hers. "But I do admire his taste.''

"Hmm. Weird.'' Then she shrugged it off and worked on polishing off her pie. "You've got yourself a very strange family, sugar.''

"Darling, you don't know the half of it.''

Later, they walked off the meal in the high heat and moist air, ducking into shops now and then to court the chill of air-conditioning and browse. When he caught her eyeing a tin of pralines, he roared with laughter.

"You can't possibly be hungry again."

"Not now," she said with a gleam in her eye. "But I will be, so why not be prepared?"

He bought them for her—not the little tin she'd looked at, but one big enough to feed a greedy family of four. And made her laugh.

She liked him, she thought. Really, really liked him. And that, combined with the sneaky animal lust she was experiencing, made for a difficult combination to resist. The first was bound to nudge her into acting on the second.

Be prepared, Cat warned herself as he pulled her into yet another shop. And get out alive.

This shop was full of trinkets and jewelry. Colored stones and crystals winked in glass cases or were draped artfully over walls and shelves. Lining the side were three curtained alcoves where the curious—and to Cat's mind the gullible—could have their fortunes told.

She wandered idly, toying with pretty dust catchers while Duncan perused one of the cases. She heard a sale ring up and shook her head without much interest. The man—she'd come to note—just loved tossing his money away.

When he tapped her on the shoulder, she turned, and he slipped a thin gold chain over her head.

"What's this?" Frowning, she scooped up the sword-shaped yellow gem dangling from the chain. It was lovely, polished to a gleam and slim as a running tear.

"Citrine. Stimulates communication—and voice projection." He smiled at her. "Excellent stone for performers."

"Get out." But her fingers had closed around it. "You don't believe stuff like that."

"Darling, I'm Celt and Comanche. I *know* stuff like that. Besides, it suits you, Catherine Mary."

He had the pleasure of seeing surprise, consternation and vague annoyance flicker over her face before she controlled it. "How do you know my full name?"

"Just one of the many other things I know. Want your palm read?"

"Now that's really bunk."

"Then it won't hurt you." He drew her to the counter to arrange payment for a reading.

"Fine. You got money to burn, go ahead."

She'd never considered herself superstitious. Never traveling without her lucky cap was just a tradition, after all. So she sat in the little alcove, smirked at the pretty young woman who took her hand and waited to be told she'd be taking a long voyage and meeting a tall, dark stranger.

"You have a strong hand," the woman said with a sweet smile. "An old soul."

Cat rolled her eyes toward Duncan, who leaned against the wall. "Yeah, I'm ancient."

"You've suffered loss, sorrow and struggle."

"Who hasn't?" Cat muttered, but the woman only stroked her palm with a fingertip.

"You use them and they've made you strong. You chose your direction at a young age, and it's rare for you to look back instead of forward. Passions, ambitions. You take care to make decisions with your head. Do you think your heart is unreliable?''

This time Cat looked into the woman's eyes. ''Whose isn't?'' she said flippantly.

''Yours can be trusted. It's a steady one. Talent. It runs deep, very powerful, and it feeds you. What you give of it, it gives back. It will take you where you want to go.'' She frowned a minute, studying Cat's face rather than her hand. ''Do you sing?''

The quick tremor came first, making her want to jerk her hand free, but she shrugged, figuring the con. ''My pal here must have prompted you pretty good.''

''You can trust him, too,'' the woman said by way of answer. ''His heart's as steady as yours, though as closely guarded. Changes and decisions, risks and rewards. It will be up to you. You don't have to be alone, unless you turn away. Family centers you. It's an anchor no matter how far you drift. You have so many places to go, so many doors opening,'' she said with a beaming smile, ''that were locked, or seemed to be.''

Her fingers played over Cat's hand, skimmed, settled. ''You aren't afraid to work and work hard, but you expect to be paid in kind. You're thrifty and wish you didn't have to be. Generous with those who matter. One will, more than others. There's only one who'll fit you, body, head and heart, and he's already in your mind.''

Cat tossed her hair back as they stepped back out into the thick air. ''That was pretty lame, Blade. How much did it cost you to set her up with what to say?''

''I didn't.'' He was vaguely disturbed over what

he'd expected to be a passing amusement for both of them.

"Get out."

"I didn't," he repeated, and stuck his hands in his pockets rather than taking hers. "I just stopped in there on impulse, figured we'd get a kick out of it."

"Hold it." She put a hand on his arm, narrowed her eyes and studied his face. Either he was a hell of an actor, she concluded, or he was as baffled as she. "Well, that was weird," she decided.

"Yeah. Weird."

They walked back toward the river in silence.

Chapter 15

They stayed two days in New Orleans, slipping away from the docks on the second evening. The celebrational Mardi Gras–style party to celebrate the journey was populated with fresh faces and familiar ones. The music was loud, the drinks colorful, the mood high.

Duncan circulated, strolling the decks, passing through lounges, greeting new passengers, chatting with those who'd remained for the week's voyage back north. But he couldn't find her.

Until he couldn't, he didn't realize that throughout his routine tour of the boat, he'd been looking for Cat.

Following instinct, he headed down to the kitchen. Dinner preparations were well underway. Pots steamed, pans sizzled, cleavers hacked. Idly, he snagged a carrot stick from a military line on a cutting board, crunching it as Charlie saluted him.

"Hey, bossman, we're busy 'round here. You come to stir a pot?"

"Just passing through. How's the redfish tonight?"

"Fresh and fine. Want me to blacken up a piece for you? Got garlic 'taters, too—less you got you a hot date." He cackled over his pots. "I hear tell we got some fine ladies this trip up. Groupa sisters, each one pretty as the next."

"The Kingston group, yep. Four long-stemmed blondes." He winked and nibbled the carrot. "I checked them out for you, Charlie. Looking for wife number four."

"Ain't gonna be no number four. I'm swearing offa matrimony."

"Heard that before. You seen Cat around?"

"She passing through, too. Girl's got her one healthy appetite." He wiggled his eyebrows at Duncan. "You hoping she take a bite outta you?"

"Wouldn't hurt my feelings. She been passing through this evening?"

"Got her some dinner before the show, like usual. She likes her redfish black and spicy, too. She took her some strawberry shortcake on up to her cabin. You maybe catch her if you got a long stride."

"I've got one," Duncan began, then felt his beeper vibrate in his pocket. He pulled it out, checked the code and saw he was needed in the casino. "But I'll just have to catch her later."

* * *

He didn't manage any free time until midway through the second show.

His pit boss was down with a migraine, and two of his best dealers were suffering from a mild case of food poisoning after splitting a bushel of crayfish. The casino was woefully shorthanded.

Duncan filled in at a blackjack table, taking on the duties of dealer and entertaining his table—one that consisted of the Kingston sisters.

They were lookers, he thought. Good-natured women with deep pockets and a lot of family affection. And not one of them could play worth spit.

"Honey, you don't want to hold on fourteen when the dealer's got ten showing. The name of the game is beat the house. You want to take me down."

"Love to." She giggled cheerfully while her sisters hooted. "Okay, handsome, hit me."

He dealt her a six, causing her sisters to applaud, then went on down the line, coaching each one.

He paid off two, raked in chips from the other pair, then dealt the next hand. Under usual circumstances, he'd have enjoyed nothing better than playing flirt-and-gamble with a quartet of attractive blondes. But his mind kept wandering...out of the casino and into the lounge beyond.

She'd be singing, standing center stage with the mike in her hand and some sexy little dress barely covering her. Her voice would be filling the room, radiating through it. Deep and rich and smooth.

He realized he didn't want to just see her, he wanted to hear her. He wanted to find a table in the back of the room, in the dark, and just listen.

"I've got twelve." The sister on the end batted

enormous baby blues and demanded attention. "What should I do, Duncan?"

"Take a chance. I'm showing nine, so you have to figure nineteen."

"Okay, but be gentle with me."

He clobbered her with a king and smiled sympathetically.

"Oh, pooh." She pouted prettily. "Maybe I'm just better at other games."

Signal received, he thought. Loud and clear. And what the hell was wrong with him? He didn't feel the least bit tempted to bounce back with a signal of his own. And felt nothing but relief when Gloria stepped beside him.

"Changing dealers, ladies," she said cheerfully. Their responding chorus of awws had Gloria chuckling. "Say good-night, Duncan."

"Good night, ladies. You've got the floor from here," he murmured to his manager.

"Yeah, under control. Why don't you go on into the lounge and take in the rest of the show—since that's where your mind's been for the last hour, anyway."

"Might just." He gave her a quick flick on her nose. "Gloria will take good care of you," he said to the table, and four pairs of big blue eyes followed him out the door.

"So, is he taken?"

Gloria arched her brows at the blonde across from her, then grinned. "Yeah, he is. He just doesn't know it yet. Ladies, place your bets." I have, she thought, and laughed to herself.

Duncan slipped quietly into the lounge, adjusting

to the dim lights and the heat of Cat's voice. She was singing about loving the wrong man, but there was as much defiance as sorrow in the vocals.

He'd meant to ease down the side and toward the back, order a brandy and sit sipping while he listened to her. But he stayed where he was, in the shadows just to stage left.

She knew he was there, would have sworn there'd been a change in the air the moment he'd stepped in. Something charged and edgy that had her skin prickling. As if to test them both, she shifted her gaze, met his, held it. Let the song pour out of her, and into him.

It wasn't until the applause sounded that she realized she'd yet to break the connection. She lowered the mike so her shaky expulsion of breath wouldn't carry, then turned a sparkling smile to the audience.

She had a patter, some that was scripted in her head, more that came as suited the mood—hers and theirs. But she knew how to play the audience and enjoyed it, because she enjoyed them.

So she would concentrate on them instead of the dangerous man standing in the shadows.

He had yet to recover his breath when she began talking, sliding into an intimate conversation with those who sat at the tables.

She charmed them, he noted, calling for the lights to spot on a couple near the front who were celebrating their twenty-fifth anniversary. She made a few jokes, just bawdy enough to have the room roaring, then cuing the music, she began to sing a suggestive version of ''Big Spender'' directly to the man.

She stroked his cheek, skimmed her fingers through his hair, slid into his lap as his wife giggled helplessly and he turned a deep pink accented with a foolish grin.

Duncan found himself grinning, too. Damn, she was good, he thought. She'd wrap them around her finger and keep them right there until she was done.

And she was doing exactly the same to him.

But the difference was, he told himself, he intended to do some wrapping himself.

Leaning back against the wall, he watched, and kept watching until the end of the show.

It made her jumpy to know he was still there, right where he'd been since he'd come in, where she'd have no choice but to pass him on the way to her dressing room.

And because she was jumpy, she was all the more determined to pretend she couldn't care less.

"You don't usually stay so long," she commented, unscrewing the top of the bottle of water she always kept close by the stage. "Spot checking the talent?"

"I wanted to see you." He said it simply because it was true—and because he knew it would throw her off.

"Well…you did." She started past, pausing when he took her wrist.

"Let's go outside."

"No thanks. I need to change."

"No, you don't. I like looking at you in that delightful excuse for a dress." It was black tonight, plunging deep, front and back.

"I'm tired, Duncan."

"No, you're not. You're revved."

He could feel the energy pouring out of her, wanted to capture it. Watching her eyes, he lifted the hand he held to his mouth. "It's warm on deck, and there's a moon. Take a walk with me. I won't touch you unless you want me to."

That was the trouble, she thought. She did want him to. Maybe it was time to stop pretending otherwise. "All right. We'll walk. I could use some air. Nice crowd tonight."

He guided her through the tables and out the doors. "You made Anniversary Boy's night. Possibly his year."

She laughed at that, shook back her hair and drew in the deep, dark scent of the water. "His wife set it up with me before the show, gave me fifty bucks to pour it on."

"She got her money's worth. Let's go up, closer to the moon."

"I hear you're a big hit with the Kingston sisters," she commented as they climbed the stairs.

"Did you?"

"They were in the lounge earlier, giggling and sighing over you."

"Nothing more rewarding to a man than to make the ladies giggle and sigh." He climbed steadily up to the third deck, pleased to find it deserted.

"I bet." She walked to the rail, leaned out. "God, this is fabulous. Really fabulous. I love the night on the river."

"My personal favorite. I've been hoping to wear you down enough to get you out here with me." He turned her slowly. "At night on the river."

"That's not where you want me, Duncan."

"Just one of the many places." He ran his hands up her arms, but didn't draw her against him. "You sang to me."

Her heart began to flutter, an uncomfortable and, she thought, idiotic feeling. "I sing to everyone. It's my job."

"You sang to me," he repeated, his voice quiet and smooth. "It made me want you so much my bones ached." His fingers skimmed over her shoulders, up the side of her throat. "And it made me see you wanted me right back."

He lowered his head, keeping his mouth a whisper from hers. "You'll have to ask me, since I promised I wouldn't."

"Do you always keep your word, Duncan?"

"Yeah." His breath fluttered over her lips. "I do."

"And I never ask," she told him, and fisting her hands in his hair, dragged his mouth to hers.

She cut him off at the knees with that wild and sudden slap of lust. Her mouth was like a flame, branding and burning and making him desperate for more. He knew if he didn't take control he'd simply snap and take her where they stood.

He broke the kiss, ordered himself to gentle the hands that had clamped on her shoulders. "My cabin's right behind us."

She angled her head, smiled slowly. Desire was a slow and steady burning in the blood. "I know."

He backed up, sliding his hands down to hers, drawing her with him. Then he circled her, freeing one hand to dig for his key, watching her face as he slipped it into the lock.

"Why don't we go inside?"

"Why don't we?" she murmured, and turned to walk into the room.

He'd left a light burning by the bed and the wide window undraped and open to the moon. Though her blood continued to pump hot and hard, she took a careless turn around the room.

There was an antique table graced with pictures framed in gleaming silver, deep-cushioned chairs in a vivid shade of blue, brass lamps with glass globes, a gracefully arched niche filled with books and more photos.

The bed was brass as well, with fluid lines and of generous size.

"Nice digs." She glanced over her shoulder as she heard the scrape of a match, and watched with both pleasure and surprise as he lit a group of slender white candles. "You're quite the romantic, aren't you?"

He blew out the match, then walked over to switch off the bedside lamp so they stood in the soft glow of shifting light and shadows. "You have a problem with that?"

"No, not particularly." But it made her just a little shaky. To counter it she curved her lips and reached back to unzip her dress.

"Don't." He stepped forward, ran a single fingertip from the base of her throat to the edge of the plunge of black silk. "I want to undress you."

She let her arms fall back to her sides. "What's stopping you?"

"Nothing." He lowered his head, nibbled gently at her neck. "Not a thing. You smell like you look."

She fought the urge to shake her head clear. "You bought the perfume...big spender."

He chuckled and lapped at her. "Taste like you look."

Her breath was going ragged despite her efforts to control it. "You've had a sample or two before."

"Not enough. Not nearly." He worked his way back up to her mouth, but barely skimmed it. "Should I tell you what I want to do with you...or should I just surprise you?"

Oh dear, was all she could think. "I don't surprise easy."

"Then let's see what I can do."

His lips brushed hers again, once, then twice, teasing hers apart. His tongue seduced hers into a lazy dance, lulling her into mists that thickened slowly, sweetly.

No one had ever kissed her like this, spent so much time, shown so much patience. And when he began to inch down the zipper at her back, she shivered in delicious anticipation.

But he didn't peel the dress away, simply spread it apart, stroking his hands over her back. He wanted time to enjoy every inch of her, every moment of this first time. Even when her hands clutched at him, her nails raked down his shirt, he took his time.

It built slowly, this pleasure, layer over layer of heat tangling with layer over layer of need. So when he slipped the dress from her shoulders, listened to it rustle as it fell in a pool, he was ready to take them both to the next stage.

Thoughtfully, he traced a fingertip along the swell of her breasts, over the top of her strapless black bra. ''Very nice,'' he said softly, then trailed that fingertip down, over her midriff, down to flick over the slim matching garter belt. ''Very, very nice.''

''Let's see if I can say the same.'' Struggling to keep her hands steady, she slipped off his jacket and began unbuttoning his shirt. The candlelight flickered over his skin, that lovely dusky gold; shimmered over the lean torso, the long muscles. She ran her tongue between her teeth, slid her gaze up.

''Yes, very, very nice.''

He swept her up, making her heart flop in her chest. ''It's about to get better.''

Chapter 16

She expected speed now, fast hands, and would have welcomed them. But when he lay her on the bed, when he covered her, when he slid down her body, those hands were slow, thorough and devastating.

He heard her moan, felt her arch, and in one blind moment dug teeth into her thigh just above the top of her stocking. When she shuddered, he ran his tongue up, over, then into her.

Shocked by the sudden change, staggered by the sharp lance of pleasure, she bowed up, opening for him, and felt herself fly like a pebble out of a slingshot.

Greedy, he took, then greedy still, he worked his way up, using hands and mouth, teeth and tongue. He flicked open the front clasp of her bra and feasted.

Delirious, desperate for more, she wrapped herself

around him, her hands as busy as his, her mouth seeking the taste of him everywhere. The breath tore through her lungs when their lips met again.

"I want you inside me." She tugged at his slacks, fighting them down his hips. "Now. Right now."

Her eyes glinted in the shifting light. Her hair tumbled like wildfire over the bed. He thought in that moment he wanted her more than he wanted to live.

"Then look at me." He panted the words, yanking up her hips. "Look at me when I am."

And drove into her.

He watched those glorious eyes blur, go dark, glassy, and swallowed the moan that trembled through her lips. Beneath him she moved, a silk-skinned lightning bolt.

Power, speed, wild and wicked energy barely tapped. Her nails dug into his back, ran over his hips, dragged through his hair as all the while that marvelous, agile body plunged with his.

He felt the climax tear through her in one long, shuddering rip, gloried in the choked sob that caught in her throat.

He thought *mine,* then his mind emptied as he poured himself into her.

Well, Cat thought when her mind could function again, she'd done it now. All those good intentions, all those sensible lectures she'd given herself—out the window and into the river.

Advantage, Duncan, she decided. Not only had she surrendered her body, but somewhere along the line she'd slipped up and let him get a good grip on her heart, as well.

And she knew just what would happen next. He'd enjoy it. They'd have a tumbling, torrid affair—discreetly, of course. He was, after all, the boss, and wouldn't want to risk gossip. Then when her contract was up, he'd wink her out of his life, perhaps adding a small, tasteful parting gift.

And that would be that.

Men like Duncan Blade didn't make serious plays for itinerant lounge singers.

So, she'd have to prepare herself. And when the time came, she'd do the winking and leaving first.

Determined to follow the rules of this particular game, she ran her hands casually down his back, then lifted her arms and stretched. "Mmm. Very nice, Blade. Very nice."

His head was still reeling. "I feel like a cartoon cat."

"What?"

"You know, one that gets his head bashed with a sledgehammer. Then he has three heads all vibrating and making that really cool sound while his eyes spin around."

She snorted out a laugh and had nearly hugged him before she remembered it was smarter to play it cool. "What happens when his head stops vibrating?"

"He does it all again." Chuckling, he nipped at her throat, her jaw, paused at her mouth with one long, slow kiss. And just as Cat's mind began to fog again, he rolled and tucked her neatly against him.

He was a snuggler, she thought, and felt that grip on her heart tighten, just a bit. "So, you watch a lot of cartoons?"

"They'll take your troubles away. Who can worry when they're in Frostbite Falls?"

"Whatsamatta U."

He laughed and gave her a squeeze. "Don't make it worse…"

"It's Badenov."

"Well, who'd've thought, the sophisticated Cat Farrell and Rocky and Bullwinkle."

"Hey, it takes a very sophisticated palette to truly appreciate moose and squirrel."

"Indeed it does." And there, he thought, was that connection again, on a different level. "My cousin Cybil and I used to have long, intense discussions on the true meaning of those opening credits. She's a cartoonist."

"Oh yeah?"

"Mmm. Clever girl our Cybil." He nudged Cat until they were face-to-face, damp bodies meshing. "Want to have a long, intense discussion?"

"We could do that." Her blood was heating again. She slid against him, scraping her teeth lightly over his chin. "Or I could get my sledgehammer back out."

"I like the way you think." He found her mouth with his, sank in. "Move your things in here."

"Mmm. What?" She jerked back, shoving at his shoulder before he could shift on top of her.

"Your things." His hand skimmed up, cupped her breast. "Move them in here."

"Whoa." Off balance, she squirmed free. "What's that about?"

"I want to be with you. What's the point of you

sleeping two decks below?" He sat up as well and began to nibble her shoulder.

"Discretion. If I move in here, the crew and passengers are going to know. It's not that big a boat."

"So what?" He gave her hips a boost, maneuvering her until her legs were around his waist and they were torso-to-torso. "We're all grown up now, past the climb-through-the-window stage." He ran his hands up her back, moving in so that he could feast on her neck. "I want you here. I just want the hell out of you."

Think, think, think, she ordered herself, even as the blood rushed to her head to roar like the sea. "You've got a bigger bed. A better view. Incredible hands," she said in a humming purr. "But..." While she still could, she laid her hands on his shoulders and held him off. "If I move my stuff in here, the cabin below stays mine. No booking it."

He looked into her eyes. "You want an escape route?"

"Tidier that way, sugar. If either one of us decides the arrangement's getting old, I just move back down. No harm, no foul."

He ignored the quick twist of annoyance and gripped her hips again. "Deal."

Then he lifted her, filled her.

It didn't get old. She kept expecting it to, at least on his part. But the longer they were together, the more they seemed to need to stay that way. She told herself it was the sex. Lord knew their hunger for each other didn't appear to be waning.

Late nights and early mornings. One sweltering

afternoon in Natchez where he surprised her with a hotel suite and they'd made energetic love in an enormous tub frothy with swirling bubbles. A hot, fast coupling against her dressing room door that had taken them both by surprise and had left her shimmering through her first show.

He still brought her flowers, and foolish little gifts. She couldn't get a handle on it. He had her, why was he still pursuing her? It had been nearly three weeks since they'd become lovers, she thought as she rolled over in the bed she now thought of as hers as much as his.

They'd cruised up the river, down and now up again, and this…connection between them remained.

She didn't have a clue what to do about it.

Enjoy, Cat, she ordered herself. Just enjoy the moment.

She stretched and thought about snuggling back into sleep. They were docked in Saint Louis, and Duncan was doing whatever it was he did on these early mornings in port. She had the entire day off, and no desire to go into the city. She'd take the afternoon to work on her demo, though she wasn't entirely convinced Duncan really meant to do anything with it.

Still, she'd taken the controls back and had fired Cicero. The moron. She'd need that demo when this gig was up. She'd have to find a new agent, another run. The salary from this one would tide her over, give her enough of a cushion to select representation with more care.

She wasn't going back to those one-night stands

in hotel bars, riding the bus from city to city and living out of her trunk in some two-bit room.

She'd had just a little too much of a taste of the good life, and she liked it.

No time like the present, she decided, and rose to dress and take advantage of the near-empty boat.

She strolled out on deck, wincing against the bright flash of sunlight until her dark glasses were in place. The heat was outrageous, shimmering visibly over the water, and had driven those who remained on board inside, where air-conditioning made life civilized.

But she liked the heat, and treated herself to a stroll before buckling down to work.

Sometimes, when she was alone like this, she liked to imagine the boat was hers. Her personal vessel with its glossy white paint and fancy rails. She hadn't realized she'd enjoy life on the river quite so much, and already knew she'd miss it dreadfully when it was over.

But nothing lasted forever, she reminded herself. So you grabbed on to all you could while you had it.

Then she turned the corner and saw Duncan in a hard embrace with a slim strawberry blonde.

Son of a bitch! Her hands fisted at her sides even as her heart slammed down to her toes. *Nobody* two-timed Cat Farrell. *Nobody* played her for a fool. She wanted to lunge forward, rip the slut's eyes out, then finish up by scooping Duncan Blade's cheating heart right out of his chest and tossing it overboard.

All that held her back was a thin, vibrating strand of pride. Damned if she'd let him know he could hurt her. So she sucked the hurt in, tossed her head and strolled toward them as if she hadn't a care in the world.

"Nice morning. You jerk."

The easy smile he'd sent her blinked away into bafflement. "Huh?"

"Who the hell do you think you are?" Pride hadn't held, after all. And there was a vicious satisfaction in jabbing him in the chest. "You think you can climb out of bed with me, then cozy up with some—"

"Mother," Duncan said quickly, grabbing Cat's hand before she could jab him again and put a hole in his heart. "And not just some mother, my mother. Mom, Cat Farrell. I was telling you about her."

"So you were." And obviously leaving out some very pertinent details, Serena thought, but she smiled and offered Cat a hand. "First I have to thank you for the compliment."

Mortified, and furiously working out why this unspeakable embarrassment was Duncan's fault, Cat took the offered hand. "I beg your pardon, Mrs. Blade."

"Oh, please don't," Serena said with a laugh. "You'll spoil it."

Some of the stiffness went out of Cat's shoulders. After all, she thought, the woman was lovely. She didn't look like anyone's mother with that gorgeous glinting hair and those exotic lavender eyes. The breezy yellow slacks and blouse set off a slim figure, and her skin was rose-petal smooth.

"An honest mistake." But Cat took her hand back

and shoved it into the pocket of her baggy shorts.
"You're beautiful."

"I like you. We've surprised Duncan, too," Serena went on. "His father and I decided to fly in and meet the boat, take a day before we head west. We have some business in Vegas."

"And that's not all." Thoroughly delighted with Cat's reaction, Duncan slid an arm around his mother's shoulders. "My grandparents are here. They're going to cruise down to New Orleans with us."

Terrific, Cat thought. God. "That's nice for you. You'll have to excuse me, I was just..." She trailed off as a man headed down the deck toward them.

He was tall, his golden skin gleaming in the sun. Dark glasses shielded his eyes and made his sculpted face mysterious and not a little dangerous. Silver glinted in a rich mane of raven black hair.

Prime, was all Cat could think. Absolutely prime. The champion of heartbreakers.

"Justin." Serena held out a hand. "Come meet Cat Farrell, the singer Duncan's been telling us about."

His father, Cat mused. Well, no wonder Duncan was sinfully attractive. He came from premium stock.

"A pleasure." Justin caught Cat's hand between both of his. "Both Mac and Duncan have told us what an asset you are to our entertainment area. I'm hoping we can book you into the Comanche Atlantic City."

She didn't dance a jig—but she wanted to. "I'll look forward to it." She had to get out of here, Cat thought, before she did something ridiculous. Like turn cartwheels. "I have some work to do. I hope I'll see you before you go."

"Count on it," Serena said under her breath as Cat walked away. Then, lifting a brow, she turned to her son. "So…"

"So, let's go inside before we melt. I want to make sure Grandma and Grandpa are settling in, and I need to get the papers Dad wants to review." Duncan took his mother's hand. "And yes, I'll tell you about it."

"Good."

An hour later Serena rattled the ice in her tall glass of cold tea and laughed. "He set you up! He just plopped her down on your boat the same way he plopped Justin down on my ship all those years ago."

"More or less," Duncan agreed. "I'm going to have to thank him for it."

"Don't. Please." Justin held up a hand. "You'll create a monster."

"Well, I can't fault his taste. She's fabulous." Behind his desk, Duncan kicked back in his chair. "Professionally speaking, she's amazing. It's a miracle she isn't topping the charts. Bad management is what I figure. But we're going to fix that."

"We?" Serena said.

"The family has connections," he said simply. "And I intend to use them. I know she grew up poor and she grew up rough, and her life hasn't changed much there. But there's no reason for that to continue when she's got a gift like she does. That's the business side. As for the personal, I just haven't quite figured it out yet. She's…unusual, and I've never felt for anyone what I feel for her.''

Frowning a little, he picked up a brass paperweight in the shape of the MacGregor clan symbol and passed it from hand to hand. Feelings were the issue, he mused. Strong and urgent, soft and sweet, a tangled confusion of them neatly winding around his heart.

No other woman, at any other time, had ever come close to taking root in his heart.

''Maybe because she's not like anyone else. I'm going to exercise our option and book her for another six weeks. Professionally, it's a solid move. She really pulls them in. Personally, it'll give me a little more time to…figure it out.''

Part of you already has, Serena thought, slipping her hand into Justin's as she studied her son's face. But your head just hasn't caught up with your heart.

She didn't have much time herself, Serena mused as she slipped away from her family to find Cat. She wanted a clearer impression of the woman who was dazzling her son. Though she'd managed to wheedle some facts out of her father—while scorching him for interfering in her child's life—she needed more.

Who was Cat Farrell, and was her heart big enough to make room for Duncan?

She laughed at herself as she reached the doors of the main lounge. Not to put too fine a point on it, she supposed she was about to follow her father's footsteps and do some meddling of her own.

Then she opened the doors and stopped. Stopped and just listened.

Cat was at the piano at the corner of the stage.

She played well, not brilliantly, Serena thought, but with enough style to give that stunning voice a path to follow. And that voice caressed the heart-breaking lyrics of ''Am I Blue'' with a power that had to come straight from the soul.

When it was done, Serena's eyes were wet.

''You should be too young to do that song justice,'' she said, smiling when Cat's head whipped around. ''But you sing it as though it was written for you.''

Struggling not to be uncomfortable, Cat turned on the bench. ''That's my job.''

''No, it's your gift. You made me cry.''

''The highest of compliments. Thanks.''

''I know I'm interrupting.'' Still, she crossed the room to sit beside Cat on the piano bench. ''I was hoping to persuade you to join all of us for dinner tonight.''

''It's a family deal.'' She knew nothing about families, and everything about being the outsider.

''We'd like you to come. You've met my father.''

''Yes, briefly, when I was in Vegas. He makes an impression.''

''Oh, indeed he does.'' Laughing, Serena shifted to noodle with the keys. ''He was very taken with you.''

After a beat, Cat nodded. ''I suppose Duncan told you that Mr. MacGregor arranged for me to have this gig.''

''For his own purposes, yes. That's The Mac-Gregor. He can't help it.'' She smiled gently. ''I hope you're not offended.''

"No. Surprised."

"Really, why?"

"I'd have expected him to browse through the debutante line for his grandson."

"And to that The MacGregor would say, 'Debutante! Hah!' A good heart and a strong spine's what he looks for, and I'd say you have both. A good mind, strength of purpose and an appreciation of family."

Cat lifted her eyebrows. "I barely finished high school, so far my purpose has mostly been to earn enough to keep from going hungry and my only family is my mother. Though I appreciate her very much."

"And to that he would say 'Cat Farrell has grit.' There's no winning with Daniel MacGregor."

Cat looked down at her hands, then at Serena's. Duncan's mother had lady's hands, she mused. A lady's face. A lady's way. She thought she was getting the drift. "And you'd like me to move along, Mrs. Blade, before Duncan starts thinking his grandfather might have a pretty good idea."

Serena stopped playing, looked over and into Cat's eyes. "Why would you think that?"

"It's obvious enough. I know what I am and where I come from. My father was an ordinary man who had the bad luck to die when he wasn't yet thirty. My mother's a waitress who never had a chance to be anything else. And I sing for my supper. You're father might be old and sentimental, but you wouldn't be."

"I see." Serena considered. "And if I offered you,

say…ten thousand dollars to move along, what would you say?''

Green fire flashed, cold and bitter. "I'd say go to hell, Mrs. Blade.''

To Cat's surprise, Serena threw back her head and laughed delightedly. "Oh, I knew I liked you—the minute you tore into Duncan on deck, I knew it. Cat, since you don't know me, I won't be insulted by you considering me a shallow snob, more interested in pedigree than my son's happiness, but…'' She paused, and her lovely eyes sobered. "You should think more of yourself than you apparently do.''

"I don't know what you're talking about.''

"I'm talking about the fact that the only one in here who's thinking of you as less than an interesting, appealing and delightful woman, is you.''

Gently now, she laid a hand over Cat's. "I love my son. He's a beautiful young man in every possible way. How could I be less than happy that you love him, too?''

"I didn't say I loved him.'' Struck with sheet-white panic, Cat yanked back and scrambled up. "I didn't say that.''

Can't be, she thought dizzily. Won't be.

"No.'' Serena smiled again. "No, you didn't. But if you ever do, I'll be very happy for him. I'll let you get back to work.'' She rose gracefully. "Think about dinner, will you?''

Serena was nearly out the door before Cat could speak again. "Mrs. Blade?''

"Yes?''

"I figured when I saw this setup—'' she gestured

to encompass the boat ''—that Duncan was a lucky man. Looks like I didn't know the half of it.''

"Oh yes," Serena said. "I really do like you." Then she breezed out, content.

Chapter 17

Cat hadn't expected to fall in love during a six-week gig on the river. And she certainly hadn't expected to find herself in love with a ninety-year-old man.

But she fell, head over heels, for Daniel Mac-Gregor.

He was a rogue, and that appealed to her own sense of adventure. He was a hothead, and she appreciated pitting her own temper against an equal. His heart was sentimental mush, his mind razor sharp. The combination was more than she could resist.

She wasn't quite so sure of Anna MacGregor. There, she thought, was dignity, serenity and that steel-and-velvet ladylike quality that could never be learned. You were born with it.

Her daughter had it, Cat mused. She imagined all

the MacGregor women did, including those who'd come into the family through marriage.

Well, she'd never be a lady, had no desire to be. She didn't intend to get anywhere through marriage. She was a solo act, and intended to stay that way. But she could meet The MacGregor head-to-head and enjoy every moment.

"You don't know one single Scottish ballad? What kind of singer are you?"

"A torch singer, Mr. MacG." Enjoying herself, Cat rehearsed in the empty lounge for an audience of one. Daniel had taken to sitting at one of the tables whenever the lounge was closed, and commenting and kibitzing on her song list.

"That means you can't have some variety?" He glowered at her from under snowy white eyebrows. "Why, there's some Scottish tunes that will rip a man's heart out of his chest while it's still beating. With that voice of yours, any man with the blood of the Scots in him would fall in love with you."

Deliberately, she skimmed a hand through her hair. "They all fall in love with me anyway."

He barked out a laugh, thumped his big fist on the table. "You're a sassy lass, Cat Farrell. Why aren't you reeling in that handsome grandson of mine?"

It was another standard question, and Cat grinned wickedly. "Because I'm holding out for you. Why settle for small fry when you can have the big shark?"

His wide face went pink with pleasure. When he stroked his soft white beard, his eyes, blue as summer, were canny. "He'll give you fine babies."

"Give you, you mean. I've figured you out, Mr.

MacG.'' She leaned over and kissed him. ''You won't be happy until you have enough great-grandchildren to fill an auditorium.''

''Anna frets for them.'' And since his wife wasn't about, he sneaked a cigar out of his pocket. ''And she worries day and night over young Duncan.''

''Your wife has a very smooth brow for such a worrywart.'' Cat picked up a matchbook, struck one and grinned into Daniel's eyes as he puffed the cigar into life. ''If you run away with me, sugar, neither of us will have a worry in the world.''

''Seducing my grandfather again?'' Duncan strolled in, feeling the lift in his heart he experienced whenever he came across them together. Which, he noted, was often.

''I might have talked him into taking me to Venice if you hadn't popped up.'' She'd barely managed to smirk before Duncan had her by the hair and was kissing the breath out of her.

''Now then.'' Daniel thumped his fist again. ''That's more like it! Keep a good strong hold on that one, lad. She's slippery.''

''I've got her,'' Duncan said easily. And he was beginning to think he meant to keep her. ''Lounge opens in twenty, Grandpa,'' he murmured, keeping his eyes on Cat's. ''Go play somewhere else now.''

''That's no way to talk to your grandfather,'' Cat said sternly.

''It is when he keeps trying to steal my woman.''

''This woman's trying to steal him.'' She tried to wiggle free and found herself firmly caught. ''Some of us are working here, sugar.''

''I'm the boss, remember? Excuse us, Grandpa, I

have to have a little business meeting with the talent here.'' As he pulled Cat toward her dressing room, he called back over his shoulder. ''By the way, Grandma's on her way here. You're going to want to lose that cigar.''

''Sweet Mary,'' Daniel muttered, hurriedly stubbing out the cigar, waving at smoke. Then he smiled sentimentally as Duncan dragged Cat away.

He was willing to take odds there'd be a wedding before summer ended.

''Duncan, I was having a conversation with Mr. McG.''

''You're having one with him every time I turn around. Can't believe the old man's beating my time.''

''I'm crazy about him.''

''So am I. But...'' He closed the dressing room door, flicked the lock, then nudged her back against the wall. Watching her, he skimmed his hands up her sides, over her breasts, down again.

''Oh well,'' she murmured as her heart rose up to pound hard in her throat. Keep it light, she ordered herself, keep it sexy. Don't think, don't feel any more than you can handle. ''Why didn't you say so?'' She wrapped her arms around him and prepared to pull him into a hot, turbulent kiss.

But he framed her face with his hands, let his mouth hover over hers, then brush, then nibble. He wanted to hear her breath catch as it did when he took her slowly under. Wanted to feel that gradual, almost reluctant melting, that fluid surrender.

Sometimes it was a fire in the blood, all heat and

flash and glory. In those moments they couldn't take each other fast enough.

Other times it was like carefree children, all wrestling and laughter.

And now and then, it was slow and tender. All heart. And that, he realized as his mouth cruised lazily over hers, was what he wanted now. He wanted her heart.

So she sighed, and she sank into his arms. And she gave what she'd never known she had to give. With him there was always more inside her, one more well of emotion to be tapped, one more door to be quietly nudged open.

She said his name as he picked her up to carry her to the sofa, murmured it as he lay down with her, moaned it as his hands began to move over her.

The stroke of fingertips over flesh, the warmth of breath mingling. Mouths meeting to slide into kisses long and deep and aching.

He felt her pulse trip under his hands, felt her heart race under his mouth. But he wanted more than excitement, more than desire. He wanted love.

"Let me in." He murmured it against her mouth. "I'll never hurt you."

But he was, even then he was. He was ripping something inside her, tearing something out of her that she was terrified to lose. She shook her head, denying both of them, but his mouth was patient, his hands ruthlessly tender.

They opened her heart, held it wide and let him tumble in.

The change destroyed her, left her helpless and floundering. He slipped into her, braced so that he could watch her face, the awareness and the confusion in her eyes.

His own heart filled to bursting. "It's different."

She couldn't speak, only shook her head, swallowed a sob as his mouth covered hers again. Unable to resist, she flowed with him, over the high warm wave. Then under.

"It's different," he said again.

She grabbed a robe from a hook, shrugged into it. Desperate for balance, she jerked the belt into place.

Suicide. Hadn't she said he was suicide? And here she was, teetering right on the edge of the cliff.

"No, it's not." She wanted to mean it. "And it doesn't have to be."

He angled his head. "Why does it scare you to know that I care about you? That you matter to me?"

"It doesn't." To settle her restless hands, she snapped up her brush and began to drag it through her hair. "Whatever you may think of me, I don't have sex with men unless I matter."

"That's not what I said or what I mean." He tugged on his slacks, then reached for his shirt. "You're good at turning the point around to suit yourself, Cat. But I'm just as good at sticking to what's important. Right now, you are."

"Well, that's fine." Her eyes met his in the mirror. "I like being important." Steadier, she set the brush down, then turned and leaned back against the counter. "You're important, too, Duncan. Is that what you want to hear? Of course you are, or I wouldn't still be with you. Don't complicate this."

"Funny, I actually think I'm simplifying it. What do you feel for me?"

"A great many things. I want you—I think that's obvious enough. I enjoy you." Smiling, she walked over to run her hands up his chest. "I like your style, I like your face and I downright adore your body."

The amusement she'd hoped for didn't flicker in his eyes. They remained steady, level and just a little cool. "And without the sex?"

"Hard to say." She shrugged, turned away to straighten the cosmetics on the counter, but her hands felt numb. "Since we're not without it, are we? But for the sake of argument..." She made herself turn back. "I'd still like you. You're a likable man. I don't make a lot of friends, Duncan. I'm not in one place long enough to go to the trouble or take the risk that friendship involves. You're an exception."

His brow winged up. Odd, he mused, to feel delighted and irritated at the same time. "So, we're friends?"

"Aren't we?"

"I suppose we are." He gave her the same easy smile she gave him. "Well, pal, we'll be pulling out of port shortly. I have to get to work."

"I'll see you around." She felt a shudder, as if some major crisis had been narrowly evaded. "Oh, and Duncan? Nice doing business with you, sugar."

He flashed a grin as he opened the door. But when he shut it behind him, his eyes narrowed, darkened, and the smile went thin.

He'd always considered himself a lucky man. But what the hell kind of luck was it for him to so suddenly fall in love, so ridiculously in love, with a woman who didn't follow any standard pattern?

Love wasn't a game he'd expected to play until he was damn good and ready. But the cards had already been dealt. He was just going to have to see that she anted up and didn't bluff him out of the pot.

Because when Duncan Blade played, he played to win.

Chapter 18

For the rest of the week he let it ride, held his cards close to the vest and let the pot build.

It wasn't exactly a sacrifice, he decided as he did his pass through the casino. The more she relaxed, the more...demonstrative she became.

And he enjoyed watching the way she flirted with his grandfather, the way she gradually warmed toward his grandmother. Once he'd come across the two of them with their heads together on deck and would have sworn the sexy Cat and the serene Anna were sharing secrets.

He needed to talk with Cat himself and hadn't managed to make time that afternoon. He'd skimmed over her contract, refreshing himself on the details of the option. It seemed only fair he talk to her before he called her agent and enforced it.

Then there was the call he'd gotten just that morning from Reed Valentine of Valentine Records. He imagined Cat was going to be very pleased with how well the demo he'd sent in had been received.

It wasn't something he wanted to tell her on the fly. Such news, he concluded, required the right setting. And he'd already taken steps to provide it after her second show.

It made him smile to think of it, so the warmth of that showered onto the Kingston sister who grabbed his hand as he passed the blackjack table.

"Oh, I'm going to miss that." She shot him her very best smile in return. "I can't believe our vacation is up tomorrow."

"I hope you enjoyed it." Which one was this? he wondered vaguely. Cindi? Sandi? Candi?

"Every minute. We're talking about doing it again next year. It's so much fun."

"We aim to please. Any luck?"

She kept her baby blues on his. "Not as much as I'd like."

He had to laugh. "I meant with the cards."

"There either, but it's been entertaining. I don't suppose you ever get to Philadelphia."

"I've been known to." Then he saw Cat swagger into the casino and everything else went out of his mind. "Excuse me."

The blonde watched him walk away, blew out a wistful sigh. "Some people have all the luck," she said to the dealer.

Cat watched him, too, studying the way he moved, the way he strode through the tables, past the machines, through the tempting, seductive sounds of money being won and lost.

Oh yeah, she mused. This was definitely his turf.

"Hey." He took her hand, toyed with her fingers. "You never come in here."

"No reason to. I don't—"

"Gamble as a rule. Ever break the rules?"

"All the time, sugar."

"Want a game?"

"I've only got twenty till cue."

"Time enough." He spotted an empty table, pleased she'd chosen the early hour to wander in. "Come on. I come from a long line of blackjack dealers."

"Sure you do."

"Well, a short line then. My mother was a dealer. That's how she met my father."

"Really?" It intrigued her enough to let him draw her over. "And who won?"

"Both of them. I'll spot you a hundred."

"I can cover my bets."

"Fine, you're on credit then." With nimble fingers he counted out and stacked her chips. "You look especially delicious tonight, darling."

What the hell, she thought, and slid onto a stool. Her midnight blue dress clung to every curve and shimmered under the lights. "Last night before we dock. I always want to leave them happy." She nudged a five-dollar chip onto her mark. "Deal 'em, sugar."

He dealt her a five and a seven, gave himself a facing ace. "Possible blackjack. Insurance?"

"I don't believe in it. Hit me." She took an eight and smiled.

"The hand is twenty." He flipped over his down

card. "Dealer has seven or seventeen, takes ten, busts on twenty-four." He slid her winnings over, slipped more cards out of the shoe. "How about a date later, beautiful?"

"Maybe." She glanced at her cards. Eighteen. And his. A six showing. "I'll hold."

"Holds on eighteen, dealer has fifteen, wins with nineteen." And grinned as he turned up a four.

"Do you often call your shots?"

"As often as possible."

He was good. She imagined he was good at whatever game he played. But then, so was she. And most often she played to survive, so she never, never wagered anything she couldn't afford to lose.

Not money, not time. And never her heart. But when she laid down her stake, she played to win. "Deal," she said, and smiled at him.

He nipped her the next three hands running and had her eyeing him narrowly.

"Nothing up my sleeve," he assured her. "We run a clean game."

"Can't beat the house."

"You don't gamble," he pointed out. "You hold too easily, aren't willing to chance the cards."

"I can't control the cards, especially if I'm not dealing them."

"Want to switch? Come on."

She started to refuse, then shrugged her shoulders. "Why not? You never know when you might need a fall-back career." Amused, she walked around to stand behind the table, scanned the casino. "Different perspective, isn't it?"

"Same game, same odds."

"Only now they favor me. I'll spot you, sugar. Place your bet."

He slid one of her chips over, waited for his cards. She looked entirely too pleased with herself when she turned up the corner of her hold card under her nine.

He had two eights. "Split. Deal me two more."

"I know how it's done," she said dryly. Then lifted a brow when he tapped on the hand now showing sixteen. "You're going to hit that?"

"That's right. A five will do." When she dealt him a four and frowned, he nodded. "Close enough. Hold here, hit there," he said, and gestured to the second hand of thirteen. She topped it with an eight and swore under her breath.

"Nineteen loses," she muttered, flipping over her queen. It wasn't just the cards, she decided. She kept losing ground to him; he kept tempting her to risk a little more. And every time she did, every time she let herself sink into him, it was harder to remember how much it cost when your hand—or your heart— went bust.

"You're good, Blade."

"That's my job."

"Well, since you've just taken me for thirty bucks in about five minutes, I'm done. At this rate I'll lose my shirt before cue."

"We can play strip blackjack later."

She laughed, and bent down to lean on the table. That was a game she could afford—where the odds were even between them. "I just came in to tell you I've got a little surprise for your grandfather at the end of the second show. Thought you might get a kick out of it.''

"What is it?"

"Come see for yourself." She slid her eyes to the side and smiled smugly at the Kingston blonde. "If you can tear yourself away from your harem."

"Sweetheart, I'm all yours."

"Right." She chuckled, patted his cheek, then straightened. "We'll settle up later. Got to go earn my losses."

She walked out with a not-so-subtle swing of hips that had him blowing out a breath. Yes indeed, he mused, they would definitely settle up later.

She finished up the second show, well aware that Duncan had slipped in and was now seated at the table with his grandparents. She'd worked out the timing with Anna, and stepped out of the lights as the crowd began to thin.

Some would remain, back at the bar or scattered at tables, but she considered this a personal performance. And one that oddly had little wings of nerves fluttering in her gut.

"Don't know what your problem is, boy," Daniel muttered. "That woman's made for you."

"Daniel." Anna only sighed. She'd come to the same conclusion herself and could have bopped him for saying anything that might tip the balance the wrong way. "Leave Duncan alone. He's a man grown."

"My point! My point exactly. When is he going to do his duty? When is he going to act like a man and settle down, I want to know? He lets that lass slip through his fingers, well, he's—he's no blood of mine. Hah!'' Folding his arms, Daniel sat back and glared.

Knowing it would make his grandfather twitch with envy, Duncan drew out a slim cigar, ran it lovingly through his fingers. Then clamping it between his teeth, he lit it, puffed contentedly while Daniel's blue eyes glittered with annoyance and desire.

''Who said I was going to let her slip through my fingers?''

''If you'd use the eyes in your head, you'd see…'' Trailing off, Daniel backtracked, sucked in air, then slapped Duncan hard on the back. ''Well then! Hah! You see, Anna, didn't I tell you the boy was bright? Didn't I tell you not to fret?''

''Constantly, Daniel.'' Adoring them both, Anna laid her hands over theirs. ''I like her very much, Duncan.''

''I know. Now keep him out of it, will you, so I can make it work.''

''Keep me out!'' Insulted, Daniel boomed the protest through the room, making the few heads left in the lounge turn. ''Why, you pip-squeak, you wouldn't be in it if I hadn't—''

''What, Daniel?'' Anna said it sweetly, with a soft smile on her face. ''You didn't interfere or meddle again, did you?''

''Ah. No, I did nothing. Nothing at all. Don't know what you're talking about. I'm just saying…what I'm saying.'' He thought it best to retire from the field. ''We should be getting along, Anna. You need your rest.''

''I'll just finish my wine.'' She lifted her glass,

shifting in her chair—the signal she'd worked out earlier with Cat.

Taking her cue, Cat stepped into the key light. "Daniel MacGregor? I have something for you."

"Well, what are you doing skulking around then? Come over here and give it to me."

"It comes from here. And from here," she added, touching a hand to her heart.

She sang for him, the old Scottish ballad "Loch Loman." Because she kept her eyes on him, she saw his begin to swim. And felt her own sting in response.

Duncan had accepted, or nearly, that he was in love with her. But as he sat there, as he saw the softness that came over her as she sang for the man who held such a large piece of his heart, he realized he'd only been falling up to that point.

Now he tumbled clean.

It wasn't the jolt he'd thought it would be. Wasn't the shock to the system he'd always imagined. It was warm and clear, with her at the core of it. He saw his life change, and was Scot enough to accept it had been heading there all along.

Now, somewhere, he had to win her.

Beside him, Daniel sniffed, fumbled for his handkerchief, then blew his nose heartily when the song ended. "Now, that's a lass," he managed. "That's a fine lass."

"I'm going to miss you, Daniel." She stepped over to bend and kiss his cheek. "I'm really going to miss you."

"There now." And to her surprise and weepy pleasure, he drew her into his lap to cuddle.

"Duncan, take a walk with me," Anna murmured. She took his hand, drawing him away from the table. "That girl needs love." She said it softly as Duncan glanced back at the couple holding each other at the edge of the stage.

"I have it for her. I just have to convince her to take it."

Anna squeezed his hand. "My money's on you."

He knew she was tired, could see it in her eyes as he walked her to their cabin. He doubted she let her emotions tip over and out very often. For a woman like Cat, Duncan imagined the experience was exhausting.

"That was a beautiful thing you did for my grandfather."

"I'm nuts about him. Seriously nuts about him." It frightened her, more than a little, that she'd come to care so much about people who could never be hers.

"I'd say the feeling's mutual. If it wasn't for my grandmother and oh, close to seventy years of age difference, I'd be worried."

She laughed, settled again, and struggled back a yawn. "I wouldn't be too sure of myself, even as things stand." She stepped in ahead of him when he unlocked the cabin, then blinked in surprise at the glow of candlelight, the glint of crystal.

"What's all this, Blade?"

"I thought you might break another rule." He moved to the ice bucket, took out the chilling bottle.

"Champagne?" She glanced at the label, whistled. "The good stuff, too. What's the occasion?"

"We'll get to that. Would you like a glass?"

"I could probably choke one down, thanks. Is this why you didn't want me to change after the show? So I'd be dressed for fancy French grapes?"

"No, I didn't want you to change because I want to undress you. Eventually." He opened the bottle with an expert twist and cheerful pop.

He poured two flutes, handed her one, then tapped rims. "To those amazing pipes of yours."

She laughed, sipped. "How could I not drink to that?"

"We're coming up on the last week of your contract."

She was grateful she'd swallowed or she might very well have choked. "Yes, I know. It's been a good run."

"I want to exercise our option."

Her heart began to beat again. "Well, I can drink to that, too."

"I wanted to talk it over with you before I called your agent."

"I fired my agent, so you can deal with me direct."

"Fired him?" Duncan pursed his lips, then nodded. "Smart move, but you'll want representation."

"They're not exactly beating down my door, sugar. I'll get to it when the time comes, though."

"I'd say it's come. Reed Valentine would like to schedule a meeting and arrange for a professional demo, in studio, in New York, when it suits you."

She couldn't feel her hands. Or her feet. She realized dizzily that all she could feel was the sudden, ferocious hammering of her heart. "Reed Valentine? Valentine Records? A meeting? With me? Why?"

"Suddenly you're full of questions." With a laugh, he toasted her again. "Yes, Reed Valentine of Valentine Records wants a meeting with you because he was very favorably impressed with the tape you put together."

"You sent it in? You sent it to Reed Valentine."

"I told you I was going to send it to a connection of mine."

Valentine Records. Now she couldn't feel her own lips. But she could feel the abrupt lurch of her stomach. "I didn't expect—I never thought…"

"Didn't you think I meant it, Cat? I don't play games like that."

"No, I don't—God, I can't breathe." She pressed a hand to her chest as if to push out air, but couldn't find any. "I can't get my breath."

Alarmed, he reached for her. She'd gone dead white. "Hey. Sit down."

"No. Yes. No. I need some air."

She shoved the wineglass into his hand and bolted for the balcony doors. Her head was light, as if she'd swallowed the whole bottle of champagne in one gulp. She couldn't get her breath because the air was trapped somewhere under her diaphragm.

She clutched the rail and leaned out, staring blindly at the slow-moving river.

"Isn't this what you want?"

With her back to him she squeezed her eyes shut, felt the tears pressing hot behind her lids. "My whole life. It's all I've ever wanted in my whole life. Just

a chance, just one chance to prove I could be somebody.''

When her voice broke, she bore down hard. "I
need a minute here, Duncan. Okay? Just give me a
minute here.''

Instead he went to her, turned her to face him and
saw her eyes were drenched. "I thought I knew how
much it meant to you.'' He said it gently, as gently
as the hand that brushed the first tears from her
cheek. "I didn't. I should have found a better way
to tell you.''

"No, it's perfect, it's fine.'' She was terrified,
down to the bone, of what he was offering. Of him.
Of everything that was pounding and beating inside
her. "If you'd just leave me alone for a minute. I
need to pull myself together.''

"No, you don't.'' He gathered her close. "You
need to let yourself go.''

Her breath hitched once, then shattered on a sob.
She clung, pressing her face into his shoulder, holding on to him, to the feeling, to the gift. "This is
everything to me. Everything. Even if they change
their minds, hate what I do, kick me out on my butt,
this is everything. The chance. I'll never be able to
pay you back for it.''

"There's nothing to pay back. Cat—''

"It's everything,'' she said again, and framed his
face as she drew back. "Everything. I'm so grateful,
Duncan.'' She let everything she felt pour out into
the kiss. "Let me show you.''

"Cat, I'm not looking for gratitude.''

"I have to give it.'' She kissed him again, hyp-
notizing them both. "Let me give it.''

Chapter 19

She'd been like a witch, Duncan thought, casting spells. Now, in the clear light of day, he was still weaving under them.

He'd wanted to tell her he loved her. Wanted to ask her to belong to him. But it hadn't seemed fair when she'd been riding an emotional roller coaster already.

He preferred to play fair. When possible.

He could wait until night. Until the air was soft and quiet, and they were alone with the river. In any case, that would give him several hours to figure out how to tell her. What words he should use, what tone.

He wished he could be certain of her, but some odds were impossible to figure.

He imagined the ring he'd dashed out that morning

to buy after seeing his grandparents off was going to weigh heavily in his pocket all day.

The best way to make the time pass, he decided, was to fill it with work.

Cat had prepared all morning, had thought it all through. There was only one possible answer. Duncan Blade had given her something she'd been working for all of her life. And he'd done it with no strings attached.

The only way to repay him, as far as she could see, was to get out of his, quickly, cleanly. No harm, no foul, she told herself as she climbed the steps to his office.

Her knees were shaking. She stopped, cursing herself as she steadied herself again, as she forced herself to admit she wasn't being noble. She was running.

She couldn't handle what she felt for him. Why the hell should she have to? She didn't know how to be in love. She'd never be able to make it work, never be able to cover her stake if she gambled here.

Smarter to cut if off clean now, before she got in any deeper, before she started to let herself believe she could be a real part of his life.

More, it would be cowardly to wait another week, until the end of her current contract, to tell him she was skipping. The decent thing, the professional thing to do was to give him time to book another act.

She wasn't going to pay him back by messing up his business. Or his life.

It was just her bad luck she'd gone and fallen in love with him.

She'd wanted to convince herself it was just gratitude, but hadn't even come close. She wanted to believe she would survive whole and intact when they parted company. But she knew better. It was her doing. She'd opened herself up for it, and now she had to pay the price.

Suddenly the thrill of attaining a lifelong dream didn't have quite the shine it should have.

But Cat Farrell stood by her word, she faced her responsibilities and she handled herself through good times and bad.

Then she stepped to his office and saw him through the window. Her needy heart collapsed in her chest.

Oh God, he was so perfect, she thought. What had his mother said? A beautiful young man, in every way. It was perfectly true. It wasn't just the looks, the charm, the snazzy clothes.

He was kind and he was caring.

He wasn't some kick-it-up trust-fund baby, cruising around on his family money. He worked, and worked hard, and had put his personal stamp on every inch of his boat.

He had integrity, he had ambition.

Dangerous Duncan. Heartbreaker, she mused. You'll forget my name before the season's over.

She drew in a breath, tossed back her hair and sauntered into his office. "Got a minute, boss?"

He leaned back, set his paperwork aside. "Oh, I think I can make one for you. How're you feeling?"

"I'm still flying. Did you see your grandparents off?"

"Yeah, they're going to spend a day in New Orleans, then fly to Boston to visit my sister and my cousins. Play with the babies. They'll catch up with my uncle Caine and aunt Diana, then Grandpa will harass my cousin Ian for a while about why he's still single—a fine young lawyer like him. There was talk about scooting up to Maine so The MacGregor could devil the Campbell side of the family for a bit."

Cat's eyes danced. "It keeps him young."

"Then he'll forever be eighteen, because he's never going to stop."

"Family's his heart."

"Yes. You learned to understand him quickly."

"I learned to love him quickly. Love all of you. Love you so much it makes me shake inside. I have an invitation," she added, and worked up a smile. "An open invitation to visit Hyannis Port anytime I like. I've seen pictures of that castle he built there. Very cool."

"Then we'll make a point for you to see it in person."

Not until she was certain she could bear it, Cat thought. Which would be approximately never. She stretched out her legs, crossed her ankles and prepared to give the performance of her life.

"I don't want to interrupt your work for long, but there's some business we need to talk about."

"Fine. I was going to catch you later, but now's as good a time as any." He flipped open a file folder and took out her contract. "It's a standard option clause, with a guaranteed five-percent salary increase when activated. Everything else remains the same as it did in the original agreement. If you're shaky about signing papers without representation, we can hook you up with a lawyer here in New Orleans, or in one of the ports going back to Saint Louis.''

''I'm not shaky about signing papers, Duncan. I never sign anything without reading it all, top to bottom. Including fine print and bottom line.''

''Smart. Then you've already read these, but you might want to read them again.''

''I don't have to. I don't want to sign.''

He held the papers out between them for several long seconds before he lowered them carefully to the desk. ''Excuse me?''

''I don't want the option enforced. I'm not interested in another run. As far as I'm concerned, when we dock in Saint Louis next weekend, I'm a free agent.''

''Take off the glasses.''

''It's bright in here.''

''You want to talk business, you look me in the eye.''

There, she thought, was that quick shift in his voice. Satin to steel. Because he was right, because it was cowardly to hide behind shaded lenses, she slipped them off, swung them by the earpiece.

He took his time, studying her face, looking for the tells every gambler recognizes. If she was bluffing, he mused, she was damn good at it. ''You want to negotiate new terms?''

''That's not what I said, and I say what I mean.'' She lifted her shoulders, let them fall. ''I've got fresh fish to fry, sugar, and you to thank for it. There's no point in me spending another six weeks singing in a riverboat lounge when I could be in New York.''

"I see. If you read your contract, Cat, you'll know that I have a right to exercise this option clause. You're obliged to honor it.''

Well, she hadn't thought he'd make it easy, had she? "I hoped you'd let me out without a hassle—for old time's sake.''

"Hope springs eternal.'' He rose, walked to the minifridge and took out a bottle of water for each of them. It felt as though someone had opened his chest and given his heart a bare-knuckled punch. ''But this is business, and has nothing to do with the fact we sleep together. Want a glass for this?''

She snatched the bottle out of his hand before she could stop herself. And the little snip of temper eased one of the knots in his stomach. She wasn't quite as cool as she wanted to be.

What was her angle? he wondered. What was the deal?

"Okay, no favors. Fair enough.'' She took a long drink. "So, sue me.''

"Let's just see if we can handle this like professionals first.'' He made his voice deliberately snide and watched her color come up. Nerves, he decided. Feelings. They were there. So he would use them. "You want to get to New York and follow through with Valentine. I can't blame you. When we hit Saint Louis, you can go—'' He held up a finger before she could speak. "I'll get an act to fill in for a week. Then you meet the boat in New Orleans, and fulfill the rest of your contract. Everybody's happy.''

"I don't like that deal.''

"Take it or leave it."

"Leaving it," she said, and got to her feet.

"Sit down."

"Don't tell me what to do."

"Business is concluded. Now it's personal, and I said sit down."

She cocked a hip, lifted the bottle and watched him steadily as she drank. "Is that what this is about, Duncan? Is your ego bruised or something?"

"Do you really think I'm going to let you walk out?"

"Yeah, because if you try otherwise, I'll bruise a hell of a lot more than your ego. Look, it's been fun, and I owe you a lot. But it's moving-on time."

"And that's what you do best? Move on?"

"Yes." Regret flickered in her eyes before she could stop it. "Sorry, I've got to think about number one here. But I won't forget you, sugar."

Then she made a mistake. She flashed a sassy smile and patted his cheek.

The smile faded quickly when he grabbed her wrist.

"You're trembling. *Sugar.*"

"No, I'm not." She couldn't quite manage to swallow, so shrugged instead. "It's cold in here, that's all."

"Like hell. Why are you shaking?"

"You're hurting me."

"No." His fingers barely encircled her wrist. "I'm not, but you're doing your damnedest to hurt *me.* Why?"

"I don't want to hurt you, Duncan." Emotion had her voice wavering. "I don't. Damn it, let me go."

"Not a chance. You want to dump me? You want to move on? No harm, no foul? You're a liar, and you're not as good at it as I'd expected you to be."

"I guess you don't have much experience being the dumpee, do you?"

His brow lifted. "Ah, now. There. There it is. You break it off and run before I can?"

"Let's just call it even."

"No, let's not. Let's just lay the cards on the table and see what we've been holding. I love you, and you're going to marry me."

"What?" If he'd dashed the cold contents of the water bottle in her face, she'd have been less shocked. "What? Are you *crazy?*"

"You're exactly what I want, exactly what I'll have, so get used to it."

"The hell with that. Who the hell do you…I can't get my breath." Struggling for air, she rapped her fist between her breasts. "Damn it."

"Funny, you had the same reaction last night when I told you about Valentine. Something you claimed to have wanted your entire life." He took a step closer while she panted. "See something else you want, Cat?"

"No. Get away from me. You're a lunatic. I need air."

"You're not going anywhere." He took her arm and pushed her into a chair. "We have a tradition in my family." Out of his pocket, he took a coin. "Heads you marry me, tails you walk."

"Oh sure, oh right." Thoroughly dizzy now, she dropped her head between her knees.

"Agreed then."

"I did not." Her head shot back up just as he flipped the coin. He snagged it, and watching her, slapped it onto the back of his hand. "Heads. I win. You want a big, splashy wedding, or something quieter?"

She stayed exactly where she was. She had her breath back now and the blood was no longer pounding in her head. He was angry; she could see that. Beyond the cocky, go-to-hell grin was pure temper. "Duncan, sensible people don't decide to get married on the toss of a coin."

"My parents did, and so will we. You don't plan to welsh on a bet."

"I don't make bets—"

"As a rule," he finished, then, putting his hands on either arm of the chair to cage her, he leaned down. "I love you."

"Get out," she managed, but weakly.

"I love you," he repeated. "That's it for me. I always knew it would be. Time, place, the woman. When it hit it'd be over for me. It's over for me, Catherine Mary. You're the one. Now tell me you don't love me."

"I don't."

"Don't what?"

"Oh, get out of my face. How the hell am I supposed to think with you pushing at me?"

"Just say it," he murmured, and brushed his lips over hers. "And make me believe it."

"It can't work."

"That's not what I asked you."

"I was doing you a favor."

"Thanks. Now tell me."

"Back off, Duncan. You're crowding me."

He smiled, stepped back. Because he'd already seen the answer in her eyes. "Okay, on your feet is more your style."

Because it was, she rose. "I want my career."

"So do I."

He meant it—she could see it. Somehow a miracle had happened and the single thing she'd dreamed of was as important to him. And so was she. That, she realized, was beyond miraculous.

She jammed her hands in her pockets. "I don't need any house in the 'burbs or a white picket fence."

"Please, that image has always petrified me."

It made her laugh, one quick gulp, then she let out a breath. "Do you mean it?"

"Absolutely. I used to have nightmares about white picket fences."

"Duncan." At a loss, she pressed her fingers to her eyes. "I'm trying to be straight with you." She dropped her hands, looked into his eyes. And everything she wanted was right there. "I need you to be straight with me because you can do more than break my heart. You can shatter it."

Tenderness welled up inside him. "I told you I'll never hurt you. I keep my word."

She took a breath, found it came easier. "You're sure this is what you want?"

"Dead sure." He took the ring box out of his pocket. "Guess what I've got here?"

"Oh God. You work fast." She glanced down at her hands. "My palms are sweating. Only happens when I'm really nervous." Absently, she rubbed them on her shorts. "Okay, sugar, you asked for it. Just remember I gave you every chance. I love you, and that's it for me, too. I guess I started heading that way when you tried to roust me at the gangplank. You looked so sexy and dangerous."

"Funny, I was thinking the same thing about you."

"Nobody's ever gotten inside me this way. I've never wanted anyone else inside me this way."

"Then we're starting on even ground." He took her hand again, opened the box.

"Oh man, you could put someone's eye out with that."

He roared with laughter, swung her into his arms for a kiss that left them both giddy. "Want to bet it fits?"

For a moment, she just pressed her cheek to his. My God, she thought, he wanted her. For keeps. "I'm not betting against the house again."

Grinning, he took the square-cut citrine out of the box and slipped it on her finger. "Smart move." He lifted her hand, pressed his lips just above the ring. "Deal?"

"Looks like." She brought their joined hands to her own lips in turn. Hers, she thought. For keeps. "But I want to see that coin."

He cocked a brow, flipped the coin through the fingers of his free hand and vanished it. "What coin?"

From the Private Memoirs
of
Daniel Duncan MacGregor

There are moments that etch themselves into a man's memory like a fine diamond cuts into clear glass. The first time he loves a woman. And the first time he sees the woman he will always love. The moment his child, taken from his mother's womb, is placed yowling with life into his hands.

And the many moments of that child's life that fill his own with joys and sorrows, with laughter and tears.

There are moments etched in my memory, too many to count, too few to take for granted. And all of them cherished.

Another moment joined them recently. I watched a lass I've come to love as much as my own stand in the gardens of the home I built with my Anna. And there, on a fine day in the last winds of summer, she joined hands with my grandson Duncan to become his.

To become ours.

And when the vows were taken, and the first kiss shared as man and wife, didn't she walk straight to me and whisper in my ear, "Thank you, Mr. MacG"—for that's what she likes to call me—"thank you," said she, "for picking me for him."

Well now, I ask you, is that a lass?

Not that I did it for thanks, but by God, it's nice to have your thought and care be appreciated from time to time.

What sons and daughters that pair will make between them. Not that there's any hurry, mind—though Anna, of course, is fretting already that they'll be slow about it.

But, well then, we've done what we can to set them on the right road.

Now I'm watching from my window here, with the last of Anna's roses clinging to their stems and waiting to be whipped away by the coming autumn winds. Time passes, no matter how we wish it might stand still for a bit.

So it's not to be wasted, is it? I've more grandchildren yet who need a bit of direction, a wee bit of a nudge, so to speak. Though we'd best not speak of it, as Anna was in a lecturing mode not long ago when I just happened to mention, in passing, that our young Ian was of an age to be thinking about his future.

Boy's a lawyer now. Seems like yesterday he was toddling along in the parlor and wanting to get his hands on his granny's good crystal vase. Always had an eye for pretty things, did our Ian.

Well, I've found him a pretty one. One I think will suit his sweet nature and soft heart. The lad wants family, make no mistake. Hasn't he just bought himself a house? What does a man buy a house for if it isn't to fill it with family?

Fine enough if he starts with furniture and doodads and the things that content a man to have about him. But it's family that makes a home.

Hasn't it made mine?

And it's the least I can do for a be-

252

*loved grandchild, give him the direc-
tion he needs to go and make his own.
   And the devil I say to those who
claim different.*

Part Three

IAN

Chapter 20

Sometimes, Ian thought, there just weren't enough hours in the day. He hated to rush, whether it was business, pleasure or life in general. But he had to admit that lately it seemed like he'd been doing nothing but tearing around. Which included pushing his way through the mad maze of Boston traffic at peak rush hour.

One more stop, he told himself, then he could go home. His new home. Just the thought of the elegant old house tucked behind dignified old maples made him smile and ignore the rude blast of a horn as traffic snarled.

He'd had two months to enjoy it, to scout antique shops and kitchen-supply departments in order to outfit each room exactly the way he wanted.

And every time he slipped the key into the lock

and walked into the gracious entry with its deep green walls and golden floors he was thrilled his days of college dorms and noisy apartment life were over.

It wasn't that he didn't like company or having people underfoot. He'd come from too large a family not to appreciate the confusion, the clash of personalities, the entertainment that came with crowds.

But he'd wanted his own place. Needed his own place. And he still blessed his cousin Julia for helping him find the perfect house in the perfect place.

Old and established was what he'd wanted, and that's what he'd gotten. Dignity and style and character. He supposed the need for such things ran with the MacGregor blood.

He'd grown up with dignity, style and character, both at home and at work. The law offices of MacGregor and MacGregor stood for all three, as did his parents, his grandparents and all the family that sprawled from them.

Now, along with his parents and his sister, he was part of that respected law firm. He intended to make his mark there, to uphold those traditions, and perhaps, in time, to follow the path of his father and uncle to Washington.

The press occasionally hinted that Ian MacGregor was being groomed for politics. They said he had the family lineage what with his father having served as attorney general and his uncle as the commander-in-chief. He had the looks, the gilt hair, the steady blue eyes, the strong features and firm mouth that made women sigh and men trust.

The tabloids had once had a field day with a shot

of him wearing nothing but a pair of bathing trunks while sailing on the Charles. The result had been a huge increase in tabloid sales and the title of Harvard Hunk, which had stuck—much to Ian's consternation and his family's amusement.

He'd handled it with humor—what choice did he have? And had thumbed his nose at those who said he was just another pretty boy by graduating magna cum laude, holding steady in the top five percent of his graduating class and passing his bar on the first run.

Ian MacGregor hit what he aimed for, and he'd aimed for the law as long as he could remember.

But honors and lauds aside, he was the youngest member of the firm, and as such, was often reduced to the position of errand boy.

His current assignment was little more.

Ian circled, scanning for a parking place without much hope. He settled for one six blocks from his objective and thought he might as well have driven home and walked from there.

Still, he took his briefcase and relaxed enough to window-shop in the artful storefronts on the way up to Brightstone's.

It was balmy early autumn, perfect New England weather, with the trees just beginning to hint at the wild color to come in the evening light of a slowly deepening sky. When he got home, he promised himself, he was going to take a glass of wine, sit on his back porch and survey his kingdom.

With his topcoat flapping in the steady breeze, he

paused outside of Brightstone's and studied the sturdy old building of weathered red brick.

It was an institution in Boston, one he regretted not having had the time to explore in the last couple of years. But now that he lived fairly nearby, he thought he would find opportunities to wander in, stroll through the stacks, the aisles, the towers of books.

Brightstone's *was* books in Boston.

He remembered holding his mother's hand when she'd shopped there in his childhood, then tucking himself into the Children's Corner with picture books. The staff had always been helpful and unobtrusive, the mood serene, the stock expansive.

And remembering the contented hours he'd experienced inside, he thought it might be a fine idea to turn one of his spare rooms into a library.

He stepped inside, pleased to see the familiar soaring ceilings with their fussy cornices, the polished gleam of chestnut floors, the grand sweep of books.

The second floor, as he recalled, would be histories, biographies, local interest, local authors. And the third, a treasure trove of rare books.

As he scanned, he noted that business was good, which surprised him a little. A year or so before, he'd read that the old Boston institution was in serious trouble and apparently unable to compete with the malls or superstores. But there were a number of customers browsing the shelves, more at the graceful old counter making purchases, and a scattering of others settled into the inviting seating arrangements tucked here and there.

That was new, wasn't it? he wondered. Those cushy chairs and thick old tables? He saw, too, a little café had been added to the rear, up a short flight of steps where he remembered towering shelves.

And the music playing quietly in the background wasn't the stern classical tunes he remembered, but something light with harps and flutes.

Interested, he wandered through, noting the Children's Corner remained as it had, but a basket of bright plastic toys and charming posters of fairy tale scenes had been added.

And here a display of eye-catching bookmarks, reading lamps, paperweights and a variety of gifts suitable for a book lover. As he wound his way through, the seductive scent of coffee reached out and hooked him.

Smart, very smart, he decided. It would take a strong will to walk out without a sample—and without a purchase. Telling himself he didn't have time for either, he headed to the checkout area and snagged the attention of a clerk.

"I'm looking for Naomi Brightstone. I'm Ian MacGregor. She's expecting me."

"Ms. Brightstone's in her office on the second floor. Would you like me to send for her?"

Well-mannered, efficient staff were obviously still the order of the day. Ian smiled, shook his head. "No, thanks. I'll go up."

"I'll let her know you're on your way, Mr. MacGregor."

"Appreciate it." He started up the sharply angled stairs and had a sudden, vivid flash of his mother grinning down at him and telling him they'd go for ice cream if he was very patient while she finished shopping.

"Rocky Road," he murmured. He'd always gone for Rocky Road, and his mother had always held his hand firmly in hers when they'd crossed the street to order cones.

Good memory, he decided, then noted that the second floor was no longer dim and intimidating. He didn't think it was only because now he was six feet tall rather than three.

Lights had been added and the shelves had changed from dark brown to a honey-toned wood. There was a pair of long, sturdy tables lined with chairs, creating a kind of study area. It was being used by what looked to be a high-school couple more interested in each other than the books opened in front of them.

Now that he thought of it, he had some fine memories of study dates as well in the less-atmospheric corners of his school library.

Something else there didn't seem to be enough hours in the day for just now, he mused. Not the studying, God knew, but the dating. He was going to have to get back in the swim before too long.

He missed women.

"Mr. MacGregor?"

He turned and watched the woman approach. She was a tidy little package, he concluded. Bandbox neat in her smart red suit and practical heels. Her hair was glossy black, subdued into a thick braid that hung down her back and left her quietly pretty face unframed.

Her lips were full, with just the slightest hint of overbite, and painted to match the suit. Simple gold hoops swung at her ears, and the hand she offered him was narrow and unadorned.

"Ms. Brightstone."

"Yes." She smiled. "I'm sorry I wasn't downstairs when you got here."

"I wasn't able to be firm on the time. It's not a problem."

"Let me show you to my office. Can I get you something? Coffee? Cappuccino?"

"Is that cappuccino as good as it smells?"

This time the smile reached her clear gray eyes. "It's better, especially if you add one of our hazelnut *biscotti* on the side."

"Sold."

"You won't be sorry." She led the way back through the stacks to a door over the café. "I'll have someone bring it up. Please excuse the confusion," she said, skirting around a stepladder and painting supplies. "We haven't quite finished our face-lift."

"I noticed the changes. Very nice."

"Thank you." She glanced back and opened another door. "We're getting very positive feedback."

Her office had the feel of recent remodeling. The walls were a soft pearly white accented with Boston street scenes done in soft, misty colors. The gleaming cherry desk was tidy, suiting her size and style. She gestured to one of a pair of cheerful striped chairs. "Let me just call for the coffee."

He took a seat and the time to study her. He knew from the paperwork in his briefcase that she was the daughter of the owners—making her in his calculations the fourth generation of Brightstone Books.

He'd expected her to be older, starchier, he realized, but pegged her in her early twenties, efficient but stylish. And built, he added, as he noted just how nicely the red suit showed off her curves.

When she hung up the phone, she took the seat across from him, folded her hands in her lap. "It'll be right up. I want to thank you for agreeing to meet me here. The store's taking all my time these days."

Her voice, he noted, was as clear and quiet as her eyes. "I know the feeling. And I'm happy to oblige. You're on my way home, anyway."

"That's handy, then. Your secretary said you had the papers for me to look over and sign."

"The partnership agreement, yes. Pretty standard, and I think we have everything detailed the way your father outlined." Curious, he opened his briefcase, stalling as he flipped through papers. "Can I assume your father's retiring?"

"More or less. He and my mother want to spend more time in their winter home in Arizona, perhaps relocate there permanently. My brother and his family already have."

"And you don't have any yen to go west?"

"No. Boston is mine." And so, she thought with a little flutter of the heart, was Brightstone's. Or it would be. "I've been taking on more responsibility for the store over the last eighteen months."

"The changes your idea?"

"Yes." Ones she'd fought for tooth and nail. "The market changes, customer demands and expectations change. It was time to catch up."

She rose at the knock on the door, and taking a tray from the boy delivering the coffee, murmured her thanks. "The café, for one," she continued, setting the tray on the desk and offering Ian his frothy coffee in an oversize cup and saucer. "It's the type of service that people want in a bookstore today. They no longer simply come for books, but for the atmosphere, a meeting place, a center." She smiled again as she sat with her own cup. "And great coffee."

"Well, I can vouch for the last of that," Ian said after a sip. "It's great coffee. And as I've gone over your files, your numbers, the profit-and-loss statements and so forth, it appears your alterations are working."

"We increased sales by fifteen percent in the last nine months." She wouldn't think, just yet, about what it had cost to make those changes that had helped generate those increases. "I estimate we'll be up another fifteen within the next six."

"I always loved to come here as a kid."

"And have you been a customer of Brightstone's within the last year?"

He shook his head. "Got me. But I will be." He set the coffee on the little table between them, then passed her the papers. "You'll want to look these over. I'll answer any questions you might have."

"Thank you." She retrieved a pair of wire-rim reading glasses from the desk. The minute she put them on Ian experienced a slow, inevitable melt-down.

Women in glasses drove him crazy.

He rolled his eyes, picked up his coffee and told himself to get a grip. She was a client.

Whose sober and intelligent gray eyes looked fabulous behind those lenses. Then there was that hotly painted and sexily flawed mouth. The lushly curved body in the trim, nearly military style suit. Sensible shoes. Great legs.

All that stop-and-go in one package would drive a saint crazy, he comforted himself. And the MacGregors weren't known for being saints.

Still, he gave his coffee his attention and tried not to think that the thick neat braid and the subtle, all-female perfume was just one more combo to add to the whole.

Besides, what was the harm in asking her out? To dinner. No, lunch, he decided. Lunch was definitely better. More businesslike. They could have lunch. A very casual, perfectly acceptable lunch—where he wouldn't give a single thought to nibbling on her neck to see if that was where her scent was warmest.

Her nails were short, rounded and unpainted. She wasn't wearing a ring, so he hoped that meant she was unattached.

He sat, waiting while she read, and planning exactly how to broach the subject of a nice little lunch later in the week.

Naomi read every line, then allowed herself a long, quiet breath. It was a momentous event for her, what these coolly legal papers symbolized. If she'd been alone, she might have clutched them to her breast and wept. Or shouted with joy. But as she wasn't, she laid them on the desk, slipped off her glasses.

"Everything appears to be in order."

"Questions?"

"No, I understand them. I minored in business law."

"Well then. You can sign them now if you're satisfied. You'll need a witness. Then I'll send them to your parents in Scottsdale. Once they're signed and sealed, it's a done deal."

"I'll just get my assistant."

Five minutes later, Naomi held out a steady hand. "Thanks so much for taking care of this for us."

"Happy to help. Listen, I have a list here. My grandfather—you've met him."

"Yes, many times." Her eyes warmed again; the hot red mouth curved softly. "He and your grandmother often come in when they're in Boston."

"A couple of first editions he's after. He asked if you'd see what you could do—since I was coming in."

"I'd be glad to. We'll go up to the third floor—and if we don't have what he's looking for, we'll do a search."

"Terrific."

She stepped forward, and he stayed where he was. When her gaze flicked up to his, held, he smiled slow and easy. "You smell fabulous."

"Oh." Her gaze dropped as warm color surged to her cheeks. The hands that had been calm and graceful fluttered once, then linked together, and she visibly shrank back and into herself. "Thank you. It's, ah, new. That is, I just…well," she said, despising herself. "We should go up."

Hell, he thought as he opened the door and let her scramble out ahead of him. Blew that one, Mac-Gregor.

Chapter 21

As far as Naomi was concerned, the Grand Canyon wasn't a big enough hole to fall into. Only the fact that she was surrounded by books—always a comfort—and performing a set task had kept her from losing it until Ian was gone. After she'd located two of the books on his list and agreed to start a search for the third, she'd formally shaken his hand, thanked him again and politely seen him downstairs.

Then she'd walked back to her office, quietly shut the door and laid her head down on the desk.

Moron. Idiot.

Would she always turn into a babbling fool when an attractive man so much as hinted at a personal interest? Wasn't that supposed to be one of the benefits in the changes she'd made in herself? The transformation from the pudgy, awkward and dowdy girl to the sleek, stylish and confident woman.

The one who'd made a fool of herself because Ian MacGregor had complimented her perfume.

A full week later, and she still wasn't over it.

She'd found the book. It sat on her desk, neatly wrapped, ready for delivery or pickup. She'd yet to work up the courage to lift the phone and tell Ian his order was now in stock.

Moron, she thought again. Idiot.

After all the work she'd done, all the effort she'd put in. Brightstone's wasn't the only project she'd taken on with a vengeance. Naomi had systematically and effortfully given herself a face-lift over the past year.

Not just the weight loss, which had started when she'd finally convinced herself to stop feeding her shyness, her social clumsiness and her dissatisfaction with her self-image by going on eating binges, and had begun a search for the woman inside.

A woman she'd found she could like and respect.

A reasonable diet, healthy exercise, had become habit once she'd understood that all she'd been doing through her miserable teenage years had been hiding.

It wasn't just her wardrobe, she thought, mentally reviewing the process, though it had taken her months to finally cull the dowdy out of her closet and replace it with flattering and attractive styles. Incorporating color for a change, she reflected, sighing as she looked down at her new teal suit. Gone were the days of sensible navy, unobtrusive brown and self-effacing gray. Of boxy styles and baggy jackets.

But that was just surface, she mused, just like the cosmetics she'd carefully learned to select and apply.

She no longer faded back into crowds. She'd taught herself how to present a reasonably attractive, competent and professional appearance.

And she had, for the most part, managed the metamorphosis from socially awkward to socially adept on the inside as well. She wouldn't allow herself to be shy, to hide in corners, to avoid people as she'd done most of her life simply because she couldn't be as beautiful or sophisticated as her mother, as outgoing and confident as her brother.

Brightstone's required a savvy, personable manager, and she had become one.

And she'd been doing so well, she thought in despair. She'd been so proud of herself. Look how nicely she'd been handling that one-on-one meeting with Ian MacGregor. Who was, she mused, just the kind of man who usually tied her tongue into slippery, tangled knots before she managed to say hello.

The Harvard Hunk. Oh yes, he definitely rated the title, she thought. He was so handsome, so smooth, and when he smiled...well, she doubted hers was the only woman's heart that beat a bit faster.

But she'd been fine. They'd shared coffee, had conversation, done business.

Then he'd given her one quick, casual personal compliment, and she'd babbled like a fool. Stuttered. Blushed, for Lord's sake. And all because he'd commented on her new perfume.

And why do you wear perfume, Naomi? she asked herself viciously. You wear it so people notice you, so that you feel both feminine and confident.

A man like him, she mused, with his looks, his

background, his charm, would be well skilled at offering casually flattering comments to women. And would expect them to respond in an easy, sophisticated—or perhaps liberally flirtatious—manner.

All she'd done was blush and stutter.

She could only imagine that Ian had laughed about her ridiculous and juvenile reaction all the way home. Or worse, much worse, he'd felt sorry for her.

Even the thought of it made her wince. She'd spent too many years of her life being the object of amusement or pity.

Even from her family—though they had always loved her. But when you were the lone duckling in a family of swans, you knew it.

Just as she knew how pleased they all were that she'd finally begun to make an effort to present a more polished exterior. Why, her mother had been almost giddy when Naomi had asked her for opinions on fashion, on cut and color. Just before they'd left for Arizona her father had given her his usual bear hug. But this time instead of calling her his sweet girl, as was his habit, he'd called her his pretty girl.

It had made her feel—foolishly, Naomi was sure—like a princess.

They'd trusted her with Brightstone's because they knew she had brains, knew she would work until she dropped. And because she'd fought a long, difficult battle to win them over to her side. Her father hadn't wanted to make the changes she'd outlined. He hadn't wanted to go to the expense, or take the financial risk. He'd wanted—quite reasonably, Naomi mused—to retire and let the store, something that had been as much burden as livelihood, slide quietly into oblivion.

But she loved it so much. And she needed it. It had been her refuge, her joy, her heart as long as she could remember. In the end, her family had understood that, and had trusted her.

She wasn't going to let them down. And she wasn't, she thought now, going to let herself down, either.

Brooding and moaning over one small stumble with Ian wasn't going to change anything. Likely he'd already forgotten it, and her. In order for her to forget it and continue on her quest to become who she wanted to be, she had to face it. Face him.

She picked up the book on her desk and headed for the door, barely stopping herself from chewing on her lipstick. She wouldn't call, she decided. She'd deliver the book personally.

When Naomi walked into the lovely old two-story brownstone that held the law offices of MacGregor and MacGregor, she told herself she was perfectly under control. She'd taken the time to freshen her lipstick in the car—because she had indeed chewed it off—and she'd taken those ten calming breaths she found settled her nerves.

Her problem, she admitted, was her own reaction to him. A reaction that had slammed into her the minute she'd seen him standing on the second level at Brightstone's, smiling at the teenagers in the study area.

It had been a similar reaction to ones she'd often

experienced in the past, whenever she saw something particularly beautiful, desirable—and completely out of her reach. A kind of low and liquid yearning.

But she'd gotten herself under control now by reminding herself—often—that all Ian MacGregor was interested in was business.

She gave herself a booster shot of that advice as she crossed the beautifully appointed reception area decorated in pale greens and creamy whites, with a low fire crackling in a hearth that was framed by a mantelpiece of rose-veined marble.

Class, she thought. Tradition. They were qualities in business, and family, she appreciated and understood very well.

She smiled at the woman manning the gorgeous satinwood desk.

"Good afternoon. May I help you?"

"I'm Naomi Brightstone. I have—" She broke off as a gorgeous whirlwind burst through the door.

"I won! Justice once more triumphs and the world is safe for our children." The woman, a staggeringly lovely brunette in a plum-colored suit, flashed Naomi a dazzling smile. "Sorry. We're usually more dignified around here. I'm Laura Cameron."

"I'm Naomi Brightstone, and congratulations."

"Thanks. Are you waiting… Brightstone? The bookstore?"

"Yes, that's right."

"Oh, I love that place, always have." Laura tucked up a strand of hair that had escaped her sleek coil on her dash inside. "And the new café is fabulous."

The quivers in Naomi's stomach smoothed out. "Thank you. We're very proud of it."

"We're handling something for you, aren't we? Or rather, Ian's handling something for you?"

"Yes. I just dropped by to—"

"I'm his sister."

"Yes, I know. Your grandfather wanted a book." She lifted the small shopping bag. "I had some errands out this way and thought I'd bring it by."

"Oh. Do you want me to take it, or did you want to see Ian?"

"Well, I…" She felt herself begin to fumble, then was both embarrassed and relieved when the cell phone in her purse rang. "Isn't that the silliest thing?" she said with a laugh. "It always gives me a jolt. Excuse me a moment."

She reached in her purse, drew out the trim little phone and engaged. "Hello."

"Naomi? Ian MacGregor."

"Oh." She felt the blood rush to her cheeks. "How odd."

"What?"

"I mean, I'm just…I have the book you wanted. I was just—"

"Great, we'll kill two birds. Your papers are in. I wanted you to know I'll be filing them this afternoon. I can swing by and pick up the book after I'm done at the courthouse."

"Actually, that's not necessary. You see—"

"It's no trouble. On my way home, remember?"

"Yes, I remember. But I'm downstairs."

"Where? Here?" He let out a quick, delighted

laugh. "Stay," he ordered, and clicked off, leaving Naomi staring bemusedly at her phone.

"That was your brother."

"Yes." Laura grinned. "So I gathered. The wonders of technology," she murmured, and wondered just what that sudden rush of color into Naomi's cheek signified.

Ian came down the steps at a jog. Oh yeah, he thought, she looked every bit as good as he remembered. He held out a hand, noted she was still holding the phone, and flashed that grin. "You can hang up now."

"Oh, yes. I suppose I can." Brilliant, Naomi. Why don't you just let your tongue fall out and swoon at his feet while you're at it? "I was just running some errands, so I thought I'd bring Mr. MacGregor's book by."

"Great. Come on up."

"I don't want to interrupt your work."

"You're not, especially." He glanced at his sister, lifted his eyebrows. "Well?"

"Slam dunk."

"Way to go, champ." He gave Laura a light punch on the arm that Naomi recognized as brotherly affection. "You can give me the play-by-play later." He took Naomi's arm and began to steer her toward the stairs.

"You must be busy," she began. The scenario she'd worked out in her head hadn't included a trip into his office.

"I've got a few minutes. It didn't take you long to come up with the book."

"We have a number of excellent sources. The price was within the range I quoted you—the upper range, I'm afraid."

"He wants it," Ian said simply, and guiding her down a hallway wainscoted in silky mahogany, gave the arm he held a little squeeze.

She still smelled fabulous, he mused, but he was going to be careful not to mention it and put her off again.

"Have a seat," he told her.

His office suited the mood of the old town house. If she wasn't mistaken, the desk under the stacks of files and spiffy computer was Chippendale and the carpet over the lovely hardwood floor a Bristol.

Oak file cabinets lined one wall, shelves of books another. The window with its carved trim looked out on the street where lovely trees were just beginning to burn with fall color.

Seeing no polite escape, she sat in one of the burgundy leather chairs. "It's a beautiful building."

"My father bought it before my parents were married. He was still working on some of the rehab when my mother took an office here. He wanted—then they wanted—the law housed somewhere with character and warmth."

"They certainly succeeded."

"How about coffee? Not that what I can serve you will come close to what you gave me."

"No, no, I'm fine. I really should—"

"I'll be filing the papers," he began. No way, he thought, was he letting her rush off before he'd had a chance to make up for his blunder.

He sat, not behind the desk as she'd expected, but in the chair beside her.

"I have copies for you," he continued, "but the originals will be in the courthouse. It's not absolutely official until I've filed them, but essentially you're now a full partner, vice president of Brightstone Books, with full executive power and authority. Congratulations."

She opened her mouth to thank him politely, then couldn't form a single word as emotion filled her throat. All she could do was shut her eyes.

"Okay?" he said gently.

She nodded her head, pressed her fingers to her lips until the first edge of the joys and fears had receded. "Yes. Sorry."

"Don't be." He took her hand before he thought about it. She looked so thrilled and terrified. "It's a big moment."

"The biggest. I thought I was prepared. I am," she corrected. "I am prepared to do the job. But it's just hearing it, knowing it's real, is a little over-whelming. Thank you so much." She managed a laugh. "I'm glad I was sitting down."

"I know how it feels. Like the day I walked into this office, sat down at that desk and knew I was a part of what was most important to me. I sat there—must have been an hour—just grinning. Euphoria and terror?"

"Exactly." Her hand relaxed in his. "It's awe-some, isn't it, to be the next step in a long flight of family tradition?"

"It certainly is. What are you going to do to celebrate?"

"Celebrate?" Her mind went blank. "I suppose I'll get back to work."

"Not nearly good enough. How about dinner?"

"Dinner? Yes, I'll fix something when I get home."

He stared at her a moment, then shook his head. Okay, he decided, no subtleties. "Naomi, I'd like to take you out to dinner tonight, if you don't have any plans."

"Oh. Well…plans. No, not really. Um…" Oh, please, please, her mind screamed, don't babble! "You don't have to feel obliged to—"

"Let me put this another way," he said, fascinated by the way warm color rose to her cheeks. "Will you go to dinner with me tonight?"

"Ah…yes, thank you. That would be nice."

"Good. Seven work for you?"

"Seven, yes, that's fine."

"Should I pick you up at the store, or your apartment?"

"The—my apartment. I'll give you the address."

"I have it—from your file."

"Oh yes, of course." Idiot. "It's not far from the store. I can walk to work every day. I like the neighborhood."

Shut up, shut up, and get out before you make a total fool of yourself.

"I should get back." She got to her feet, jerking to a stop when she realized her hand was still caught in his. "To work. At the store."

Her eyes were huge, lovely and, for reasons that baffled him, full of nerves. "Are you okay?"

"Yes, fine. Just fine. Thank you."

"I'll walk you down."

"No, no, don't bother." Desperate now, she tugged her hand free. "I know the way."

"Naomi," he said before she could get out the door.

"Hmm?"

"The book?"

"Book? Oh." Cursing herself, she turned back and handed him the bag she still carried. "Silly of me. I forgot all about it. Well, goodbye."

"See you tonight."

"Yes, tonight," she managed and escaped.

Ian slipped his hands into his pockets and rocked back on his heels. Funny, he mused, she hadn't struck him as a scatterbrain. He supposed the finality of the partnership agreement had muddled her mind.

Or, he considered, he made her nervous. Now wouldn't that be a nice little side benefit? He wouldn't mind making the pretty and efficient Naomi Brightstone nervous. Not a bit.

Strolling over to the desk, he buzzed his secretary and asked her to make reservations for dinner for two at Rinaldo's at seven-thirty. Then, tucking the paperwork into his briefcase, he headed out to the courthouse, whistling on the way.

He couldn't remember ever looking forward to an evening more.

Chapter 22

Ian was just knotting his tie when the phone rang. He ignored it, not wanting to take time for conversation. He still had to go by the florist's on the way to Naomi's apartment.

But when he heard "Why the devil aren't you home?" delivered in a booming voice rich with a Scottish burr, he grinned and snatched up his portable.

"Well, I am home, but not for long."

"Can't any one of my grandchildren stay put?" Daniel demanded. "Gallivanters, the lot of you. Your grandmother doesn't get a moment's peace worrying over you."

"Oh?" Ian stuck his tongue in his cheek. "I thought she worried I never got out, always had my nose in a law book."

"That, too," Daniel said, without missing a beat. "The woman frets night and day. When are you coming out to see her?"

"Grandpa, I was there last month for Duncan's wedding, remember?"

"So? That was last month, wasn't it? What's wrong with this month?"

"Not a thing. I'll come out soon."

"See that you do. Do you think I want your granny nagging me half to death? Now what are you up to?"

"I'm up to going to dinner with a pretty woman, thanks to you."

"Me? Me? Why, I haven't done a bloody thing. Don't you be telling your grandmother I have, either. All I did—"

"Relax," Ian said with a laugh. "I wasn't accusing you of meddling. It's just a happy coincidence. You asked me to have Brightstone's find your books while I was there for my meeting with Naomi."

"And what if I did? A man's entitled to his books, isn't he?"

"Yes, Grandpa." Ian raised his eyes heavenward. "Naomi dropped the Walter Scott off at my office today—right after her paperwork came through. So instead of the phone call the papers would have generated, your book got me another personal meeting. And I asked her out. So…thanks."

"Ah, well then." In his office in Hyannis Port, Daniel grinned like a maniac. The boy was sharp, he thought, but not quite sharp enough to match his grandpa. Hah! "That's fine. She's a nice young woman, little Naomi. Got manners, got brains."

"It's just dinner, Grandpa. Don't get started."

"Started on what? I'm only saying it's fine you're having dinner with a nice young woman. What's wrong with that, I'd like to know?"

"Nothing, not a thing." Ian glanced at his watch. "And I've got to go or I'll be late."

"Then what are you dawdling for? On your way, lad, and call your grandmother before she pines down to the bones."

Daniel hung up, then rubbed his hands together. Well, he thought, that was easy.

Naomi agonized over what to wear, then went through another period of misery over what to do with her hair. In the end she settled on a simple black dress with a scooped neck, snug sleeves and straight skirt, and left her hair loose.

She thought—hoped—it looked sophisticated and just casual enough to indicate she hadn't agonized. She added her grandmother's triple strand of pearls, slid her feet into high black heels that would cause her feet great distress before the evening was over but made her feel powerful, then spritzed on the scent that Ian had complimented.

"There," she said to her reflection. "You're fine. You're ready, and you will not be stupid. A very nice man is being considerate enough to take you out to dinner to celebrate an important moment in your life. That's all there is to it. Oh God!" she said when she heard the knock on her door. "All right, okay." And closing her eyes, she took those habitual ten steady-ing breaths.

She was steady and smiling when she opened the door. And if her heart sighed at the sight of him— handsome as a fairy tale prince—she managed to maintain her composure.

"How lovely."

"Thanks, you too."

She laughed and didn't feel so foolish. "I meant the flowers."

"Oh, these." He glanced down at the spray of pink roses. "I guess you want them."

"Yes, I do." She gathered them into her arms. "Come in, I'll put them in a vase. Just make yourself comfortable."

It would be easy, he decided. Her living space was attractive, efficient and simple. Like her office, he thought. Like her. He approved of the strong col-ors—deep greens and mauves—the traditional lines of Queen Anne and Chippendale, the femininity of the accent pieces and the art.

She came back with the flowers, pleased that though they were the first given to her by a man who wasn't a family member, she'd only mooned and fluttered over them for a moment.

Later, she promised herself, she would spend all the time she wanted mooning and fluttering.

"They really are lovely, thank you."

"So are you, and you're welcome. I like your space."

"Oh." Grateful her hands didn't bobble the vase as she set it on a table, she straightened. "I wanted something close to work—and I don't need a lot of room. I know one of the newer complexes might have been more convenient, but I love old buildings. All their eccentricities.''

"So do I. I just bought a house a few months ago. The floors creak, the plumbing rattles and the cellar's damp as a tomb. I love it.''

"Sounds like the one I grew up in. I still can't drive by it without getting sentimental. Would you like a drink before we go?''

"No, thanks. You'll need a wrap. It's getting breezy.''

"I have one.'' She turned and opened the closet off the short hallway.

Testing, Ian stepped up behind her. She was just congratulating herself for behaving normally when she turned, bumped into him, jerked back as if her heels had become springs, and all but fell into the closet.

He took her arms to steady her, smiled slowly. Oh yeah, he thought, he made her plenty nervous. And wasn't that delightful? "Sorry,'' he lied without a qualm. "Didn't mean to startle you.''

"I didn't realize you were behind me. I was just…getting my coat.'' She yanked it up between them and very nearly rapped him in the chin.

"So I see.'' He took it from her. "Why don't I just help you on with it?''

She doubted, sincerely, that the heart was designed to pound quite this hard. She despised the clumsiness, berated herself for it, then remembered that there would have been a time when she'd have sought comfort against the embarrassment in a jumbo bag of potato chips.

Now she turned, ordering herself to breathe as he slipped the coat on for her.

With more speed than grace, she ducked away, grabbed her purse. "Shall we go?"

It was easier in the restaurant, with the soft glow of candlelight and the silky taste of good wine. He was wonderful to talk to, to listen to. And she was quietly amazed they shared so many interests.

"I like the spirit and the charm of traditional music," she said. "That's why I like it playing in the store. It think it lifts the customers' moods without being intrusive."

"Did you make the Celtic festival last summer?"

"I spent nearly an entire day there."

"Me, too." He offered her a bite of his grilled portabello mushroom. "Wonderful music—and the dancers, amazing."

"I love to watch the step-toe dancers." Without thinking, she leaned forward to take the offered bite from his fork. "Isn't it odd how something that disciplined and precise can be sexy, too? Mmm." She swallowed. "That's very good."

"Want some more?"

"No, I'm fine. Just a weakness for Italian food."

"Me, too. I make a pretty terrific chicken *picata*."

"You like to cook?" She tried to imagine him puttering around in the kitchen, then decided not to risk the rise in her blood pressure. "So do I. And I'd put my clam sauce against your *picata* any day."

"We'll have to have a cook-off." When she only smiled vaguely, he warned himself not to move too fast. His grandfather wasn't the only MacGregor who could scheme, he thought. And he already had a plan in mind.

"Actually, Naomi, I have a little business proposition for you."

"Business?" She gave him a blank look as their appetizer plates were removed and the entrées served.

"One I hope will be as much a pleasure for you as it will be for me. I want to remodel one of my spare rooms into a library. I have a design in mind that I wanted you to look at and offer suggestions on. Then I'd hoped you could give me some help with setting up my collection."

"Yes, of course." She fought off a wave of disappointment, telling herself it was better this way. Of course he was interested in her on a professional level. What else could she expect? "You're interested in rare books, for investment purposes?"

"No, not necessarily. I want a library, not a museum. I want a comfortable room, and I want the books varied. I don't want anyone to feel as if they should sign a waiver if they take a book off the shelf. I'd want to start with my personal favorites—most of which I own already. Then I'm willing to explore."

"I'd love to help you. If you could give me a list of what you have—and what you're looking for—we can start there."

"Great. Can you make time to look at my space and review the design?"

"All right. Let me know when it fits into your schedule."

"How about Saturday, say six?"

She was too surprised, and too dazzled by his smile, to do anything more than nod.

The wind was up when he pulled in front of her apartment building, rustling energetically through the trees. Moonlight splattered over the streets and sidewalks, and the music he'd tuned in on the radio was quiet and dreamy.

It was, to his mind, a perfect evening.

The subtle fragrance she wore drifted through the closed car. She'd relaxed again, he thought, becoming particularly animated and easy when they'd continued to discuss books. He had to congratulate himself on finding the perfect ploy.

Not that it was precisely a ploy, he corrected. He wanted the library, after all, and she was the logical source for the books. He believed strongly in enlisting experts. It was just a delightful side benefit that she was a lovely woman who stirred his interest on more basic levels.

And if he wasn't mistaken, he stirred hers as well.

"This was wonderful." She turned, absently brushing the heavy fall of hair back from her face. "Thanks for helping me celebrate."

"My pleasure."

He slipped out of the car, rounding the hood to open her door. She didn't fumble with her seat belt, but it was a close thing. Before she could tell him there was no need to walk her to her door, he'd taken her hand.

Not her arm, Naomi thought with sudden, skittering panic, but her hand. He was holding her hand as they walked, and that was more personal, more... intimate.

Was she supposed to ask him in? Impossible, out of the question. She hadn't figured it into her evening plans, so wasn't prepared for it and was bound to do something humiliating.

"I imagine you want to get an early start tomorrow," he commented as they stepped inside the building foyer. "Your first full day as partner."

"Yes." She nearly dissolved in relief at the lifeline he'd tossed her. "I do. There's a staff meeting, and I have to discuss a new author-signing policy with my events coordinator. We're holding our first children's story hour of the fall on Saturday."

"Not just selling books, is it?" Idly he rubbed his thumb over her wrist and found to his pleasure that her pulse was rabbiting.

"No." Her pulse had nothing on her stomach as they climbed the stairs to her door. "It's...a good bookstore needs to be a community center. I want—we want—to be able to offer services and events that interest all age groups. Well..." She turned at the door, startled when he took her other hand and held her there. "And we're sponsoring three different reading clubs. They hold regular monthly meetings in the—in the..." What the hell was it called? "Café," she said on an explosion of breath.

She tugged one of her hands free, yanked her purse from under her arm with some notion of digging out her keys. "So, well, thank you for a lovely dinner."

She dropped the keys, nearly bumped heads with him as they both bent to retrieve them, then jerked up straight as a flagpole.

Ian debated a moment, then, handing her the keys, took her face in his hands to hold her in place. "Let's try it this way," he murmured, and laid his lips gently on hers.

She didn't move a muscle, which made him wonder if he'd misread that tangle of signals. Then her lips parted under his on a sharp intake of breath, and he couldn't resist.

His hands slid into that thick stream of hair. A low hum of pleasure sounded in his throat as he skimmed his tongue over hers, drew her closer.

The world had been none too steady under her feet in any case. Now, with his mouth moving warm and easy over hers, it just dropped away.

The keys slipped out of her hands for a second time, landing with a musical crash as her fingers clutched at his arms, curled into his coat. Then slowly, swaying, she leaned into him.

Rainbows, misty at the edges, circled in her head.

He drew back, watched those heavy gray eyes, blurred now, flutter open. Watched that mouth, with its seductive, heavy top lip, tremble on an unsteady breath.

He skimmed his hands down to her shoulders, and felt her shudder. "I have to do that again."

''Oh, well.'' She stared at him, so obviously staggered, he smiled. ''All right.''

His mouth took hers again, a little deeper now, a little hotter. He felt the same sharp stab of desire he'd experienced with the first taste. She gave a sexy little sigh that had his blood simmering.

He steeped himself in the taste of her, surrendered to that singular scent that had teased his senses since the moment he'd met her. She clouded his brain.

The hesitant brush of her fingers on the back of his neck, the slow yielding of her mouth under his, rattled him. Well aware that he was close to asking for more, he drew back.

Saying nothing, he bent down to pick up her keys, then unlocked the door for her. ''Good night, Naomi.'' With his eyes on hers, he pressed the keys into her hand.

''Yes, good night. Thanks.'' She all but staggered into the apartment and, without turning, shut the door in his face.

He stood there a moment, wondering if he'd made a mistake by kissing her—or had made one in stopping. Then he heard it—the musical clink of her keys hitting the floor yet again.

Grinning widely, he strolled away. No mistake either way, he decided. And he planned on kissing the very interesting Miss Brightstone again. Very soon.

Chapter 23

"**D**on't you have *any* chocolate?"

As he stirred his pot of red sauce, Ian glanced back over his shoulder at his cousin Julia. She was, he thought, as pretty as ever, impatient as always and grandly pregnant.

"You ate it all the last time you were here."

Eyes sharp, Julia continued to root through his cupboards. "You could go to the store now and again, couldn't you?"

"There's fresh fruit in the fridge, but unfortunately it's not chocolate covered. Here." He gestured her over with a jerk of his head and held a hand under the bowl of a wooden spoon. "Try this."

Deciding beggars couldn't be choosers, Julia walked over and, resting a hand on the wide shelf of her belly, sampled the sauce he offered. "It's good. Where's dessert?"

He laughed and set the spoon aside. "Doesn't Cullum ever feed you?"

"It's not me. Butch here wants chocolate." She patted her swollen belly. "I'm just the delivery chute. Not even a candy bar?"

"Sorry. I'll stock up. With Travis it was ice cream, wasn't it? Gallons, as I recall."

"He still loves ice cream," she said with a soft maternal smile. "His first words were 'fudge ripple.'" When Ian laughed again, she cocked her head. "You're in a pretty chipper mood, pal."

"There's a woman."

"Yeah, that's the usual answer. Brightstone?"

"That's the one. She'll be here shortly, so…"

"Cullum and Travis will be along to pick me up. I won't cramp your style. Where's the final design for the library?"

"Upstairs. I was looking at it last night."

"Well, let's go get it."

"I appreciate it, Jules." He swung a friendly arm around her shoulders as they headed down the hallway to the front stairs. "Between you and Cullum, this house has really come together."

"You haven't exactly stood around with your hands in your pockets. You've done a nice job here, Ian. I know a lot of people think that it's impractical for a single guy to tie himself up with a big old house like this."

"But not you."

"There's nothing like a house, the possibilities within that structure and what you make of them." She ran her fingers over the newel post of the silky oak banister. "This place feels like you. Open, easy, sturdy, with one eye on the future and the other on the past." Then she sighed. "And I don't think I'm walking up those steps. I'd have to walk down again, and I'm having a little trouble seeing my feet these days."

"I'll bring the design down. Why don't you go sit in the parlor?"

"Don't need to sit." She pressed a hand to the small of her back to relieve some of the pressure. "Need chocolate."

"Next time, I swear."

While he headed up, Julia wandered. She'd been perfectly sincere when she'd said the house felt like her cousin. It pleased her that she'd helped him find it, had been able to watch him fall in love with it, and that she and Cullum had been able to add their expertise and experience in rehab to make it home for him.

Ian, she knew, needed home.

"Easy, Butch," she murmured, rubbing her side as the baby inside her kicked restlessly. "Daddy'll be along, and he'll get us a nice big box of double fudge brownies."

At the sound of the doorbell, she moved as quickly as Butch would allow.

Naomi's first impression when Julia opened the door was flash. The kind of style that came from the bones out and still had the power to make her sigh with envy. A curling mass of red hair tumbled around a face that glowed with health. Warm brown eyes both welcomed and appraised.

"You must be Naomi. Hi, I'm Julia, Golden Boy's cousin."

"Yes, I know. I recognized you. I heard you speak at the Women in Business lunch a couple of years ago."

"Oh yeah. Well, I was a bit trimmer then." She patted her belly and stepped back. "Come on in. Ian just went up to get a copy of the design for the library. My husband and his crew are going to do most of the work."

Pretty, Julia mused. A little shy. Very well turned out. Gorgeous body, fabulous hair, quiet eyes. Details, she thought, amused, were what her cousins Laura and Gwen would want. "So, you've taken over Brightstone's."

"I'm managing it now, yes."

"You got chocolate mochas in the café?"

"Yes. They're wonderful."

Julia moaned. "Easy, Butch. He's desperate for chocolate," she explained with a grin when Naomi looked a bit panicked. "He's got another two months to cook in here. Don't worry."

"He wants chocolate?" Only slightly baffled, Naomi glanced down and watched Julia's stomach ripple under the long, forest green sweater. "I have some M&M's."

Julia reached out, took a firm hold of Naomi's arm. "Don't toy with me."

"No, really. I always carry something in case I miss a meal and need a boost." It was something else she'd learned—not to deny that need for comfort, just to regulate it. She opened her purse and took out a small bag.

"If you let me have them," Julia said in a quietly urgent voice, "I'll name the baby after you. Boy or girl, it's Naomi."

"That's what you told me when you wanted my caramel sundae when you were carrying Travis," Ian commented as he came down the stairs.

"Isn't your name Travis?"

Chuckling, Naomi passed the bag of candy. "Enjoy."

"I'll never forget this," Julia promised as she ripped open the bag and dug out a handful. "Um. Yes. Good. See, he's happy now. Field goal."

"He's kicking? Cool." Delighted, Ian laid a hand on his cousin's belly and grinned. "Wow, from mid-field and right through the goal posts. Check this out," he said to Naomi, and before she could blink he had her hand pressed to Julia under his.

The first wave of embarrassment never managed to crest as the strong, lively movements under her palm shot a thrill straight to her heart. "Oh! That's marvelous."

When her gaze lifted to Julia's, something passed between them that only women know.

"There's Cullum." Julia tilted her head as she heard the two short toots. "I told him to beep the horn if Travis fell asleep in the car seat. We'll look over the plans tonight, Ian." She took them, tipped up her face to kiss him. "Nice meeting you, Naomi." She rattled the candy in the bag. "And thanks."

"Too bad the kid zonked out," Ian said to Naomi

as he watched his cousin walk to the waiting car.
"He's great. Not even two years old, and he can talk
your ear off."

"You like children."

"Yeah." He shut the door, closing the bright autumn breeze out, when the car drove off. "A lot. In
my family, you'd better. We're loaded with them,
and there's always another on the way. Two right
now with Jules working on her second and my cousin
Mac and his wife expecting their first. Thanks for
coming," he added, then took her by the shoulders
and kissed her.

When she stepped back abruptly, he arched a
brow. "Problem?"

"No, no, nothing." Except she'd managed to convince herself that he'd only kissed her good-night
after their date because it was what people did at the
end of an evening.

"All right. Let me get you a glass of wine."

"I shouldn't. I'm driving." But somehow he was
guiding her down the hall. "I thought we'd just look
over your—the room you want to outfit, and then..."

She caught the glorious scent of sauce simmering.
One step into the kitchen, she saw the beautiful,
warm slate counters, the cheerful pots of herbs on
the wide window ledge, the trim brick hearth.

"You're expecting company," she said, noting the
size of the saucepan. "I won't keep you long."

He'd started to pour from the bottle he'd left
breathing on the counter, and now just stared at her.
"Ah, Naomi, I asked you to come. You're who I
was expecting."

"Oh."

He finished pouring the wine, offered her a glass. "I figured the least I could do, since I was putting you out on a Saturday evening, was give you a meal."

"You didn't have to go to all that trouble. I don't mind coming by. I'm interested in your library project."

"Uh-huh." He leaned back on the counter. "Am I going to have to dream up an excuse whenever I want to have dinner with you?"

"I—no. Hmm." Stumped, she looked down into her wine.

"Maybe I should ask if you're only interested in my library project or if you're at all interested in me." He watched her gaze shoot up, and what he saw in those lovely gray eyes had him stepping forward. "Or maybe I should just tell you I'm very attracted to you. That I enjoy your company," he added, taking the glass out of her numb fingers, setting it aside. "That I want to spend more time with you." He lowered his head to rub his lips over hers. "That I want to get to know you." Nibbled on them. "That I just want you."

A soft, weightless white cloud seemed to drift over her brain. "Want me to what?"

With his mouth still on hers, he opened his eyes. Drawing back slightly, he shook his head, then began to trace quiet kisses along her jaw.

Then his mouth came back to hers, and the sudden sharp lance of heat pierced through the cloud. Her lips parted on a gasp of shock; her hands fluttered up to grip his shoulders.

Wanted her? *Her?* she thought just before her system went berserk. Her legs dissolved, her bones melted and the blood sang under her skin. One wild wave of sensation swamped her, tumbled her so that she clung to him, certain she'd be swept away.

He hadn't meant to move fast, but her sudden vivid response slammed into him. He spun her around so he could press her back against the counter and devour that wonderfully lopsided mouth.

Desperate to touch, he ran his hands up her hips, along her sides until he could fill his hands with those fabulous breasts.

Her heart seemed to heave against his palm.

"Why don't we get to know each other better later." Wild with need, he attacked her neck with his teeth. "Everything—life stories, hopes and dreams, likes and dislikes. Damn, Naomi, I've got to have you."

"Yes. No. Wait." It terrified her, this fierce and violent hunger inside her own body.

"Let's go with yes."

"No, please." She lifted her hands to his chest, felt the tension vibrate. Looked up into his eyes, saw the desire swirl. "Please," she said again, but didn't start to tremble until he'd stepped back. "I'm sorry."

"Don't be. We're moving a little fast." But he picked up one of the wineglasses and drank deeply. "I figured we were going at the same pace."

He was angry, she thought. Trying not to be, but there was temper stirring in his eyes. "No, I am sorry. I misunderstood why you asked me to come over, why you…''

''Did you misunderstand why I kissed you the other night, the way I kissed you?'' She was right, the temper was bubbling. ''The way you kissed me?''

''I don't know.'' Her voice went sharp as she clutched her arms and fought against a miserable combination of embarrassment and confusion. ''I just don't know. I don't have any experience with this. I'm sorry, I've never done what you seem to want me to do.''

Rising temper died in simple shock. ''You haven't ever? Ever?''

''No.'' Embarrassment won. ''I have to go.''

And because he was still reeling, she managed to dash by him. ''Naomi, wait. Damn it.'' He caught her in the hall. ''Just wait,'' he ordered, taking her upper arms. ''Give me a minute here, will you?''

''I'm not going to apologize again,'' she said between her teeth.

''No, I am, if you'll just give me a minute.'' He let her go to rub his hands over his face. He needed to settle, and quickly. To get beyond the surprise, the guilt, and God help him, the arousal her announcement caused him.

''I'm sorry.'' She'd never been touched. Good God, he'd taken her in a series of quick, greedy bites. ''Naomi, I'm sorry I moved in on you that way. I must have scared you.''

''Some. Yes.''

''I won't scare you again.'' He touched a hand to

her cheek, doing his best to make the gesture un-
threatening. ''And I won't push you. Why don't we
just take a step back?''

She studied him a moment, then closed her eyes
and took her ten calming breaths. ''What kind of step
back?''

''We'll take a glass of wine upstairs, look at the
space for the library. I'll show you the design. Then
we'll have dinner.''

''You're not angry?''

''No, of course I'm not angry. I'm hoping you
won't be. Will you stay, give me another chance
to...get to know you?''

''Yes, all right.'' She smiled a little. ''I'd like to.''

''Good. I'll get the wine.''

He started back to the kitchen, resisted rubbing a
hand over the knot of desire tangled in his gut. It
would take time, he told himself, to earn her trust.
He didn't think it would help the situation to tell her
that he only wanted her more now that he knew he'd
be the first to touch her.

''Be careful, MacGregor,'' he murmured as he
picked up the glasses. ''Be *very* careful.''

Chapter 24

It was pointless to be embarrassed that she'd confessed her complete lack of experience with men. A sharper woman would have said she wanted more time, or she wasn't certain she wanted to have an affair.

Some, Naomi imagined, would have enjoyed that flash-point kiss, indulged in others, then coolly left the man dangling.

Later, darling. Maybe.

Such smoldering promises would be delivered in a husky voice, with a throaty laugh, while keeping a man at arm's length with a tantalizing skim of beautifully manicured nails along the cheek and a sultry sweep of long, thick lashes.

Naomi decided that was a female skill she couldn't even pull off in dreams, much less reality.

But there was no use being embarrassed that she'd simply blurted out she'd never been with a man.

In any case, she thought, it had lightened the tension in the air that evening.

She supposed it was the politician in his blood that had enabled Ian to smooth over the awkwardness so quickly, so completely, and take her upstairs to show her the room he intended for his books.

By the time they'd reached it, no one would have imagined the two of them had just shared a violent embrace in his kitchen.

She was having a hard time imagining it herself a few days later.

Better that way, she told herself. Imagining it too well would only cause that restless stirring inside her again. Work was a much better way, a much more productive way, of spending her time.

With her hands folded in front of her, she stood at the rear of the events area she and her staff had worked so hard to create for Brightstone's new monthly Women's Evening. The guest author was keeping the audience well entertained with off-the-cuff stories and short readings from her book *Dates from Hell…And How to Survive Them.*

Spontaneous laughter had drawn a number of other midweek customers over to stand behind the rows of chairs. Business, Naomi predicted, would be very brisk during the after-lecture autographing.

Unobtrusively, she slipped over to the signing table, to fuss where no fussing was needed. The books were cleverly stacked; pens were at hand. The flower arrangement was in place and would be a gift to the author after the evening was over. There was a pitcher of ice water, and the author would be offered her choice of beverage from the café.

As far as Naomi could see, her very first Wednesday evening program was a huge success.

With a murmur to her events coordinator to make certain the author's autographing would be announced over the loudspeaker at the end of the lecture, she turned. And rammed head-on into Ian.

"Sorry." He took her arms to keep her from overbalancing. "I seem to have a habit of sneaking up on you."

"I wasn't looking...." She stared into his eyes, and suddenly she could imagine very well, all too well, that staggering kiss. She could all but taste it.

Then he gave her arms a light, somewhat fraternal squeeze and let her go.

"You pulled in a crowd tonight."

"Yes." She glanced behind her as the audience erupted with laughter. "Shelly Goldsmith."

"I saw the ad in the paper. Clever idea, the women's night. Yours?"

"I worked on it with my events coordinator. Did you come to hear the lecture?"

He lifted a brow as the applause rang out. "If I did, I'm a little late."

"Oh. Excuse me." She hurried to the front, slipped up to the podium to shake the author's hand.

Handles it well, Ian mused. Professional, polite, but warm. The "thank you" into the mike was neat, cheerful and included an invitation to the audience to have their books signed by the author.

He kept out of the way while Naomi settled her charge, offered her something from the café, then flicked a single glance at a hovering assistant, who dashed off to fetch the coffee. Then she took a moment to chat with Goldsmith, bending down to speak quietly with a smile.

Efficient, personable. Incredibly sexy in the trim, moss green suit with her hair—all that terrific hair—coiled in a neat roll at the base of her neck.

Her very tasty neck.

And he had to stop thinking that way.

He'd known she'd be busy. It had been his intention to go straight home after work. He'd had no business detouring by the bookstore…just for a look at her.

Hadn't he vowed to give her plenty of space? And here he was, only days after he'd nearly devoured her in his kitchen, jumping back in and sniffing around her like a puppy.

It was demoralizing. It was stupid.

It was irresistible.

He gauged the line forming at the table, decided that the efficient Ms. Brightstone would stand by her author for the duration. So he took himself off to wander.

She saw him go out of the corner of her eye and tried not to let her shoulders slump. It was likely he'd just dropped in for a book—it was a bookstore, wasn't it? she reminded herself viciously. He'd seen the crowd and had come back to satisfy his curiosity.

Now he'd find his book and leave. And all she'd managed to do was trip over his feet.

Pulling herself together, she turned to chat with some of the waiting customers.

It was after nine before the event wound down. Naomi considered it a very productive two hours—which had taken more than forty man-hours to create. And worth every minute, she decided after personally escorting her featured guest to the door.

Now all she wanted was a quiet place to sit down and close her eyes for fifteen minutes.

"Nice job." Ian had waited her out, but hadn't wasted time. He had a loaded Brightstone's shopping bag weighing down one hand.

"I didn't realize you were still here."

"I was going to browse." He grinned and shook the bag. "At this rate, I'm going to have to add more shelves to my library design."

"Brightstone's appreciates your patronage." She smiled when she said it and managed to stop herself from fussing with her hair. "Did you find everything you were looking for?"

Found you, didn't I? "It looks that way. And as an extra service, I did some spying for you."

"Spying?"

"Well, eavesdropping, anyway. You have some very satisfied customers. There was a group of women scouring the new fiction section. They were pretty chirpy about tonight's event, and already talking about making an evening of it next month."

"Wonderful. That's what we're after."

"Are you done, or are you going to be tied up for a while?"

"No, that was it." She blew out a breath. "Thank God."

He chuckled. "How about I buy you some excellent Brightstone's coffee?" He watched her blink, hesitate, and shoving guilt aside, he pushed. "I really hoped I could show you the changes we've made in the design. I think we've got it now."

"I'd love to see them. Do you want to go upstairs?"

Where he could be alone with her? Not a good idea, he decided. "The café's fine with me."

"All right. But Brightstone's buys the coffee. It's the least we can do for such a good customer."

She led the way, noting that the Children's Corner needed to be tidied. If Ian hadn't been with her, she would have stopped and stored the scatter of toys and books herself.

"Tired?" he asked as they climbed the short flight to the café.

"Hmm? No, actually, I'm a little wired, I suppose. I authorized the advertising and promotion budget for this new program. I could almost see my father wincing over the phone."

"He's given you pretty much a free rein, hasn't he?"

"Yes. He trusts me." Her voice warmed on the words. "It's going to be very nice to let him know he didn't make a mistake."

She scanned the café, pleased to see it was nearly filled to capacity, and smiled broadly when she spotted a table of women bubbling with laughter as one of them read a portion of Shelly Goldsmith's book aloud.

"Here." Ian took her elbow and steered her to one of the few empty tables. "Lucky to find one. It looks like Brightstone's Café is a happening place."

"Yes, it does. Sometimes I come through here and I get giddy and weepy at the same time. Silly," she said quickly, annoyed with herself for saying such a thing to him.

"No, it's not. You're making your mark, Naomi. You should be proud of what you're accomplishing. I watched you working. You're very good at your job."

She wasn't sure which thrilled most, the compliment or realizing he'd watched her. "It's all I've ever wanted to do. When I was little, I'd come in here with my father. I'd wander the stacks, tuck myself into corners, sit behind the checkout counter. My poor mother used to buy me dolls, and I'd only use them as customers and clerks when I played bookstore."

And pretend to feed them the candy I stuffed in my face, she remembered, because I knew she was disappointed I couldn't be the pretty, frilly little girl she wanted.

"Some of us are born for something," he murmured. "This is yours."

"Yes, this is mine." And her days of hiding in corners were in the past. She glanced at the waitress who hurried over. "Busy tonight, Tracy."

"We haven't stopped hopping since five-thirty. What can I get you, Ms. Brightstone?"

"Two cappuccinos," Naomi ordered, glancing at Ian and receiving his nod.

"You got it. You should try a slice of that Chocolate Sin, Ms. Brightstone. It's awesome, and you've been on your feet for hours."

"Oh, I—"

"We'll split it," Ian said, flashing a smile at the waitress. "Thanks."

"Six million calories," Naomi muttered, and Ian laughed.

"Honey, odds are you've already burned them off during the event. Where do you get your looks?"

The "honey" had thrown her off, and the sharp veer in topic finished the job. "Excuse me?"

"Your coloring. You have hair like my mother's—that thick, dense black. Is Brightstone Native American?"

"Yes, actually. There's some Cherokee on my father's side, mixed with all manner of others. Some Italian, some French, some English, then English and Welsh on my mother's. She likes to say her children are hybrids."

"I have Comanche through my mother, but Laura got the coloring."

"She's beautiful, your sister."

"Yes, she is."

"Your whole family's dazzling. Whenever I see a picture in the paper, or a clip on the news, I'm staggered. You take after your father. I suppose one day you'll be a mix of the distinguished statesman and the Harvard Hunk."

When he winced, she simply goggled. Had that

actually come out of her mouth? "I'm sorry. What a ridiculous thing to say."

He angled his head, amused that she was more embarrassed than he was. "So I'm not a hunk, and have no hope of achieving distinguished status?"

"No, of course you are, and…" She simply shut her eyes and wondered if the Grand Canyon might be a big enough hole, after all.

He laughed until his sides ached, and caused the waitress who brought their drinks to grin in delight. It was about time, as far as Tracy was concerned, that Ms. Brightstone got lucky. And it was looking as though she'd hit the jackpot.

"I'll never live down that picture." Ian sighed and stirred his coffee. "What was I, twenty-three, twenty-four? Out for a sail and minding my own business. Guy takes his shirt off to catch some rays, and snap! He's immortalized."

"It must be intrusive…the press."

"I grew up with it." He scooped up a forkful of the creamy chocolate confection on the plate between them and offered it. "You get used to it."

"I'm not sure I could." Because he didn't seem offended, after all, she accepted the bite. "I've been dealing with the media for over a year now, promoting the store, giving interviews, that sort of thing. It's necessary for the store, but I can't say I'm used to it."

"Doing it well's often the bottom line." He sampled the chocolate himself. "This is very well named. 'Sin.'" He tormented himself by imagining the taste of her mixed with the chocolate.

It made her stomach jump. "You're going to have to sin by yourself." She picked up her coffee. "I'm resisting."

"One more," he murmured, sliding the fork into the dessert, lifting a tempting bite to her lips. And he was pleased to see, when she took it, that she could indeed be tempted.

He also decided that if he wanted to survive the evening, he'd better shift into business mode. "So, let me show you what I've got. Tell me what you think."

He opened his briefcase, took out the scale drawing of the proposed design. "I'm handing it over to Cullum tomorrow. He can get started right away."

"You move quickly."

"Usually," he muttered, then spread out the drawing.

Naomi took her glasses out of the little case in her pocket, slipped them on and made Ian's mouth water. Then she leaned forward, bending over the drawings, and drove him slightly mad as her scent slipped into his senses.

"Oh, these are wonderful. Just wonderful. You put in the library ladder and the console."

"They were good suggestions. Thanks."

"I'm so glad I could help. This is going to be fabulous. You have a wonderful space for furniture, too, and with the fireplace here, a perfect spot for enjoying the books you're going to display."

He imagined the two of them doing just that. Sprawled together on the sofa in front of a roaring fire, with a nice bottle of red, and music playing quietly in the background.

He'd rub her feet, he thought. Then start nibbling until he'd worked his way up to…

Hold it, he ordered himself, and resolutely shoving the image aside, cleared his throat. "Any changes you'd make?"

Oblivious, she continued to study, shaking her head. "No. I think it's absolutely perfect as it is. I love it, Ian."

"Good. So do I." He wanted to touch the hand she had on the table, stroke a fingertip over her knuckles, down her wrist.

Down boy, he thought, and comforted himself with Chocolate Sin.

The discreet announcement that the store was closing in fifteen minutes had Naomi looking up. Where had the time gone? "I didn't realize it was so late."

"Do you have anything left to do?"

"No. And I actually don't have to be in until midmorning tomorrow. My little treat for the last few twelve-hour days."

"Want to go to a movie?"

"A movie?"

"We've just pumped in all this caffeine." He smiled easily, noting how quickly her eyes could go wary. If she was going to learn to trust him, to become used to him, he was going to have to start nudging her into his company on a regular basis. "Neither one of us are going to sleep for a while yet. Why not take in a movie?"

"Well, I suppose…"

"Great." Moving quickly now, he folded the drawing. "You walked to work, right? My car's just down the block. I'll drive you home afterward."

He was already on his feet, the bag and his briefcase in one hand, and his other held out to her.

Chapter 25

He was a patient man. He knew how to wait. He understood and appreciated the value of building foundations, developing relationships, bonding friendships.

He enjoyed taking his time, holding on to moments, planning days. He found those times, those moments, those days he managed to spend with Naomi very precious. And he certainly valued learning more about her, having conversations about family, about work, about mutual interests.

He wasn't an animal, after all, whose only goal in life was sex. He was a civilized and reasonable man who found pleasure and contentment in the company of a woman he liked, respected and enjoyed.

And he thought if he didn't get his hands on Naomi Brightstone soon, he'd go completely insane.

She was fascinating, fabulous and so unwittingly sexy he spent half his time with her quivering like a stallion wild to cover a mare. And the other half in dazzled delight at having found her.

He was careful not to touch her—oh, a few brotherly pats or pecks, but nothing that came close to that hot-blooded embrace in his kitchen. He wasn't about to risk scaring her off.

And as he'd gotten to know her over the past weeks, he'd realized that she was a great deal more shy, more vulnerable and more insecure than he'd assumed when he'd met her.

They went to concerts, to films, for long walks. They cooked a few meals together and spent ridiculous amounts of time on the phone late at night.

He realized he hadn't experienced such an intense, wonderful, innocent and sexually frustrating relationship since high school.

And when once or twice he tested the waters, she'd shied back like a rabbit under the gun and had left his gut grinding.

It reminded him, forcibly, that if they did become lovers, he would be her first and would have not only the pleasure, but the responsibility of that.

It wasn't a simple matter, or one to be taken lightly, or quickly. But he was a patient man, Ian assured himself, as he surveyed the nearly finished library. He had always been able to work steadily toward what was really important.

This was important in its own way, too, he thought, running his fingers on the freshly waxed trim of one of his custom-designed, built-in units.

The creation of something that was well thought out, that was right, that would last. Cullum did beautiful work, he mused. Precise, creative. The cherry wood gleamed, its corners softly curved, almost fluid.

Shelves stood at varying heights, as Ian had wanted to avoid the look and feel of uniformity. He wanted nothing rigid or forbidding about the room. Between the two tall windows he'd set a huge, festive, ornamental lemon tree in a brass pot. A gift from his parents. They always knew what suited him best, he thought, smiling as he trailed a fingertip over a glossy leaf.

He'd already arranged the seating area. A long, take-a-nap sofa in cheerful blue, a pair of wide chairs, low tables that invited the occupants to put up their feet and relax. Naomi had helped him choose the lamps, he recalled—the charming die-cut tin shades, the romantic globes—on one of their shopping forays.

The stately pewter candlesticks that graced the mantel were heirlooms, housewarming gifts from his grandparents. The bronze-colored mums that stood in a Wedgwood vase between them had come out of his own garden.

There was a great deal of himself in the room, Ian realized. And pieces of those he loved.

Including Naomi.

He sat in one of the oversize chairs, dragged his hands through his gilt-edged hair. There was no point in turning away from it, he told himself. He was in love with her, was nearly sure he'd fallen flat on his face in love the instant he'd met her.

He believed in such things—in love at first sight, in fate, in mating for life. He wanted such things, Ian admitted. Even during his college years, when he'd played as hard as he'd worked, he'd always had an eye focused on what was ahead for him.

His career and where he wanted to take it. His life and where he needed it to go. And that was home, marriage, family, children.

Pushing out of the chair, he began to pace. He couldn't use his feelings to pressure Naomi. He felt dead certain that if he told her he loved her, she'd let him make love with her. From there he could persuade her to move in with him, then nudge her gently into marriage.

And he'd have exactly what he wanted.

Which said nothing of what she wanted. He jammed his hands into his pockets and stared out the window. It had to be her decision.

She didn't know what she was supposed to do. Naomi pulled up at the address Julia had given her and studied the gorgeous old brick house. A house only blocks away from Ian's.

She wanted to be with him. As much as it scraped at her heart, she wanted to be where he was.

He'd be arranging his books today, she thought with a sigh. Books they'd pored over together; books she'd helped him select. He'd asked her to come by and be part of the final stage of the library. He was so sweet about it, she thought with a sigh.

But she'd already agreed to come here and join what Julia called Girl Day.

Naomi had become so fond of Julia over the last few weeks, as they'd consulted on Ian's library project, that she hadn't been able to make excuses.

She took the glossy white bakery box and climbed out of the car. And crossing to the house through the Sunday sunshine, she smiled. Well, after all, she'd never been part of a Girl Day before.

When she'd been a teenager and the other girls were riding in herds, having slumber parties, talking about boys and clothes, she'd stood on the outside, unable to break into that lovely haze of young femininity. Telling herself she didn't want to.

But, of course, she had.

Now, at least for a day, she'd have a taste of it.

Casual, Julia had said, and Naomi tugged at the hem of her red sweater before she knocked.

"Hey!" Julia homed in on the box even as she grabbed Naomi's hand to pull her inside. "What'd you bring?"

"Brownies."

"I love you. And you timed it perfectly, as we've just put all the midgets down for naps."

"Oh, I was hoping to see Travis."

"You will. He and Laura's Daniel never stay down long." She pulled Naomi into a beautifully finished parlor as she spoke. "You met Laura, right?"

"Yes, hello."

"Hi, glad you could come by." Laura sat on the floor eating from a bowl of potato chips. "What's in the box?"

"Brownies."

"Oh God. Gimme."

"Don't be greedy," Julia returned. "And this is our cousin Gwen."

"I've heard lots about you." Gwen rose out of her chair where she'd been studiously painting her toenails. "I'm in your store all the time. Branson's doing one of your author events next month."

"He's wonderful! Branson Maguire's one of Boston's best and brightest," Naomi replied. "I have all of his books in my personal collection—signed by the author."

"Did you know the psycho in *Do No Harm* was based on Gwen?" Laura commented.

"Not the psycho part," Gwen said with a laugh. "Just the dedicated-doctor part. We've got hot chocolate. Chocolate mousse, chocolate drops and chocolate-covered pretzels."

"Julia chose the menu," Laura put in.

"Butch did." Setting the box down, Julia opened it. "And he's going to really go for these. Have a seat, Naomi, and pull up some calories."

Within an hour her system was jangling with caffeine, her stomach groaning from overindulgence she hadn't allowed herself in over three years, and she'd laughed more than she could ever remember.

The girl she'd once been wouldn't have been able to indulge herself only once. She wouldn't have been able to sprawl comfortably on the floor and talk about so many wonderful and foolish things, or to feel a part of the whole.

Before and After, she thought, and nearly laughed

at herself. When was she going to remember, to really accept, that she was firmly rooted in the After?

Here, she thought, in the time it took to demolish a boxful of brownies, she had somehow made three friends.

"Mmm." Julia licked chocolate from her fingers. "Wait till you see Ian's library," she said to Gwen. "It's great."

"Cullum did a fantastic job on the built-ins." Laura poured more hot chocolate.

"Hey, I helped design them." Julia jerked a thumb at Naomi. "And so did she."

"I didn't do that much. Ian already knew what he wanted."

"He get the books in yet?" Julia wanted to know.

"He's doing that today."

"So...how are the two of you getting on?"

"Oh, fine. He's a wonderful friend."

"Friend?" Laura choked out a laugh. "I wouldn't say the looks he was giving you the last time I was over were pal to pal. Looked to me like he wanted to start gnawing at your neck."

"He doesn't think of me that way."

"Since when?"

Naomi shrugged and decided one more chocolate drop couldn't hurt. "He did, but now he doesn't."

"Excuse me." Julia held up a hand. "Are we all friends now?" Without waiting for an answer, she nodded. "Good. Naomi, are you out of your mind?"

"I don't know what you mean."

"Ian's gone over you, honey. He's sunk, he's

gaga. Name your terms. Gwen, you haven't seen it, but you know our boy, Ian, right?''

"Know him and love him," Gwen said, and stuck out her bare feet to admire her toes.

"Well, in your medical opinion, knowing the patient well, what's your diagnosis on a guy who spends all his free time with one woman, talks about her constantly, goes into daydreams with a dopey look on his face and cooks cozy dinners for two?''

"Hmm." Gwen pursed her lips, wiggled her toes. "In medical terminology that would be gaga.''

Julia patted her belly to soothe the actively kicking Butch. "See?''

"He moons at the office, too," Laura commented. "And I heard him tell his secretary last week to hold all of his calls while he worked on this brief—unless it was Ms. Brightstone.''

"Terminally gaga," Gwen said with a sober nod. "A heartbreaking condition that has so far baffled medical science.''

"But he's not." Unsure whether to laugh or moan, Naomi dug into the chocolate drops again. "He treats me like a sister.''

"A very sick man," Gwen murmured. "If you'd care to share more details, I'd be happy to try to suggest a course of treatment.''

"He kisses my cheek," Naomi muttered, while a frown slowly formed on her brow. "Pats my head. Once in a while he looks at me, and I think, oh boy, here it comes. Then nothing. Before I told him I'd never had sex, he kissed me brainless, but now...oh!'' She moved quickly, rapping Laura on the back as Ian's sister choked. ''Are you all right?''

''Oh, poor Ian!'' Then Laura burst into wild laughter.

Baffled, Naomi stood, looking around the room as her three new friends howled until tears ran down their cheeks.

''Sorry, sorry.'' Laura pressed both hands to her heart. ''I doubt it's funny to you—or him—but we're his family. We have to laugh. He must be suffering the torments of the damned. Gwen?'' Helpless, Laura waved a hand for her cousin to take over.

''He's terrified of you,'' Gwen told her. The thought made her smile. And she remembered how sweetly, how romantically Branson had become her first.

''That's just silly.''

''No.'' Sympathetic now, Gwen held out a hand. ''He wouldn't want to push, not a man like Ian. He'd be afraid he'd make the wrong move, frighten you, hurt you. And if he's as attracted as I think he is, those brotherly pats and pecks aren't easy on him. He's waiting for you to make the next move, for you to be sure it's what you want. And that's exactly as it should be.''

For ten staggered seconds, Naomi stared at the three grinning faces. ''I thought he just wasn't interested that way, after he found out I didn't have any experience.''

''He'd never pressure a woman, Naomi.'' Laura gave her hand a squeeze. ''And the more he cares, the more careful he'd be.''

"You really think..." Naomi trailed off and smiled dreamily into space.

"Oh-oh, Dr. Maguire, I think we have another case of gaga." Julia grinned and winked at her cousins. "This could cause an epidemic."

It was dusk when Naomi stopped her car in front of Ian's house. The lights were on, glowing in welcome through the windows. Was he still up in the library, she wondered, arranging his books? Was he wondering if she'd call or drop by?

Did he want her to?

Or was his family wrong? Was it exactly as she'd assumed, and he thought of her as a friend?

Maybe he wasn't alone.

That thought sneaked into her brain and had her gripping the steering wheel. He was so attractive, so charming, so...everything. There had to be a dozen women he could summon with one crook of the finger. Beautiful, experienced, sophisticated women.

Why would he be waiting for her?

"Stop it, stop it, stop it." Annoyed with herself, she thumped a fist on the wheel. "That's the way you used to think. You're different now."

She'd made herself different. Maybe it was still a work in progress, but she had indeed made progress. She was reasonably attractive when she took time to work on it. She could hold up her end in conversations. She owned a business, for God's sake. She had employees, and none of them thought of her as a wishy-washy add-on.

Three incredibly delightful and intelligent women

now considered her a friend. Oh, she would treasure that, Naomi thought, closing her eyes. She would remember this single foolish afternoon all of her life.

And those three women knew and loved Ian, didn't they? Why should she question their opinion?

And why didn't she stop being a sniveling coward, get out of the car and see for herself?

"Okay. All right. We're going."

She drew calming breaths as she walked to the door. But they didn't seem to do the job. Caffeine overload, she decided, and bracing herself, rang the bell.

He answered in bare feet, faded jeans and a ragged Harvard Law sweatshirt. And his quick smile of greeting warmed her shaky heart.

"Hi. I didn't think I'd see you tonight."

"I should have called. But I was just over at Julia's, and—"

"Girl Day, yeah." He grasped her hands, drawing her inside out of the chilly twilight. "They do that every couple of months. What the hell do you do on Girl Day?"

"Paint your nails, eat chocolate. Talk about men."

"Yeah? What do you say about us?"

"Ah…could I have a drink?"

"Sure, sorry. Come on up. I've got some wine in the library, and I'm dying to show you what I've done."

He could have eaten her up. Her cheeks were rosy, her eyes dark, and the oversize sweater made his fingers itch to find her under it. So he kept his hands in his pockets as they walked upstairs.

"I've been at it most of the day," he went on. "Once I got started, I couldn't stop." He stopped a short distance from the open door. "Close your eyes."

When she obeyed without question, simply stood there, eyes shut, his hands fisted in his pockets. It took some effort to unball them, to lay them lightly on her shoulders and guide her into the room.

"Okay. Open up."

When she did, her hands went straight to her heart. "Oh, Ian, it's wonderful. It's more than wonderful." Eyes shining, she turned to look around the room, where the beautifully trimmed, built-in shelves were lined with books. Old worn spines, new glossy ones, embossed leather and tattered covers.

"Perfect. And your library ladder arrived! I just love it." She turned in another circle, then beamed at him.

"I wanted you here." His heart had circled with her, and now beat uncomfortably in his chest. "I wanted to see how the room would feel with you in it. Just right." He dug his hands into his pockets again, dragged them back out. "Let me get you that wine."

The hands still held against her heart dropped to her sides. She gathered all her courage. "Ian, do you want to go to bed with me?"

He bobbled the glass, splashed wine on his shirt, swore. *"What?"*

"I don't mean to be rude or to put you in an awkward position. It's just that I'd like to know if you're still attracted to me in that way or not. If not, then that's fine, but if you are, and you've just been trying to be considerate because I haven't been with a man before, you could stop now. I'd prefer you to stop being so considerate, if that's what you're being.''

She ran out of breath, and words, and compensated by shrugging as he stood staring at her, a bottle of wine in one hand, a half-empty glass in the other, and a good splotch of cabernet sauvignon spreading over his beloved Harvard Law sweatshirt.

Chapter 26

He set the bottle down. "You don't want me to be considerate?"

"No. Not really."

He put the glass beside the bottle. "You don't want me to keep my hands off you?"

A shivery thrill ran up her spine. "Not if you still feel, um, interested."

His throat went bone-dry. This was the woman he wanted, and she was offering herself to him, as she'd done with no other man. Could he be careful enough to show her what there could be between the two of them?

He had to be, because nothing had ever been more important.

A smile was slowly curving his lips as he walked toward her. "The witness is required to answer the question. Yes or no. Do you want me to keep my hands off you?''

''No.'' She had to tilt her head back to keep her eyes on his.

''Thank God.'' Then he was sweeping her close, pulling her to her toes, and his mouth captured hers in a long, draining kiss that had her heart flopping helplessly in her chest.

''Does that answer your question?'' he murmured, shifting his attention from her mouth to her neck until little startled sounds hummed in her throat.

''What question?''

''Do I want you? Do I want to make love with you?'' Lord, she was delicious. ''In case you missed my answer the first time, let me just repeat myself.'' His lips skimmed over her jaw, then settled warmly on hers. ''Got it now?''

''Yes.'' For balance, for pleasure, she linked her arms around his neck. ''Yes, I've got it now.''

''You've been making me crazy for weeks.'' He circled her, slowly, toward the door.

''I—'' The concept shocked and delighted. ''Really?''

''Being considerate was killing me.''

''I thought you'd decided we'd just be friends.''

''We are friends.'' He kept circling, a long slow dance, down the hallway, into his bedroom. ''That only makes me want you more.''

''No one ever has.'' Emotion swam into her eyes as she laid a hand on his cheek. ''I don't know what to do about it.''

''I'll help you with that.'' He turned his head so that his lips brushed her palm. ''Trust me, Naomi. I won't hurt you. And if you want me to stop, I'll stop.''

"I won't want you to."

He left the light burning. Though he wished he'd lit a fire, wished there were candles flickering, he didn't think he could let her go long enough to tend to it.

She was trembling lightly, but those lovely gray eyes were steady on his. The trust he'd asked for was in there. He swore that, whatever his own needs, he wouldn't break that trust.

His mouth was soft on hers, drawing her in with care, with warmth. "I love this part of you." He caught her top lip between his teeth, chewed gently. "It's so sexy."

Her eyes blinked open, the aroused surprise in them pulling a groaning laugh out of him. "Don't have a clue, do you? Pretty Naomi. I've been dying to bite your lips."

So he did, pleasing himself, destroying her until the pressure building inside her threatened to erupt. With a muffled cry she threw her arms around him. And her mouth went wild.

Pure hot lust burst in his blood, rattled his brain. Slow down, slow down, he ordered himself. Her response might have been the answer to every sexual dream, but she was still untouched.

And he'd given his word.

He softened the kiss, soothing her lips now as he began to unwind the braid at her back. He wanted her hair in his hands, tumbled over his bed, wrapped around him. The weight and texture of it, the scent enthralled him.

Combing his fingers through it, he stepped back. Then, keeping his eyes on hers, he lifted her sweater up.

Her first instinct was to cover herself, but he caught her hands in his. Struggling for air, she felt the heat rise up to flush her skin as his gaze swept down, lingered, came back to hers.

Nerves and needs jangled inside her as he skimmed a fingertip over the swell above her bra. Her hands curled at her sides before she ordered herself to relax, to be brave enough to do what she wanted. After a shaky breath, she gripped the hem of his sweatshirt and drew it up over his body.

"Oh. My." He was beautiful. Lean muscles, smooth skin. Without thinking, she laid her hands on his chest. Then snatched them back when she felt him quiver.

With a strained laugh, he brought her hands back. "Step out of your shoes."

Oh, his heart was racing, she thought. And his chest was so…hard. "My shoes."

"Step out of them."

"Mmm." Fascinated by the feel of him, she splayed her fingers over him as she obeyed. Then her body jerked when he unhooked her trousers.

"Relax." He murmured the word, bringing his mouth back to hers, taking her swimming into another kiss as the trousers slid down. While his mouth continued to play on hers, he lifted her, laid her on the bed.

She felt the heat from his body over hers, the coolness of the spread beneath her. And as her heart plunged, she felt the smooth, lazy glide of his hands.

She stirred under him, yearning toward......something. But before she could reach it, she was floating, drifting into dreams at the urging of his mouth and hands.

He'd never taken more care with a woman. Never felt the need to take so much. He wanted to give her every pleasure, awaken her to her own desires. It was easier than he'd believed to bank the fires within himself, to let them simmer.

Her eyes were closed, her breathing deep. But he could feel her heart trip beneath his mouth as he tasted her. The low and mindless moan she gave when he slipped her bra aside sent an echoing shimmer into his gut.

She slipped into his hands, firm and full. Her hips arched instinctively as he skimmed his thumbs over her nipples. He watched the stunned pleasure flicker over her face, her lashes flutter, then lift, to reveal eyes gone storm dark and clouded.

She sucked in a ragged breath. "What should I do?"

Her hands were roaming restlessly over his back, driving him wonderfully mad. "Enjoy."

His mouth lowered, his breath skimming over the sensitized skin of her breast, his tongue flicking erotically, tortuously, until her hands clamped on the back of his head to bring him to her.

With lazy tugs and pulls he set out to destroy her, reveling in her shocked gasps, her trembles. He let her taste fill him as his hands roamed down, stroking closer and closer to the heat.

Just a brush of fingertips and slow, openmouthed kisses over her shoulders, her breasts. Just a slide of his palm along her thigh. He cupped her, gently, intending to give her time to get used to this new intimacy.

She exploded beneath him, her body bucking, his name bursting from her lips, and the heat flooding out of her into his hand.

Her reaction ripped through him, forcing him to bury his face in her hair and for the first time fight viciously for control.

Her body went lax and her breath remained shallow and fast. Nothing had prepared her for that long, glorious shock to the system, for the tidal wave of hot, liquid pleasure. Delirious from it, she turned her head, hands pulling at him until she could find his mouth with hers.

His skin was damp, slippery. Oh, she loved the feel of it. Wanted more, and raced her lips over his neck and shoulders even as her hips began to lift and press, lift and press against him.

Her body was full of storms ready to break, her mind whirling with them.

He rolled with her, struggling back from the edge, holding himself in check long enough to strip off his jeans and protect her. Fighting the beat of his own blood so he could take her back up slowly, drench her in pleasure until he knew she was close to flying again.

And as her body bowed, as that moan of release sounded in her throat, he gripped her hips and slipped into her. The resistance of innocence made him shudder, and made him gentle. He took her mouth, swallowed her single, sharp cry and made her his.

Only his, he thought, as he filled her for the first time.

She quivered still, cradled in the circle of his arms. He held her there, stroking her hair and waiting for his own system to level out.

"You okay?"

"Mmm," was the best she could manage, and made him smile.

"How do you feel?"

"Ah, thickheaded, floaty, a little drunk." She sighed. "Incredibly relaxed. Not awkward at all. I was sure I'd feel awkward. Did I do everything right?"

He lifted a brow. Her voice was slurred and sleepy. "No. You were a huge disappointment to me. I'm afraid I'll have to ask you to leave now."

Her head snapped up, her eyes wide in a face still glowing. Then she saw his grin, blinked. "I could probably do better with practice," she said, stunning herself.

"Hmm. Well, maybe I'll give you another shot at it. Pretty Naomi." He cupped her cheek and touched his lips to hers. "Want that wine now?"

"All right." She couldn't have cared less about wine, but thought it would give her a chance to recover from the quiver it gave her when he called her pretty.

She pretended not to watch him as he climbed out of bed and walked naked from the room. But when he'd gone, she patted a hand to her heart. How in the world, she wondered, had she managed to engage the interest of a man who looked like *that?* Who had such intense physical beauty along with such intense kindness?

Better not to question it, she told herself. Then, realizing suddenly that she was naked, too, she tugged up the tangled sheets and spread just as he came back into the room.

He stood there a moment, then shook his head. "Why the hell hasn't someone gobbled you up before me?"

She flushed, only adding to the sexy, tumbled image she projected. "I guess no one ever really tried."

With a laugh, he carried the wine and glasses to the bed. "Get serious. You must not have been paying attention."

"No, I've always been clumsy with boys. Men. Males." And because she was starting to feel clumsy again, she gratefully took the wine he offered.

"Honey, I'd say the males you've come across have been the clumsy ones, if none of them managed to get ahold of you." With a fingertip he drew the sheet she held to her breasts down an inch. "You have an amazing body."

"I always wanted to be tall and slim." Trying to relax again, she sipped her wine. "But I started, you know, developing early. It was very painful."

"Why?"

"Oh...I suppose you have to be a girl to understand what it's like to be an adolescent and suddenly..."

"Grow beautiful breasts," he finished with a smile. "But boys really like breasts, Naomi. We consider them one of nature's finest miracles."

She laughed a little. "I spent years trying to hide mine."

"Still are," he pointed out, then tugged the sheet down to her waist, grinning when she sputtered. "Much better. How's your wine?"

"It's fine." Resolutely, she pulled the sheet back up. She couldn't possibly sit there drinking wine while uncovered. "I'm sorry about your shirt. You could probably get most of the stain out if you soaked it now."

"I'm keeping the stain to remind me of a monumental night in my life."

Delight shone in her eyes. "That's so sweet. How could you possibly be interested in me?"

Even as she prepared to saw off her tongue, he angled his head, gave her a long considering look. "You have breasts."

Her eyes widened; her mouth dropped open. Then she caught the gleam in his eyes and burst into laughter. "Well, lucky me."

His fingertip skimmed over the curve of her shoulder, down her throat, lowered to toy with the sheet again. "After you finish your wine, I think we should have that practice session."

"Oh." He wanted her again. Life was so suddenly full of miracles. "All right. But I'd like to move into the library this time." It was her turn to see surprise light in his eyes. "You see, I do really well around books."

The image that brought into his mind had him going rock hard. "Naomi?"

"Yes?"

"Finish your wine."

She had to swallow first, then tipped back her glass and drained it. "Done," she announced.

It was a wonderful thing, Ian mused, to lie in the dark with Naomi curled against him in sleep. This was what he wanted, now, tomorrow, forever. It was almost ridiculously simple how she slipped into and completed his life.

He could imagine them there, in that big bed in the sturdy old house, year after year. With children sleeping, safe down the hall, a dog snoring on the rug.

Life would be busy with her career and his, a family to raise, a marriage to nurture, but they would do it.

His parents had. And it was what he'd seen in them, seen between them—what that bond had given him and Laura—that he wanted now for himself. For Naomi.

All he had to do was take his time, move slowly. Caution and care had brought her to him, after all. He'd given her the space to move toward physical intimacy. And she'd come to him not only willing, but eager.

It stirred his blood to think just how eager.

He'd give her a few weeks, then persuade her to move in with him. Step by step, he told himself. That was the way to handle it. He could control his impatience, his needs, when the rewards were so rich.

He'd give her room, he thought, even as he drew her closer. Then they'd have a lifetime together.

Chapter 27

Ian hung up the phone and shook his head. His grandfather was certainly keeping in close touch lately. That made the third call in less than two weeks.

He really had to make time to get to Hyannis Port soon, Ian decided, turning back to his computer to study the wording of the writ he was composing. He'd love to take Naomi there for a quick weekend.

But…

He didn't have a doubt in the world that if The MacGregor liked the looks of her, he'd start meddling. Hinting none too subtly about weddings, about duty, about continuing the MacGregor line. Ian grinned, changed a phrase on the screen. Little did The MacGregor know that was exactly what his grandson had in mind.

And Ian wanted to keep it that way.

He glanced up at the knock on his open door, lifted a brow at his mother.

"Busy?"

"Not too."

She walked in, tall, slim, her dark hair swept back from a strong and beautiful face. Then she dropped a load of files on his desk. "Gee, now you are."

"Not the Perinsky matter."

Diana smiled cheerfully at her son's distress. "Got it in one. This time she's determined to sue her neighborhood market for not carrying her brand of tea. Claims it's violating her civil rights."

He thumbed through a file. It was full of the paperwork Mrs. Perinsky loved to generate. Old bat, Ian thought, but not without some reluctant affection. "Laura's so much better with her." He lifted hopeful blue eyes.

"Mrs. Perinsky likes you best." With a laugh, Diana leaned a hip on his desk. "I think she has a thing for you, sweetheart."

"She's a hundred and fifty, at the very least."

"And hasn't forgotten the thrill of having a handsome young man at her beck and call. I know it's a pain, Ian, but she's been a client since before you were born."

"Since before *you* were born," he muttered, and made Diana laugh again.

"Nearly, but in any case, she's just lonely and looking for attention. You'll give her a little, eat some of her cookies and talk her out of filing a nuisance suit against her very harassed grocer."

"I can do that. But then you'll owe me."

"Would a home-cooked meal balance the scales?"

He considered. Anything involving Mrs. Perinsky required stiff payment. "Maybe if it was a pot roast with the works, it could come close."

"I think we can arrange that. Sunday work for you?"

"It would if you could stretch it to include one more."

"Naomi?"

"Yeah." Since they hadn't really discussed it, or her, Ian studied his mother's face. "Is that all right with you?"

"I like her very much."

"I'm in love with her."

"Oh." Helpless to stop it, Diana felt her eyes fill, and held up a hand. "I'm sorry."

"Hold it." Alarmed, he got up to shut the door, then hurried back to take his mother's shoulders. "I thought you said you liked her."

"I do. I do." Diana waved her hand, then laid it on his cheek. "You're my baby." Straightening, she rested her cheek on his, remembered a hundred sweet and foolish moments. "My baby," she murmured again. "Oh, Ian, I'm happy for you."

"Could've fooled me."

"No, I am." She gave a watery laugh and drew back. "But there's a place inside me where you'll always be my little boy. And another that's so incredibly proud of the man he's become."

This time he rested his cheek against hers. "You'll make *me* sloppy in a minute."

She wrapped her arms around him in one fierce hug. "I know there were other girls, other women." She took a deep breath, let it out in a sigh and stepped back.

"Me? Girls, women? I don't know where you got such an idea."

She laughed again, easier now. "Maybe it was the way they kept popping up at the house, or answering your phone at college. But…" She framed his face with her hands. "This is the first time you've ever looked at me and told me you were in love. So I know it's real."

"It is. Very real."

"She's a very lucky woman." Diana kissed him lightly. "And I say that without any prejudice whatsoever."

"So maybe you could drop a few comments about what a terrific guy I am when we come to dinner."

"I think I could do that."

"But subtly. She shies easily and I don't want to scare her off."

Surprise had Diana lifting her brows. "You haven't told her how you feel?"

"I'm working up to it. I've got it planned out."

"Ian, if I have one criticism of you, it's that you tend to plan things just a bit too carefully. Or perhaps," she said with a gleam in her eye, "the word should be *plot*. À la Daniel MacGregor."

"Works for him," Ian said cheerfully. "And won't it take some of the wind out of his sails when I present him with the woman I'm going to marry before he manages to get his hand into it?"

Diana pursed her lips, recalling the list of books Daniel had given Ian to purchase, when it would have been a simple matter for Daniel to pick up the phone and order them himself.

"Won't it just," she murmured, and decided to let her baby have his illusions.

Naomi arranged the display of Branson Maguire's latest thriller personally. She felt she had a special interest in him now, as she'd become friends with his wife and family. She'd even cuddled his children.

They were such pretty girls, she mused. Just as Laura's boys were a handsome delight. And Travis. Well, Naomi had to admit she had a special fondness for Julia's energetic young son.

She'd always been good with children, Naomi thought as she studiously arranged copies of *Killer Run* in a dramatic spiral tower. One of her first adult duties at Brightstone's had been to handle the children's area and the weekly reading hour.

Still, she'd rarely allowed herself to think of what it would be like to have children of her own. As she was now.

If she didn't do anything to ruin it, Ian could fall in love with her. It wasn't impossible. Nothing was impossible any longer. He wanted her, and she knew he had strong feelings for her. There was no reason those feelings couldn't blossom into love.

The kind of deep, stirring, consuming love she felt for him.

Then one day he might take her face in his hands

as he sometimes did, look into her eyes and say it. *I love you, Naomi.*

"Naomi?"

The brisk tap on the shoulder had her coming back to earth and staring blankly at Julia.

"Did you have a nice trip?"

"Oh." With a laugh, Naomi shook her head to clear her thoughts. "My mind was wandering. Julia! You're due any minute. You shouldn't be out driving around."

"God, you sound like Cullum." Julia rolled her eyes. "And you'll be pleased to know that he's out looking for a parking place. He let me off at the door so I could waddle inside. Which is how I maneuver these days." She pressed a hand to her lower back.

"You know if you'd wanted anything from the store I'd have brought it to you."

Touched, Julia smiled, and her eyes softened. "I know. You're an absolute sweetheart, Naomi. But I wanted to get out for a bit. I was feeling restless," she admitted. "And very likely driving Cullum insane. He had the bright idea to distract me with a chocolate mocha."

"Well, let's go into the café and get you one."

"Yeah, let's. This looks great, by the way," she added, gesturing to the display. "Bran will have them lined up around the block."

Naomi glanced over the nearly completed display as she took Julia's arm. "We're counting on it. Have you read it yet?"

"I can't seem to concentrate long enough to read. It was the same way right before Travis was born.

I've got it in my bag for the hospital, though. As soon as I give birth I can curl up like a cat for hours at a time.''

"You'll love it. It's a heart pounder."

"Maybe I should pick up a couple other books while I'm here." Still pressing a hand to her back, she frowned around the store that suddenly seemed to hold entirely too many choices. "I'm not in the mood to shop."

"Would you like me to pick a few out for you?"

"Yeah, fine. Whoa!" She jerked to a stop, shoving a hand against a shelf and knocking a trio of books to the floor.

"Is he kicking? Do you want to sit down?"

"No, he's not kicking. He's knocking to get out. No wonder I've felt so snarly all day."

"Get out?" Fingers of panic tickled up Naomi's throat as Julia bent over and panted. "You mean *out?* Now?"

"Not right this minute," Julia managed, a bit surprised at how strongly the contraction came on. With Travis they'd been mild initially before building to flash point. "But pretty soon. Oh hell, I'm not going to get that mocha, after all."

"You need to sit down. To sit." Desperate, Naomi searched the store she knew like the back of her hand because she'd completely forgotten where the closest seating area was located. "Over here. You just sit and do...whatever. I'll find Cullum."

"Good idea." Julia lowered herself onto a pretty love seat. "And Naomi? Tell him he better hurry. I don't think Butch is going to waste any time."

* * *

Two hours later, Naomi was pacing a hospital waiting room crowded with MacGregors. She didn't know how they could be so calm. How they could sit there chatting, laughing, telling family stories.

Her own stomach was tied in knots and her palms were sweating.

Ian's mother sat curled up in one of the chairs, talking cheerfully on the phone to the former president and first lady. Julia's parents were on their way to Boston, and getting periodic updates on the progress via cell phone.

Caine was on his own phone, laughing as he spoke to the soon-to-be great-grandparents.

And Ian, she thought as she peeked into the corridor again, was nowhere to be found.

But she spotted Gwen coming out of the birthing room and pounced before she could remember she wasn't family. "How is she? What's happening?" Her eyes widened as she heard a stream of violent cursing coming through the door.

"Don't you tell me to breathe, Murdoch, you bonehead. I know how to breathe. You try it!"

Gwen chuckled, patted Naomi's white cheek. "She's doing great. It's going to be a quick one, and there aren't any complications. Fetal heartbeat is strong. She's fully dilated, completely effaced."

Keeping a hand on Naomi's shoulder, she smiled at the crowd of faces in the waiting room. "I'm going back in. She's ready to start pushing, so get the cigars ready."

"Shelby, did you hear?" Diana laughed. "No, I'll

stay right here on the phone. She's nearly there. Yes, I know. Gwen will tell her you love her.''

"On my way," Gwen promised, then waved down the corridor. "Ian."

"Did I miss it?" He was slightly out of breath from the run from the parking lot and up the stairs. The elevators were too damn slow to suit him.

"Nearly." She pulled open the door of the birthing room, letting out the next stream of abuse.

"Don't you tell me not to push yet, you sadistic moron. You're fired."

"That's the third time she's fired her OB with this one. She made it to five with Travis." Obviously amused, Gwen stepped in and shut the door.

"She must be in pain." Naomi wrung her hands. "She must be terrified."

"Terrified? Julia? Not in this lifetime."

"Oh, what do you know?" Naomi rounded on Ian, making him take a step back and causing both him and his family to eye her with surprise. "You weren't even here. Where have you been?"

"Ah, trapped with an irritable old woman and her endless supply of stale sugar cookies. I broke out as soon as the message got to me. Want some water, Naomi?"

"No, I don't want any water." She slapped his hand aside, then marched down the corridor. When she reentered the waiting room, she caught sight of the sea of faces watching her, most of which hadn't manage to hold back grins.

She flushed, stammered. "I—I'm sorry. I'm so

sorry. I've never been involved with anything like this. I'm nervous. Why isn't anyone else nervous?''

"We've been going through this pretty regularly for the past few years,'' Ian told her. "Honey, why don't you sit down?''

"I can't.'' But she did close her eyes and take her breaths. Ian counted with her to ten. "I am sorry,'' she continued, looking at him again. "I shouldn't have snapped at you like that.''

"You're allowed to snap when you need to. I was hoping you'd be here.'' He put an arm around her shoulders and led her to an empty chair. "I called the store when I got the message about Julia. Wanted to let you know what was going on, and your assistant filled me in. They've got a pool going.''

She found herself sitting. He was clever that way. She tried to stay still, but couldn't. "Do you think it'll be much longer?''

"Hard to say. Seems to me Travis took her, oh, about a decade.''

"Fourteen hours,'' Laura corrected. "Three hours less than it took me for my first, an hour longer than it took for my second.''

"Same thing,'' Ian decided, remembering that with Laura's first, he'd been just as terrified and fidgety as Naomi while he'd waited out the birth. "Rounds out to a decade for me.'' He glanced around the room. "Where's Bran?''

"He drew the short straw,'' Caine said with a grin. "He's got all the kids. He asked us to pray for him. Here you go,'' he added, and neatly wrapped Naomi's hands around a cup of tea.

"Oh, thank you." Too embarrassed to tell him she didn't want anything, she sipped dutifully, listened to the chatter, the quick laughter, and didn't realize her stomach had calmed until she'd emptied the cup.

"Ladies and gentlemen." Gwen stood in the doorway again, her face damp with sweat and bright with joy. "I'd like to announce the appearance of Fiona Joy Murdoch. Arriving into this world at 4:43 p.m. at eight pounds even. Mother, father and daughter are doing beautifully." Tears spilled over. "Absolutely beautifully."

Then everyone was talking at once, rushing for hugs, weeping without shame. Naomi found herself kissed, squeezed and swept along. When Ian's father offered her a cigar, she stared down at it dumbfounded.

Then Ian lifted her right off her feet. "Isn't this great?"

Chapter 28

They were the most incredible family, Naomi thought. And they'd let her be a part of it, let her share one of their miraculous moments.

She'd been able to stand at the glass and stare at the beautiful new baby in Cullum's arms. When Caine had announced they were all going out to celebrate, she'd been dragged right along with them.

No one looked at her as if she were an outsider, as if she didn't belong.

They were open and loving, and most of all, honest. And, she admitted with a weight of guilt, she hadn't been, not really. Not with Ian.

When she agreed to go home with him that evening, she was prepared to be.

"There'll be another wave of family in by tomorrow," he said as he unlocked the front door. "You can count on it. Headed up by The MacGregor himself, who'll puff around for a bit, then sniffle over the new baby. Then, if D.C. and Layna get here by then, he'll want to know why the devil they haven't started a baby of their own."

He thought it best to prepare her for what was bound to happen. "Then he'll start on you."

"On me?" Miserably nervous, she wandered into the parlor, fluffed pillows that didn't need fluffing.

"Why a pretty young lass like you isn't married. Don't you like babies? What are you waiting for then?" He laced his speech with a thick Scottish burr and really hoped she'd smile.

But her eyes were gray and serious as she turned to him. "Ian, this isn't right. For you, your family. You're all so kind to me."

"What's not right about that?"

"I haven't been honest. You don't even know me. You're not attracted to me."

"I beg to differ," he murmured, and started toward her.

"No, don't. Really." She pressed her hands to his lips and prepared to confess. "I shouldn't have let you think this was me." She spread her arms, dropped them. "I'm working on making it me, but it's just not fair to you."

"Naomi, I don't know what you're talking about. I'm looking at you. I'm holding you," he added when he took her shoulders.

"Only because I've changed the surface. Even two years ago you wouldn't have looked twice at me. Why would you? No one ever did. Pudgy, working my way up to fat because eating was easier than accepting, really accepting, that I'd never be like my mother, no matter what I did.''

"Like your mother?'' He was baffled by the sudden passion in her voice.

"Slim, beautiful, completely, naturally female. I could never be that, so I just...ate and hid at the bookstore.''

"Naomi, a lot of kids go through a pudgy stage—''

"It wasn't a stage. It was a condition, and only a symptom of what I was inside. I was drab and dowdy and clumsy. And I only worked to be otherwise because I started to loathe what I was doing to myself. I wanted to find what was really inside and try to like who that was.''

"And you have. There's nothing drab or dowdy about you.''

"But there is!'' Impatient, she pushed away. "I still can't figure out what to wear in the morning unless I check my computer.''

"Your computer?''

Oh, it was mortifying. "I have my wardrobe filed on my computer, with cross references for the right accessories, right down to shoes and shade of lipstick. And I keep another file so I know what I've worn when and where so I don't repeat myself too often.''

"Really?'' He cocked his head. "That's brilliant.''

"Brilliant? It's ridiculous. Any normal woman just goes to her closet and takes something out. Last week we had a power outage and I couldn't boot my home computer. I nearly called in sick because I panicked." She huffed out a breath. "It's pathetic."

"Not that you don't always look fabulous, but I don't think you need to worry about it quite so much."

"You couldn't possibly understand. You're beautiful, you grew up beautiful and confident and personable. My parents are absolutely stunning people. My brother looks like a movie star. Then there's me."

"Naomi." He took her shoulders again. "You are a beautiful woman."

"No. I can be very presentable if I'm careful. I'm content with that. Actually, I'm thrilled with that. And I think with more practice it won't be such a worry to accomplish."

"You really believe that, don't you?" Vaguely annoyed, he pulled her into the hall, turned her firmly around—to face a mahogany-framed mirror. "What do you see there?"

"You." Her heart simply rolled over in her chest. "Just you. No one ever wanted me before you."

For the first time the full impact of that got through, and began to worry him.

"I've never felt this way about anyone else," she murmured, compounding what he was beginning to recognize as guilt. "My whole life I've felt one step behind, and I never thought anyone would care enough to let me catch up."

"Naomi."

"Let me finish." It was terrifying to turn, to face him. "I don't want you to go on thinking I'm something I'm not, when part of me is still the awkward girl who had exactly two dates in high school—and both of them friends of my brother's who felt sorry for me. And the young woman who spent her entire college career buried in books because it was the only place she felt comfortable. It often still is.''

She drew a deep breath. ''You were the first man to give me flowers, the first to make me dinner, the first to just sit and listen to me, and to look at me when you did.'' Her voice broke and had her fighting to finish. ''You're the only man who's touched me, kissed me.''

Her first, he thought, in every way that counted. Not just physically, but emotionally. She'd been sleeping like a butterfly, waiting to break free, to spread her wings. And he'd snatched her out of the air before she'd ever really felt the power.

Oh God, he thought. What had he done? What was he going to do? ''I'm not the only one who'll want to. And you're wrong if you think this isn't who you are.'' He ran his hands up and down her arms. ''This right here. You've just started to see her for yourself.''

He drew her close, rested his cheek on the top of her head. And realized he was going to have to do more than give her time. He was going to have to let her go, and hope that when she really saw herself, accepted herself, she'd come back.

He gave her arms a quick squeeze, then forced himself to take a step back. ''You're a beautiful woman, Naomi, and a fascinating one.''

''You're the only one who ever thought so.''

Hearing her say it, seeing the glimmer of tears in her eyes as she did, ripped him to pieces. "I don't think you were paying enough attention. And you know, it occurs to me that I've been monopolizing all your free time for the last several weeks."

"My free time?"

"I hadn't thought about the fact that you were just getting the alterations in the store finished, then helping me with my library."

He spoke lightly as he walked past her into the parlor. He could give her six months, he told himself viciously. Six months, then by God, he was going for her. She'd better be ready.

"I haven't given you much of a chance to settle into this new life of yours." To give himself something to do, he crouched and began to lay a fire. "We've been moving along pretty fast here. Maybe we should slow down."

She opened her mouth, closed it again because the violent kick to her heart had robbed her of breath. "I'm afraid you're going to have to be more specific, Ian. I don't have enough experience in relationships to be certain I understand the underlying meaning."

That, he thought, as he struck a match, stared at the flame, was exactly the point. "No underlying meaning, Naomi. Just slowing the pace, maybe taking a breather."

"You don't want to see me anymore?"

"Yes, I still want to see you." He watched the kindling catch hold, but the flare of heat didn't warm him. "I'm suggesting that our relationship doesn't have to be exclusive." He rose, turned, certain that knowing he was doing the right thing for her would eventually cure this sickness that churned in his gut. "You should see other people."

"Other people," she murmured. Other women, she thought. He wanted to see other women. Of course, she should have expected it. "I suppose that's very sensible. Very reasonable." A brittle smile curved her lips. "Aren't we lucky I've always been a sensible, reasonable person? I imagine some women would be angry, or at least annoyed with a suggestion like that. But then, I'm not like a lot of other women, am I?"

"No, you're not." He said it quietly. "You're one in a million."

She let out a short laugh. "One in a million," she murmured. But still not quite good enough. "Well, it's been a long day. All this excitement. I'm tired. I'm going home."

"Naomi. I don't want you to go tonight."

She studied him a moment, with the fire flickering behind him. "And I don't want to stay." She walked toward the hall, made it to the doorway before she turned back. "I was honest with you, Ian, as I should have been all along. So I'll finish this by being honest. I'm in love with you. And I have been, all along."

She went quickly to the front door and out before he could say anything kind that would make the ache inside her any worse.

"I know." He let it out in a sigh to the empty house. "But you never really had a chance to be otherwise. Now you do."

* * *

He was unhappy for a day, miserable for two
more, then surly for the best part of a week. But he
didn't pick up the phone. He didn't call her. He
didn't give in to his own needs and drive to her apartment and beat on her door.

He'd worked it out, damn it. Six months and
time's up, he thought, staring out the window of his
office, as he seemed to do much too often lately.

She'd have six months of freedom, to figure out
who she was and what she wanted. Six months to
see other men.

And if any one of them touched her, he'd…

No, that was the whole point, he reminded himself.
How could she know she loved him—really loved
him enough for a lifetime—if she'd never been ro-
manced, touched, loved by anyone else?

His lips curled at the knock on his office door. He
wanted to ignore it, or better yet to shout out, "Go
away, damn it. Can't you see I'm sulking here?"

"What is it?" he snapped out.

"Now that's a fine way to talk," Daniel said as
he shoved open the door. "Is that how you behave
with clients, Mr. Counselor-at-Law, or is it just family that rates?"

"Sorry." Ian walked over to accept his grandfather's bear hug and his grandmother's warm kiss.
"Had something on my mind."

"We won't keep you." Anna aimed a warning
glance at her husband even as Daniel took a seat and
made himself at home. "We just wanted to say goodbye."

354 The MacGregor Grooms

"Goodbye? You only got here a few days ago."

"Woman can't stay still," Daniel muttered.

"You want your own bed as much as I do," Anna said with a laugh. "We're going by Julia's to see the baby first, then heading back home."

"I'll miss you."

"Then why don't you come visit more often?" Daniel thumped his fist on the arm of the chair. "Too busy flitting around with some pretty young woman to take time to visit your poor old grandparents."

"I'll come up in a couple weeks. I'm not so busy flitting just now."

"And why the devil not? Where's Naomi?"

"At work, I imagine." Ian angled his head. "Why?"

"Every one of the family's talking about her." Daniel tapped his fingers together. "Except you, that is. Why is it I haven't seen the two of you in the same place since I got here, when talk is you've been in each other's pockets for weeks?"

"Because we're taking a break from each other."

"Break? Break! Why in bloody hell would you do that? You're perfect for each other. That girl's made for you, you dunderhead. She's smart, got a nice sweetness about her. Comes from a fine family, good strong stock. And don't let that quiet nature fool you. There's a sturdy woman in there, the kind who stands firm."

"You seem to know quite a bit about a woman you've met a handful of times in a bookstore."

Daniel glowered. "Know her family, don't I?"

"Oh, Daniel." Anna sighed, shaking her head. "I should have known."

"Known what?" His eyes twinkled an innocent blue.

"You set me up, after all," Ian said, and sat on the edge of his desk. "'Fetch me these books, will you, laddie, and see if little Naomi will help you with it.'" With a half laugh, Ian gazed at the ceiling. "I never saw it coming."

"So what? All I did was send you on an errand. If you didn't like what you saw—as if any kin of mine would be so stupid—you buy the books and you're on your way. Seems to me," Daniel continued, a canny smile in place now, "that you liked what you saw just fine and dandy."

"Yes, I did."

"So what do you have to say about it?"

"Thank you."

Daniel blinked rapidly, narrowed his eyes in search of the trap. "Thank you?"

"Thank you for having the good taste to recognize the woman I hope to marry."

"Hah!" With surprising speed for a man of his size and age, Daniel lunged out of the chair to clasp Ian against him. "That's a fine lad. See there, Anna, this one knows how to appreciate his grandpa's wisdom. That's why he's always been my favorite."

"Julia was your favorite two days ago," Ian reminded him. "I heard you tell her so."

"Well, she'd just had a baby. Needed some coddling. But you now." Beaming, he leaned back, then the smile faded. "What do you mean, hope to marry?

You are or you aren't going to marry the lass—and I expect to hear that you are because you're not a pinhead.''

"I'm giving her some time. A few months. Afterward, I hope to pick things up where we left off.''

"Time? A few months?'' Daniel roared out the words. ''He's a pinhead, after all! What the devil kind of thinking is this? Go get the girl, for sweet Lord's sake.''

"Daniel, leave the boy alone.''

"The hell I will,'' he boomed at his wife, then gave his current favorite grandchild a light cuff on the side of the head. ''Are you in love with that pretty young lass or aren't you?''

"Yes, damn it.'' Ian's temper was a rare thing, but it could roar as fiercely as his grandsire's. ''Enough to know what she needs and to give it to her. You got it started, and I'm grateful. But I'll handle it from here.''

"Handle it? Bobble it's more likely. Why—''

"Excuse me,'' Caine said at the top of his voice from the doorway. ''This is a place of business, the last I looked. Family fights aren't allowed in the schedule until after six p.m.''

"Do you know what this boy's up to?'' Daniel shouted. ''Your own son? Gets his hard head from you, that's where he gets it. You'd best be talking some sense into him, or I wash my hands of it.''

"What a fine idea,'' Caine said pleasantly. ''Why don't you go wash your hands of it, and I'll talk to my son.''

"See that you do.'' Daniel sniffed. ''Let's go see

Julia—who has more sense than a radish, unlike some of my grandchildren—and that precious baby. And you…" He cuffed Ian on the side of the head again. "Stop being a pinhead long enough to go get the girl."

Caine kissed his mother, then his father, grinning as Anna pulled a still-blustering Daniel from the room. Then he closed the door, chose a chair and continued to grin as Ian rubbed his head.

"Got a hand like a brick, doesn't he?"

"He hasn't boxed my ears since I was twelve." Then Ian worked up a smile. "I miss them already."

"I know what you mean. Sit down, Ian." Caine's face sobered. "The MacGregor called it right. It's time we talked. I'd like to know just what's going on and why you've been baring fangs at everyone within reach for the past week."

"I've got things on my mind. I'm not required to be pleasant every damn hour of every day."

Caine only lifted a brow. "I said sit down. You'll save yourself a headache if you remember The MacGregor isn't the only one who can box your ears."

Chapter 29

Ian sat, but he didn't like it. Saying nothing, he drummed his fingers on his thigh and met his father eye-to-eye.

Stubborn, Caine thought, with admiration. It had always been one of his son's finest qualities, this bullheaded, straight-ahead attitude. It was rare for him to pick a fight, and rarer still for him to walk away from one.

"What's going on between you and Naomi?"

It was just like his father, Ian thought, to zero in on the point. "I'm nearly thirty," he returned, annoyed by the stiffness in his own voice. "I'd think that would be my business at this point in my life."

"Absolutely." Caine's agreement was pleasant. "Until it spills over into MacGregor and Mac-

Gregor business. You haven't been at top form the last few days, Ian.''

"I'll work on it."

"I'm sure you will. But in the meantime…" Caine reached over, laid a hand over his son's. "Tell me where it hurts."

"Damn it." As his emotions rushed to the surface, Ian shoved himself out of the chair. "Damn it. I'm doing what's right, what's best for her."

"Which is?"

"Stepping back."

"Is that what's best for you, Ian? You're in love with her. That's not a question," Caine added. "It's all over your face. I know how it is. I feel the same way about your mother."

"I know. I've watched it all my life. I won't take anything less. Give anything less." He dragged his hands through his hair. "I'm giving her some time, some room. She has to know what she wants."

"And she doesn't? You've asked her?"

With a long breath, Ian sat again. "She'd never been with anyone before me."

"I see." Considering, Caine studied his own hands. "Did you seduce her?"

"No, I backed off. It had to be her decision— she had to feel ready. What else could I do?"

"Nothing, being you. Now it worries you, the fact that you're the only one who's touched her."

"I thought I had a handle on it. But it's not just that she hadn't had sex. She hadn't had *anything*. Anyone. All at once she's standing there telling me that she's a fraud, that I'm only attracted to her because she'd developed this new image. And it all comes tumbling out of her. She tells me she was pudgy and plain, that she hid behind that, because she didn't feel she measured up to the rest of her family. She's barely even dated, never had a chance to see or experience anything. She's just starting to realize her own capabilities, her own powers, and there I am ready to scoop her up, tuck her into marriage, children, the whole deal before she's even seen what's out there.''

''So...you told her you loved her enough to give her that chance?''

''If I'd told her I loved her she wouldn't have listened to the rest.'' He brooded over that fact. ''She thinks she's in love with me.''

''Only thinks?''

''How the hell would she know?'' Ian tossed up his hands and pushed himself out of the chair again.

''Interesting question. How do you know you're in love with her?''

''Because I've never wanted to spend my life with anyone else. Because I can see how it could be with us in a year, in ten years. In fifty.'' He circled the room, then stopped in front of his father. ''You can see I'm right, can't you? It wouldn't be fair to take advantage this way, to ask her to marry me before she'd had time to live a little more.''

''Does it matter what I think?''

"Of course it does."

"Then I'll tell you." Caine rose, laid a hand on his only son's shoulder. "You're a pinhead."

"What?"

"As much as it pains me to agree with The MacGregor on this, I have no choice. You're a pinhead, Ian. You're not giving the woman you claim to love nearly enough credit to know her own mind and heart. You're making a decision for her you have no right to make. And it's my considered opinion, though it again pains me to echo my father, that your best course of action is to go get the girl."

He wasn't convinced the men in his family were right, but Ian planted himself in front of Naomi's door in her apartment building and waited for her to get home.

He considered going to the bookstore, but discarded the idea. If they were going to discuss their future, it shouldn't be done in a place of business.

Yet, as the hour grew later, he began to worry that he'd taken the wrong tack. At least he'd have found her in the bookstore. Now he didn't know where the devil she was.

So when he heard her footsteps on the stairs, he sprang to his feet.

She stopped dead in the hallway when she spotted him, then shifted her briefcase from one hand to the other and came forward.

"Hello, Ian."

"You worked late." She wore the same scent. That same wonderful scent.

"Yes, I did." She took her keys out, slipped them into the lock.

"I'd like to talk to you. Can I come in?"

"Now's not a good time." It would never, ever be a good time, when just seeing him hurt this much.

"Please." He braced a hand on the door to keep it open. "Naomi, we need to talk."

"All right." She could handle it. She'd promised herself she could. "But you'll have to make it quick. I need to change."

"For what?"

"I have a date." It was a terrible lie, one she was sure she would be ashamed of later. But for now pride was much more vital than honesty.

"With a man?"

The absolute shock on his face had that pride rearing up and showing teeth. "I tried dating baboons, but we didn't like the same films." Moving briskly, she set her briefcase aside, hung up her coat. "What can I do for you?"

Marry me, bear my children. "I didn't make myself clear the other night."

"Oh, I think you did."

"No, I didn't explain to you the what, or why."

"I understood perfectly." And she wanted to hate herself, and him as well, because she was so pathetically in love with him. "I told you that what you saw when you looked at me wasn't what was underneath. You agreed, and that was it.''

"No, I—God, is that what you thought? Naomi, I'm sorry." He reached for her. She stepped back. "That's completely wrong. I handled it badly. Let me explain."

"I'm a little pressed for time, Ian."

"Your date will just have to wait," he snapped, and jamming his hands in his pockets, stalked around the room while she lifted her eyebrows and watched him. "After you'd finished, after you told me you'd never been with anyone…"

"You knew I'd never been with anyone."

"I don't mean just the sex!" He all but snarled it this time, and had her eyes narrowing. "God. Sex is just a part of things. There's companionship, there's fun, there's sitting around talking half the night, watching bad movies. All the things you do when you're dating. The things you've never done with anyone but me."

Certain he was under control again, he turned back to her. "I wanted to give you time so that you could think it through, so you could be sure you wanted to keep doing all those things with only me."

"Give me time?" She wished she could come up with one of those cold, go-to-hell laughs, but only managed a derisive snort. "You told me you wanted to see other women to give me time?"

"I never wanted to see other women!" He shouted it at her, then yanked his temper back. "I thought you should see other men. Which, I can point out, you don't seem to have much of a damn problem with.''

''You wanted me to see other men,'' she said slowly, staring at him.

''It's not what I wanted—are you insane?'' His eyes went to a bright and burning blue. ''It's what you needed. How the hell could I ask you to marry me when you didn't have a single point of reference? Nothing to compare what you thought you felt for me to? I was trying to be fair to you.''

''Fair to me? *Fair* to me?'' Fury danced over her shattered heart, gleefully scattering pieces. ''You decided what was right for me, and that was to break my heart?''

''No, to protect it. To protect you.''

''From what? From you? From myself? How dare you make those decisions for me.''

''I didn't. Exactly.'' He could feel himself slipping down a very big hole. ''I only wanted to... Maybe I should take the Fifth,'' he muttered.

''Oh, I could hit you. I could actually hit you.'' She had to turn away before she did. Violence was a new and unstable emotion rushing through her. ''I've never hit anyone in my life, but boy, I could. I wonder how it would feel. Damn it, don't touch me,'' she warned when she sensed him moving in her direction. ''Or I'll find out how it feels.''

Since he'd only heard her use the mildest oaths a handful of times since he'd met her, it became clear just how angry she was. ''Naomi—''

She whirled back before he could get another word out. "You must think I'm a moron."

"Of course I don't. I only—"

"A poor, pitiful excuse for a female who can't trust her own mind, her own heart." She stalked around the room, her movements as stormy as her eyes. "I suppose the only way I'd know if I loved you was to have wild sex with a dozen other men first. Or two dozen? What number did you have in mind?"

"I don't want you having sex with anyone!"

"Oh, that's right. It's not about sex. Well, let me get something to write on and you can explain to me exactly how many romantic dinners, late night dates, drives in the country or whatever I'm to have before I can be considered competent enough to decide what to think and feel."

She'd actually opened her briefcase and taken out a pad before his temper frayed the rest of the way. "Okay, that's it. That's enough." He snatched the pad out of her hand, heaved it. "I don't give a damn what's fair to you or what isn't. I'm not spending the next six months waiting until you've had your little fling."

"Six months. Was that the cutoff? You certainly had it all worked out, didn't you?" Joy was bubbling up along with the fury. The combination made her feel dizzy. And it made her feel powerful. "Well, maybe I'll see you in April then."

She started for the door, intending to fling it

wide. And ended up with her back against it and Ian's furious face close to hers.

She'd done that, she thought with a rush of wonder and delight as they glared at each other. She'd made him so angry he was snarling. She'd made him love her until he was all but incoherent with it.

As clumsy as she was, she realized. How perfectly wonderful.

And she'd done it by doing nothing more than being who she was.

"I said forget it." He grasped her hand. "You can just forget all of it. I'm not living without you. Not for six months, not for six damn hours. You're going to marry me, and if you figure out later it moved along a little too fast for you, that'll be your hard luck."

"All right, fine."

"And you might as well pack your things right now, because—"

His mouth opened and closed, giving her the first glimpse of what it was like to completely stun Ian MacGregor. It was, she decided, a marvelous feeling.

"All right, fine?" he managed.

"Yes." Riding on the new crest of power, she grabbed him by the lapels. "You idiot." And pulled his mouth down to hers.

He reeled with the impact, snatching her up, holding her hard against him so their hearts beat strongly, one against the other. "Just recently, the correct affectionate family term is pinhead."

"Pinhead," she murmured, delirious with love. "I'm so angry with you." Her mouth raced over his face, came back to cling to his.

"I know. I can tell." He chewed restlessly on her top lip. "Go on and stay mad for a while. I deserve it."

"Okay."

"I love you, Naomi." He caught her face in his hands, drew back so she could see his eyes. "I love you."

She closed her eyes, wallowing in the warm flood of emotions that streamed through her. Then opening them, looked into his and smiled. "Say it again. Just like that, would you?"

He kissed her first—her brow, her cheeks, her lips. "I love you, Naomi. It's not just the way you look—though God, you look good. It's the way you are. It's everything you are. I started falling the minute I saw you, and I haven't stopped yet."

"So did I, in exactly the same way, for exactly the same reasons. Oh, Ian, I've been so unhappy without you."

"Maybe it'll help to know I haven't had a decent night's sleep since you left."

"It does." Her lips curved when he laughed. "I hope you suffered. And I'll remind you of how much you suffered the next time you try to decide what's best for me."

He combed his fingers through her hair. "I'm what's best for you."

"Yes." She rested her head on his shoulder, wondering why she'd ever questioned how perfectly it would fit there. "Yes, and as it happens, I'm what's best for you. I want our life together, Ian."

"Let's go home then, and get started on it."

From the Private Memoirs
of
Daniel Duncan MacGregor

They say as a man grows old his memories of years past stay clear as crystal while those of last week fade into the fog.

I still remember, like yesterday, the first time I saw my Anna. Oh, I remember that cool, disinterested look she gave me. Hah. Didn't stay disinterested for long, now did she? I was a young man then, full of piss and vinegar. A big strapping man from Scotland at a fancy society dance where I'd gone hunting for a woman to take to wife.

And there was Anna, in her pretty blue dress. She was mine from the first minute—though it took some time to convince her of it.

I remember that night as if it just happened. The lights, the music, the colors. I remember the scent in the air when I brought Anna here to this cliffside where I would build the house we'd live in. And I remember the feel of the earth in my hands when I planted a young sapling to celebrate the birth of my first son. So they're right in that. The memory of an old man is long.

But I remember last week just as clear, so what the hell do they know?

My grandson took him a wife last week. And I can tell you the scents in the air of the church, the colors of the light that streamed through the windows, the full rich sound of the music that swelled when little Naomi stood at the back in her glittering white gown, with a bit of MacGregor tartan showing and the MacGregor veil covering her shining black hair.

Brides glow. They say that as well. And so she did. It's love that brings that shining beauty to a woman's face. And one more in love I've yet to see.

And Ian, handsome as a prince as he waited for her. They don't say a man glows, but perhaps they should. I can't think of another word for the look on his face as he watched her walk to him.

And not being such a pinhead after all, what did he do? He took her hand, and the other as well, and as the music died off, and before the priest could open his mouth to start the business of it, Ian said, ''I love you, Naomi,'' his voice as clear and strong as the bells that rang after the deed was done.

And if there was a dry eye in the whole of the church at that moment, well, it wasn't Daniel MacGregor's.

It's been a good year for the family. With three weddings and a baby. I've done my best, and my best is better than most. Now the year's nearly done. I'll watch the snow fall awhile, and sit with Anna by the fire and listen to the wind howl at the windows.

And if I do a bit of planning, a bit of plotting while I sit with my feet up and *a glass of whiskey in my hand, what's wrong with that?*

There's another year coming, after all. And I've more grandchildren yet.

* * * * *

And there's another brand-new
MacGregor story to come!

Look out for

The Perfect Neighbour

by
NORA ROBERTS

On sale in Silhouette Special Edition®
in March 2000!

Turn the page for an exciting, sneak preview…

THE PERFECT NEIGHBOUR
Nora Roberts

Cybil dropped the hand she'd lifted to ring his buzzer. "Thank God you're home."

His mood wavered as his thoughts zoomed right back to the dream, and the barroom floor. "What?"

"You have to do me a favor."

"No, I don't."

"It's an emergency." She grabbed his arm before he could walk by. "It's life and death. My life and very possibly Mrs. Wolinsky's nephew Johnny's death. Because one of us is going to die if I have to go out with him, which is why I told her I had a date tonight."

"And you think this interests me because…"

"Oh, don't be surly now, McQuinn, I'm a desperate woman. Look, she didn't give me time to think. I'm a terrible liar. I mean, I just don't lie very often, so I'm bad at it. She kept asking who I was going out with, and I couldn't think of anybody, so I said you.''

Because she'd meant it when she'd told him she was desperate, she darted in front of him to block his path.

''Kid, let me point out one simple fact. This isn't my problem.''

''No, it's mine, I know it, and I would have made something better up if she hadn't caught me when I was working and thinking of something else.'' She lifted her hands, pushed them through her hair and had it standing in spikes. ''She's going to be watching, don't you see? She's going to know if we don't go out of here together.''

She whirled away to pace and rap her knuckles against her temples as if to stimulate thought. ''Look, all you have to do is walk out of here with me, give an appearance of a nice, casual date. We'll go have a cup of coffee or something, spend a couple of hours, then come back—because she'll know if we don't come back together, too. She knows everything. I'll give you a hundred dollars.''

That stopped him. The basic absurdity of it pulled him up short at the head of the stairs. ''You'll pay me to go out with you?''

''It's not exactly like that—but close enough. I know you can use the money, and it's only fair to compensate you for your time. A hundred dollars, McQuinn, for a couple hours, and I'll buy the coffee.''

He leaned back against the wall, studying her. It

was just ridiculous enough to appeal to a sense of the absurd he'd all but forgotten he had. "No pie?"

Her laugh erupted on a gush of relief. "Pie? You want pie? You got pie."

"Where's the C note?"

"The…oh, the money. Hold on."

She dashed back into her apartment. He could hear her running up the steps, slamming around.

"Just let me fix myself up a little," she called out.

"Meter's running, kid."

"Okay, okay. Where the hell is my…ah! Two minutes, two minutes. I don't want her to tell me I'd hold on to a man if I'd just put on lipstick."

He had to give her credit. When she said two minutes, she meant it. She ran back out, her feet in another pair of those skinny heels, her lips slicked with deep pink and earrings dangling. Mismatched again he noted as she handed him a crisp hundred-dollar bill.

"I really appreciate this. I know how foolish it must seem. I can't stand to hurt her feelings, that's all."

"Her feelings are worth a hundred bucks to you, it's your business." Entertained, he stuffed the bill in his back pocket. "Let's go. I'm hungry."

"Oh, do you want dinner? I can spring for a meal. There's a diner just down the street. Good pasta. Okay, now. Pretend you don't know she's keeping her eye out for us," she murmured as they walked to the entrance. "Just look natural. Hold my hand, will you?"

"Why?"

"Oh, for heaven's sake." She snatched his hand, linked her fingers firmly with his, then shot him a bright smile. "We're going on a date, our first. Try to look like we're enjoying ourselves."

"You only gave me a hundred," he reminded her, surprised when she laughed.

"God, you're a hard man, 3B. A really hard man. Let's get you a hot meal and see if it improves your mood."

* * *

The Perfect Neighbour
will be on sale in March in Special Edition®
—don't miss it!